Bittersweet

P.D.R. Lindsay

ISBN: 978-0-9941194-7-6

Bittersweet

In the British army of 1872, corrupt young officers play games of a different kind. Their favourite is to rape young society women in their homes. The rogues make a competition out of it. The more girls the regiment savages, the more different ways they do it, the greater their merriment and cheers for the winning regiment.

But the victims go through hell. They can't tell anyone, not even their mothers and suffer the shame. Their families suffer too. Banker Bryce Ackerman loses the love of his life to the scoundrels, but he won't leave it alone. Bryce follows the thugs to India, where two of the marauding regiments are posted. Trying to run the rapists to ground, he learns their treachery is deadly and their evil courage more monstrous than he expected. Along the way, he must confront his own sexuality. Is he a gentleman always, or is he too a predator?

Life in the British Raj in Colonial India heightens all his senses, good and bad, as he chases down the brutal and dark side of manhood, as he tries to bring Justice to places where Justice had been absent.

DEDICATION

To Subhankar, Vinay and Jyotirmoy
and all the staff and crew of ABN Rajmahal
who took me on the Ganges river trip
my hero made and showed me his world.

ACKNOWLEDGMENTS

Dawn Keur for her marvellous covers
My son-in-law and daughter for their I.T. skills.

CONTENTS

A beginning and an end

Port Of London 1872

Aimée

Bryce doesn't know I am here. The dockside is crowded with people and I am sheltered by my husband and family. We all wish him well and hope for his success. I am even unchristian enough to hope dear Bryce will deal roughly with the Major and that foul man will know what retribution is.

We trail slowly behind him and I smile. Bryce Ackerman is what is popularly called a big bear of a man. He is broad. From the rear view his back is an expanse of best black superfine broadcloth which would wrap round me twice. He is tall, over six feet, but the breadth of his shoulders means you don't see him as tall until he stands near and looks down with an eyebrow quirked and his mouth corners turning up in the beginnings of a smile. His feet balance him in size. His fashionable button boots are solid black leather, specially made, polished and comfortably wide for those great feet, and he plants them firmly as he walks. But he rolls a little as he moves his bulk, more a sway than a sailor's roll, and it does make him look like a bear.

Yes, I still love him, oh not in that way, now we share memories of a lost love, but the terrible events of the last two years have so changed me, and him, that what we, and our families planned as a joyous June wedding two years ago became impossible. I have come through the events and been tempered by them into a sword blade determined to fight for all those young women who have suffered as I did. I have found inner peace now, that Quaker inner spirituality like my husband's, and a different kind of love with that gentle man. I pray that Bryce will find some of this peace too and rid himself of the unnecessary guilt he feels as he hunts down the villains in India.

We watch him board the ship and I am grateful that my husband understood my need to come and that the messages and gifts we have left in Bryce's cabin are my final farewell.

"Come Aimée." He turns me away from the ship. "Time to go home."

I smile, take his arm, and don't look back.

Where are the villains?

Calcutta 1872

~ 3 ~

Bryce Ackerman

The shock of India, sensuous beguiling, erotic India never wore off. I would that it had, for it made me understand something of the sexual tensions the man I wanted to kill possibly suffered under. I had no wish to feel sympathetic towards the bastard who had robbed me of my fiancée and left her distraught.

Thwarted love and revenge was not a good package to carry in a country so riotously sensual and shameless, especially the thwarted love. But I trusted that my personal anguish, as well as my self-discipline, would overrule a young man's natural but improper sexual urges. But anger now, that was an emotion harder to control.

I ached with anger when I thought of that major and blamed my rage on the evil influences of pagan India. Unfairly perhaps, but India, for many an Englishman, even the well brought up Victorian gentleman, offered constant temptation. The Indian culture turned him into an erotomaniac. Although it wasn't so much being driven mad by the passion of love, rather driven mad by the sexuality of the place. Pure lust surged everywhere in all that I saw.

India oozed eroticism. You couldn't escape it. Everywhere naked humanity, bodies freely displayed. Daily one saw underdressed females, ordinary Indian women who looked like some man's fancy piece. Daily one saw native men whose male attributes are carefully and visibly wrapped, or barely tucked out of sight. And if you averted your eyes from them, the religious statues of flower bedecked phalluses set within a representation of the female sexual organs, erotic scenes carved large and in exquisite detail on what seemed like every temple, or vividly painted on house walls in red, ochre and yellow, surrounded and overwhelmed you. It was hot sexuality at every turn. But never talked about, never discussed by the British. The only comments might be how uncomfortable the place was as far as living a good British life went.

'The heat you know.'

Yes, but which heat?

My maternal great-uncle, the Nabob, a man of the old school, and never mealy-mouthed, felt free to talk on whatever amused him. I sought his advice before leaving England and he warned me about India. He'd made a comfortable fortune there early in the century and fondly remembered the exploits of his harem. According to him an Indian woman was trained in matters sexual, taught to please a man and herself. And yes, he did keep a harem, some five or six handsome young women of amazingly sensuality, so he told me, with a wink and a leer. He was not a man to subdue his passions, and it was permissible, in his days of the old John Company, to fraternise with the natives. Not so today. The now properly named East India Company, and the British government, forbade such intercourse.

I had no intention of finding out, or collecting a bibi khana of native women. I came because I'd been forced to seek justice for my Aimée and those other young women so badly wronged. One might well say to what purpose when the damage done cannot be undone. Yet those young ladies and their families needed justice, needed to see the perpetrators punished, particularly as they were deceived and betrayed by men who maliciously broke the social conventions, and violated the sacred trust of the home. Indeed I was the only one free to find the villains who had destroyed so many lives, whose actions had consequences which spread like an insidious London smog, sneaking tentacles in so many places, affecting so many beyond the original victims. My work for the family bank could be shared among my brothers, and my parents and my fiancée's actually sent me to find and punish the villains.

It had been a delicate business. A young gentleman like myself could not walk up to unknown unmarried young ladies and ask if they had been raped. My beloved Aimée and her sisters began the task, the gentle hints, the quiet questions. It became easy, so Aimée said, to see without needing to question. A missing daughter, one never spoken of, a mother pale faced and pining. And, dear God, there were many other victims in such distress, whose families did not know what had been done. My mother and her Quaker friends provided refuge and comfort to terrified young women, and aid to their mothers. They asked more questions of more families and we discovered the bastards had not confined their actions to the north but marauded in the southern counties too.

Fathers, if they knew, were my responsibility to examine and fortunately few discovered what had happened to their or other families. Too many who did find out thought only to protect their 'good' name by casting out the violated girl. All had to be secret, hushed away, daughters hidden, disgraced, never to be spoken of. Such attitudes increased my fury as the investigation took me all over Northumberland, Durham and a wintery Yorkshire. Revenge was a strange and foreign emotion for me. I preferred to control the dangerous uncivilised feelings of anger, hate, jealousy, or revenge. Yet now I burned and fretted with anger and longed for revenge, with a fierce desire to hurt, maim, kill, which frightened me, but drove me on in pursuit.

I found that the villains I particularly wanted had vanished, returned to India. Fifteen months of the most delicate and tactful work in England it had taken to track them down, discover who some of them were, their families and their regiments. For a long time I believed I was hunting a whole army of men. Finally it became clear that there were two groups of officers, and now the devils had gone. Both sets of officers came from regiments currently stationed in India. Therefore to India I went, to follow the blackguards and seek punishment for them, knowing that there would be scant help from their regiments and their commanding officers, who should have been ashamed to shield such men.

April is not the best month to arrive in India. If I'd had my choice I'd have waited for the cooler months, but I did not have a choice; enough time had been lost. I reluctantly left the ship for the land and travelled up river to Calcutta by a craft very like a Thames lighter. The river bobbed and bounced with boats, brightly painted boats, little fishing boats shaped like crescent moons, cargo boats of odd shapes and patched colours, and ferries so overloaded they almost spilt people into the murky water. Colours so strong they shouted, noises in a multitude of discordant keys and searing spicy scents to clog my nostrils, after grey foggy London it was a sensual attack which left me blinking and sneezing.

I stood on the small deck, my clothes clinging damply, listening to the peculiar shouts and cries of the sailors. The heat felt tangible, like a fuzzy woollen blanket wrapped round my head. Each breath came with an effort to pull in the oxygen through the layers of air, as though a weight oppressed my lungs. Yet it wasn't as oppressive as the weight on my heart whenever I remembered my beloved ex-fiancée, my Aimée, whom I had lost forever.

Calcutta's overlarge population and huge government buildings crowded around me, made me feel like one of those ugly creatures in a Brueghel picture, a soul tortured in the furnaces of hell. It felt hotter than hell to a big, cold loving fellow like me. I started in the administration building, trying to find the officials who could give me an appointment with the senior magistrates, or some legislator. Both this building and the building where all the clerks worked, the writers' building, were of ruddy orange brick, grandiose in design with twiddles and curlicues, designed to impress and awe the native peoples. They weren't a bad design, very British in fact, but I had expected something more oriental. The General Post Office also loomed large on the city streets, with a tall brick tower and huge arched entrance. I used it daily sending promised postcards to my nieces and nephews as well as brief letters to the families who sent me.

I dripped and melted, struggling around those government buildings for three days until I found the right people. Lesser officials tried to help, more senior ones were either too busy or absent. However one outraged father who sent me was a member of parliament and on the committee examining finances and government spending in the Raj. His letters of introduction and a document with ministerial names and seals attached finally allowed me to access the senior magistrates. To them I presented the legal documents it had taken so long to put together.

The most senior scanned my papers, tossed them on the desk for the others to see. "You are requesting an investigation of officers in our most highly regarded regiments?"

"Yes."

The four men exchanged glances in which incredulity, outrage, and horror played fleeting parts. "For the seduction of a few female servants and some merchants' daughters?" Senior Magistrate, Lionel Torrington, achieved a sneer worthy of a musical hall villain and even flicked the points of his moustache. I allowed that comic picture to cut the edge off my anger, steady my voice.

"No. For disgraceful social behaviour, as visitors, in the violation of social customs, and acceptable behaviour; for invading, without invitation, family homes; and the despicable dishonourable act of rape forced on young girls not yet out, and on their older sisters." I curled my lip in contempt at his attitude.

The other three, having thoroughly studied the documents I had given them, muttered together, shook heads. One spoke, his voice toned with disbelief.

"No family would go through this…this court case and hearing…back home. The shame, the disgrace…."

"Whose shame? Whose disgrace, Mr Orr? Have you read the statements. How one officer would be talking to and entertaining parents whilst elsewhere in the house, the school room or breakfast room, two officer would be holding down a young lady and allowing a third to rape her before they took their turns?"

More muttering between the four.

"I'm sorry," Senior Magistrate, Lionel Torrington, wasn't and didn't sound it, "but we have no reason to…" he paused. "Why are these events supposed to have happened? There is no reason or explanation for the officers' behaviour. It seems to me to be a political attack on some of the sons of the most honourable families in Britain."

"Oh, it was a competition, sir. A major apparently led the young officers in similar outrageous episodes here in India, choosing middle class Anglo-Indian girls to rape. The men were never brought to justice. As the officers were to be home on leave he proposed to make their efforts a competition this time. The winning team of officers would be the one who raped the most young ladies and their prize was to be a special dinner in their mess with the 1857 vintage champagne."

Disbelief won. Four facial expressions flitted through shock, revulsion, and finally set in disbelief.

"No," Mr Orr sounded triumphant. "My son is with one of the regiments you name and no such dinner has been held."

"Those documents in front of you do not lie."

Lionel Torrington flung the papers back at me. "I am sorry but we cannot help you."

Two more days it took to find a magistrate of sufficient lineage, pedigree and courage to help me haul two distinguished scions of English aristocracy – hah! – from their cosy sinecure in Calcutta when they should have been on duty with their regiment. A word in those official ears, a presentation of documents and statements, a tense meeting, a swift judgement, and one small part of the affair reach its conclusion. Two of the gang of rapists, the Honourable Francis de Beauvais, and Honourable Peregrine Wutherford-Hey were to be sent home as prisoners. Sylvia's father and Dorothea's demanded trials.

I'd watched as the two Honourables listened to the magistrate, Sir Cuthbert Broadbent, laughing as he read out their crimes. My hands I fisted behind my back as they refused to believe that they would be called to account for their actions.

"What have we done but pleasured a few doxies?" the Honourable Francis de Beauvais asked, shrugging his shoulders and smirking. "They let us take their garters willingly. "

The Dishonourables had no idea that they had given the Magistrate an opportunity to acquire more proof. The garters were collected and their commanding officer had little choice now but to allow the men to be returned to England and a trial.

Honourable Peregrine Wutherford-Hey snorted. "My father will soon stop this." Outrage raised his voice. "What father would put his family through a trial?"

I remembered Sylvia's father, the M.P. and his determination. "One who believes that justice is for rich and poor and for his daughter and the bastard she bore."

He sniggered and I remembered Sylvia's face when her father's words set out her future and she realised she would never marry the man she loved, never live a comfortable life again, and never return home. I hit him. A fist to the guts and an uppercut to the chin. I hurt my hand but, despite the fuss and scandalised reactions, I would have done it again.

Sylvia's story: don't make me a victim

Yorkshire 1870

~ 11 ~

"Visitors, Mama." Here they came again, despite the bitter Yorkshire cold, riding down the mossy gravelled driveway. It puzzled me and it puzzled Mama.

"The County have never bothered us before and certainly not since your Papa became the member for parliament and pipped their lordships' choice. And here are the younger sons and even an heir or two, visiting. It's most peculiar."

We'd been out when they first called, but their cards had amazed us. Now here they were again. Mama moved into the bay window and frowned at the small group of well wrapped riders, hats firmly over ears to keep off the nippy January wind, trotting briskly to the stable yard. I admired their glossy coated horses moving so smoothly and easily, not a bit like our dear old plodders.

My sisters, both younger, and both social butterflies, seized Mama by each arm. "Pipped, Mama, such slang language." They tutted and teased her, flustering her into blushes.

"It's because we entertain all the young people in our community," said Charlotte as they swung Mama away from the bay window. "That's why they have come."

"And I did suggest to them, when we met briefly in church, that they come visiting if they sought some younger company," Eugenie said as they settled Mama in her chair by the fire, plumping her skirts around her to fluff out like a sitting hen. "After all we do have a rambling old house which is more fitting for amusing parlour games than the grand homes these young men come from."

Mama frowned. "You are too forward, Eugenie. We live a country quiet life. We do not have a town life in London…" She frowned down my sisters' impertinent mutterings of "London…we long for London…seasons, parties, balls….."

"Oh, Mama," sighed Charlotte.

"Girls, your father has to be in London for Parliament but he needs to be here in his electorate, and he prefers the country life." She rose and patted Charlotte's cheeks. "Be good." She smiled at us as she returned to the window, fidgeting her fingers amongst her shawl fringe. "I wish your father was here to quiz these visitors. We do not know them. They may be officers in respectable regiments, but it is most bold of them to come without introductions, and more than a little arrogant."

"They did leave cards," I reminded her.

She observed Eugenie's grimace and raised eyebrows as she tried to convey some message to Charlotte. "Please keep your amusements limited to parlour games in the drawing room, and only those fit for strangers." She frowned as severely as she could. "No Squeak Piggy Squeak, or Tiddlywinks, but I will allow Consequences, Twenty Questions, and I Spy."

"Oh, Mama," from Eugenie this time, "Charades please, do let us play Charades."

"You may only play Charades, Blind Man's Bluff and Snap Dragon with my approval, and I shall monitor your games myself."

"Oh, Mama." This from both sisters who liked to gently flirt, were excited by our handsome, aristocratic visitors, and had been whispering about them ever since they glimpsed the young men in church.

She relented a little. "Well, well, girls, we have few enough visitors in the winter…"

"Or anytime," Eugenie whispered in my ear.

"…if I approve you may ransack the trunks in the attics for costumes." She received a kiss on each cheek before my sisters swished away, their petticoats peeking under raised skirts as they darted out.

"And you, Sylvia, my wise child, I trust you to see that your flibbertigibbet sisters do not harm their reputations . No more than squeezing hands, no kisses on the sly or sliding away on their own with one of those young men."

"Dear Mama, as if they would."

Mama knew her giddy girls and raised an eyebrow.

"Mama, how can I if they plot and contrive together?"

She blew me a kiss. "Fret not, my pet. Today it will be tea in the drawing room with the vicarage girls and polite introductions. If I invite these young men to our weekly supper party then you and I simply organise everyone into little groups, say four or five, for games and perhaps, but only perhaps, for Charades."

She noted my questioning face, for Mama usually played chaperone discreetly, from a distance.

"Oh yes, I shall be there to help you." She sent me a loving look. "Now I must inform the kitchen quickly or we will have nothing fit for these young men to take at tea." She bustled off, but turned at the door. "Enjoy yourself, Sylvia, my dear, you are too solemn and your sisters will behave. I shall be there." She whisked away.

I found Eugenie and Charlotte upstairs, primping in their room. The scent of rose water told me that. I waited in the doorway as they twirled lacy shawls over their arms and set their skirts to rights.

Eugenie whirled up to me. "What do you think?"

"Very pretty, you giddy misses." They were pretty too, Eugenie, dark and curly haired like papa and Charlotte, fair and lustrous like Mama. "I suppose you have already brought a trunk down with costumes?"

Charlotte tapped the old trunk beside the door with one foot as she danced round the room. "If they like us enough do you think they would invite us to London?" She was only seventeen and a young seventeen.

I shook my head.

Eugenie sighed dramatically, hands clasped to bosom, eyes raised to the ceiling. "Handsome young men, parties and balls, and not just the curate, the doctor's boys or the farmers' sons," she declaimed like an actress in a melodrama, throwing her arms out in a wide gesture of frustration.

I laughed. "Come, our guest will be in the drawing room with Mama. You are attractive enough to dazzle them, even if your elegant frocks and lace shawls are our creations and not a London modiste's. They will never know."

My absurd sisters entwined their arms around my waist, kissed my cheeks and waltzed me through the door and to the top of stairs.

The vicarage girls had arrived, stood in the hall shedding warm layers of cloaks and heavy shawls, woollen bonnets, mittens and scarves. We ran down the stairs to greet them.

Millicent, Julia and Dorothea were sixteen, eighteen and twenty one to our fifteen, seventeen and twenty. That made us near enough to be close friends if we so desired, and we did. We had shared early lessons with their father, shared governesses later on, and then shared the music, singing and painting tutors. We ran in and out of each other's houses as children, but now we were young ladies our house was deemed larger and more comfortable for social events. They had five brothers and no private income, but were blessed with good looks and the promise of a dowry from their mother's elderly aunt. This gave them an added confidence and charm when meeting young men. I envied them their sang froid.

"Who are the visitors?" Dorothea hissed in my ear as she hugged me.

"We don't really know. We think the ones who left their cards, the ones from Beauvais House."

Her eyes widened, her mouth rounded in a soundless 'Oh.'

"Come and meet them."

In the drawing room Mama was pouring tea and organising the toasting of crumpets and muffins at the fire. The young men seemed most obliging. They smiled at us and apologised for not rising, but they thought we would understand that toasting crumpets and muffins needed care if they were not to incinerate them to an inedible state. They certainly organised themselves well, working as a team, two toasting, two supplying and the last, who indeed piled on the butter. He kept giving us sharp sideways glances and dripping butter onto the hearth.

They tossed names at us, smiling with charm and ease of those who are county, nobility, and rich, those who never experience social difficulties. There was an Honourable Francis, an Honourable Peregrine, and three plain misters, Mister David, Mister Leonard and Mister Ewart. Mister Ewart had flaming red hair and a marked Scottish brogue. The others were all brown haired, of varying shades, and spoke with the clipped London accents of the privileged southerners. They were officers in the Darkshire Regiment, stationed in India, home on leave.

I followed my father's politics, quietly of course, and was not prepared to like these aristocratic brats, but they aimed to please. I couldn't think why. The Honourable Francis's father had called my papa 'a street cur, a radical swine not fit to be a member in the House, and a disgrace to Parliament.'

Mama succumbed to their manners and compliments within ten minutes, and she was not easily fooled. I watched closely, but never surprised a scornful look at our old fashioned furniture or quick amused glimpses between them over our country talk. Indeed they joined in, but, to me, it felt like some carefully patterned conversation they had spoken before.

The Honourable Francis held a long conversation with Mama and myself on the origins of the Chinese silk wallpaper on the drawing room fireplace wall, which she had so carefully preserved and cleaned. Perhaps it was that he seemed too eager to please, but I did not like the practised smiles he sent my way. By the time tea had been drunk, and the food eaten down to the last potted shrimp sandwich and slightly singed crumpet, we relaxed, were all enjoying their company, even I smiled. When they rose to leave in proper fashion, only a little over the correct length of time, Mama invited them to return on the morrow to our weekly winter supper party.

"Nothing very grand," she warned them, "but this end of January is dull after Christmas festivities so we liven the month for you young people with music and singing once a week."

"And Charades perhaps, Mrs Courtland?" That was the Honourable Peregrine asking, with a sketch of a bow and fetching smile. "We do enjoy playing games, particularly Charades. We have some wonderful costumes we brought from India." He turned and inclined his head in our direction. "I am sure the young ladies would delight in silk saris."

My sisters exchanged eager glances, but Mama, in her sweet motherly way, merely said "I will see." and the young men had the sense not to press, although they seemed disappointed. They bowed politely and allowed me to show them to the front door. They departed, Mister David muttering to the Honourables about wanting Charades for their ...but

Mister Ewart said goodbye to me loudly and I did not hear the rest of the comment.

Back in the drawing room, under Mama's watchful eye, I restrained Eugenie and Charlotte from immediately blurting out personal remarks about the visitors, as Dorothea hushed Millicent. We waited until their horses trotted down the drive before venturing on polite comments about well-mannered young men which Mama would approve. More impolite comments about their handsome physique would come in our bedrooms tonight as we brushed hair and whispered.

The room seemed empty and much larger without all that muscular and energetic presence but Mama filled it again, pacing, preoccupied. "I do wish your father could be here. I am not sure he would approve."

In the general outcry I thought of a word we could use in Charades which would let us wear saris for every one of the four syllables we would act out. I looked forward to it.

How dare they?

Word spread. At breakfast the following morning Mama received two notes from families in the village. By luncheon she had received a note or message from all of those in our circle. Even the curate begged to join us. The lure of Indian costumes was as great as the lure of meeting the young men from the House.

Mama looked round the table with a severe face. "Who has gossiped?" She directed her gaze at Eugenie, then at Charlotte.

"Housemaids talk more than younger sisters," my sisters exclaimed with indignation, casting glances at me. I certainly hadn't spoken to anyone outside the house.

Mama, reckoning up the numbers, looked distracted, called up Cook. Cook called upon the heavens and then us. We spent the afternoon, not in pampering ourselves, but in the warm and spice scented kitchen, making little cakes, shortbreads, gingersnaps and fruit loaves. We helped Mama use her carefully cultivated potted plants and some ivy off the outer house wall to decorate the tables. Only then were we allowed an hour to make ourselves beautiful.

"Sylvia?"

I paused, looked back at Mama.

"What would your father say to all this? I do so hope I'm not breaching his trust allowing this party."

I thought for a moment, smiled and shook my head. "He might not approve of those young men, Mama, but he would enjoy the party." I hurried after my sisters.

– · –

Our neighbours came early and some brought thoughtful gifts of food, bread, cold chicken, a joint of beef, pickled lemons and cherries. Useful things for the days after the party. They were good folk for all my sisters complained of their dullness. I would rather have thoughtful kindness than excitement, but then I had the beginnings of an understanding with the eldest son of an established yeoman farmer's family. My John stood steady and kind, slow to speak but thoughtful. When he spoke it was to the point and coherent. Also he listened to me and respected my opinions. A rare trait I'd noticed in young men.

The visitors arrived at the same time as John and his fourteen year old sister, Elise, in a swirl of cold damp air and the scent of snow. Our tweeny maid, Abigail, took outer clothing in mountains which nearly buried her and sprinkled her with a dash of snow. I hastened to greet the young men formally before joyfully welcoming John and his sister. I ushered them through to the drawing room, and before the whispers began Mama introduced the visitors. They bowed and presented her with a magnificent Indian shawl, then turned to all our guests and going amongst them, introduced themselves again, catching and repeating names as they shook hands. I watched as they took pains to gently flirt with each of the young ladies.

The Indian shawl, a Kashmir one, so soft and smelling of sandalwood, provoked great admiration. Mr Ewart slipped into the hall, collected a sari from the large box they had carried into the house, and displayed it in a splash of rustling slithering glory. It was a magnificent gold and yellow creation, the gold being real gold thread embroidery, tiny gold mirrors and golden sequins, the yellow being a glossy silk which glimmered in the candle light. It was exotic, an artist's creation, not a piece of seamstress's work, and every one of us young ladies longed to wear it.

We sang for our supper. The visitors, the doctor's sons, the farmers' boys sang cheerfully, with gusto. Their shyer sisters were all really too young to be included, but, as Mama said, how could we exclude them from the excitement? What was usually an orderly party turned into a romp. After the country dancing spilled into the hall, some of the young ladies went beyond Mama's sight. She called for supper, had Dorothea and I collect the over-excited young sisters whilst she spoke to older brothers. Supper became a prolonged meal as the visitors actually took it in turns to carry servings to the little sisters, which caused much fluttering and blushes. I wondered what they wished to demonstrate as they seemed set on flirting only with the little sisters.

After that civility Mama organised us. She thoughtfully split everyone into groups. Older brothers had the managing of younger sisters and each group consisted of no more than five people. She then allowed each visitor to choose which group he would join. I rather thought that Mama did not permit those young men to be together so that the lovely Indian clothes would be available to five groups not one. Discreet and clever of Mama.

"You must use a two syllable word and so may only perform two scenes."

Sighs and gentle protests greeted this announcement.

"I did promise your parents to return you in good time," she told the disappointed damsels with a sweet voice but immovable expression. No one tried to persuade her.

"You may work upon your charade down here in any of the reception rooms. Gentleman needing to disrobe are free to use the guest room at the top of the stairs. Ladies, please use Eugenie's bedroom at the far end of the passageway upstairs." She smiled. "Sylvia will aid the young ladies and John will valet the young gentlemen."

Dear Mama was so careful to protect our good names and manage any giddy behaviour from the younger ones. John, standing beside me, turned his head in my direction and pulled a rueful face. I lowered my gaze but couldn't prevent a rueful smile back.

The Honourable Francis chose our group. He already had a two syllable word to act, and so I accompanied Mister David and Mister Leonard as they took the box upstairs.

They paused on the landing, looking round.

"If you could leave the box here…" I began.

"May I suggest," Mister David said, "that we leave the saris, wraps and women's garments in your sister's room?"

It seemed a good idea so I escorted them to Eugenie's room. They handed me saris, enormous lengths of cloth - I'd no idea they were so long - glorious shawls, heavy silk wraps and shift like tunics they claimed went over rather flimsy pantaloons, again in silk, but soft fine silk. Against the dark furniture and heavy pine green winter curtains the clothes made a rainbow of brilliance. I lit all the candles to enjoy the display, and noted the strange, strong scents from the clothing, not unpleasant, rather exotic perfumes hinting of hot house flowers and heated summer nights. A breath of India perhaps, like the sandalwood on the shawl? Behind me Mr Leonard fiddled with the door, I heard the lock click in and out.

I turned. He smiled. "Interesting house," he said.

"These saris are so beautiful. Don't your sisters claim them?"

Mister Leonard swopped a look with Mister David. "Oh, we spoil my sisters with silks by the mile and silk embroideries, which they prefer. We find that having a boxful of such costumes ensures a successful social life when we are in unfamiliar places. Everyone loves Charades." Both young men glanced at each other, smiled at me. "We love Charades."

I led them back to the guest room and they watched me spread turbans, baggy overshirts with matching trousers and Indian military uniforms, jackets and caps, on the bed. Mr David twiddled the door handle this time. Mr Leonard idled by the bed. Looking at the costumes I understood Mama's restriction on the words. We would be scrambling up and down to get into these costumes in decent time. Certainly we young ladies would have to have help changing. I wondered if I ought to withdraw from my group and play the personal maid, but when we returned to the drawing room the Honourable Francis had a part ready for me.

"I need you to play the Maharani, the princess." He took my hand and bowed over it.

My John grimaced and departed upstairs with Elise. Those of us remaining set an area for performing.

"May we use the hall and stairs?" Mister Ewart begged.

It was a fair request as our hallway was large, the stairs central and designed so that the first three steps were wide and broad, leading onto a small landing, and then the flight of stairs ran straight up to the upper landing. Mama agreed and permitted the banisters to be used for fixing screens and old sheets for curtains so that we had a stage with hidden entrances and exits. Even the top of the stairs remained hidden behind screens, allowing us to come and go unseen. Our aristocratic visitors seemed uncommonly handy at making a stage, and pleased with privacy they achieved.

Mama gave us ten minutes to compose our plays, five minutes to perform and five to change. Upstairs became a confusion of people. Saris were not easy to put on and keep on. We ladies soon found it difficult to dress and attend all the performances. The gentlemen were not much quicker.

Our group performed first. As I struggled to manage the wonderful material and wrap myself in a glorious dark green and gold sari, I tried to make a plan to see all the young ladies costumed and performing in time, especially as there were only seven saris and every young lady wanted to wear one. Wearing a sari meant removing one's dress and some petticoats, winding oneself into the material and trying to fix it in place without sticking pins to damage the magnificent cloth. The visitors kindly suggested that all the young ladies could try on the saris after the Charades had been guessed and were being judged. The judging would take some time as a group won points for a correct guess of each part of the word, the whole word and for their own performance. Mama had to make note of the scores and add them up. She always tried to be fair, but it took time.

Once I'd played my part I found myself running between the top of the stairs and Eugenie's room, assisting a little sister, admiring her and then shooing her out. Organised it was not, chaotic certainly. Finally the last little sister departed downstairs where most people waited in the hall to listen to Mama's results and her awarding of amusing favours. I sighed, the rush had ended. I turned to descend and found the Honourable Francis hovering beside my bedroom door. The Misters popped out of the guest room. Julia, Charlotte and Dorothea stood trapped between this bulk of looming masculinity. They had intended, I knew, to try on those saris again, or perhaps those rather scandalous tunics and pantaloons.

Charlotte asked, giving them her best hopeful expression and pleading blue eyes. "Might we try a sari again?"

"Oh, I say," Mister David shook his head, "we have to pack up ready to leave now."

Nods and murmurs from the others.

"But," the Honourable Francis said "How if we leave a sari for you? Perhaps you, Miss Sylvia, would choose it?"

Gasps from Julia and Charlotte. Dorothea looked amazed.

I felt the heat of a blush rise as I tried to explain. "I am sure Mama would not permit such a valuable gift."

We young ladies looked at each other and at the visitors.

"What if Miss Julia and Miss Charlotte ask your Mama?" That was the smooth tongued Honourable Francis. "They might even gain permission to try the saris on again."

"Good idea," said Mister Leonard.

The men crowded us closely, and I caught the Hon Francis flick a glance at Julia.

"Go now," I told Julia and Charlotte. "Wait until Mama has finished, bring her a cup of tea, and ask then. I am sure that our visitors can spare us those few extra minutes."

The girls didn't argue, the thought of owning a sari filled their giddy heads, and they sparkled with joy. They turned and Mr Leonard stepped to one side.

"Certainly we can wait for your Mama to be persuaded, young ladies. Leonard will escort you." The girls whisked around and departed with Mister Leonard as escort.

"Not quite as we planned, eh gentlemen?" Mister Ewart declared, which I thought strange, but he was ushering Dorothea to the guest room. "If you could help us fold those uniform jackets, Miss Dorothea.

We are not used to doing without a valet." His hand rested firmly in the small of her back as he moved her down the passage. Mister David followed close behind.

"But John…" I began and found myself gently guided into Eugenie's room.

"Your friend?" the Honourable Francis asked. "He is downstairs."

The Honourable Peregrine – the silent one - opened the door and I was…not pushed…more guided in physically by both men closing round me and advancing so that I had to move or be knocked over.

The Honourable Francis closed the door, and the Honourable Peregrine inclined his head to look me up and down in what appeared to be an inspection. "Which sari will it be?" Hurry do, m'dear. Try it on."

"I beg your pardon?"

He advanced. "You won't mind the two of us will you? After all you did send - your sisters wasn't it? – away and robbed me of the rather luscious blonde piece. I fancied rogering her." He looked me up and down. "You're not as pretty but you'll do."

By now I had retreated until the edge of the bed stopped me, and I hastily stepped sideways, only to be caught between the dressing table and the writing desk.

"Undress please. We never rip clothes."

Dazed and scandalised though my stunned brain was, numbed still by shock my tongue, my legs had their own sense and leapt me up on to the bed. I ran down its length and jumped for the door, only to be caught by the Honourable Francis as I reached the handle. He locked the door.

"No," I cried. "Let me out, at once, do you hear?"

The villain held me tightly, pressed me close to him. I kicked his shins and tried to cry out, but one hand constrained my head so that my face was forced into his jacket, a wedge of its cloth stopping my mouth. I could scarcely breathe, never mind call for help. I tried. Only mumbled noises resulted.

My head was released. I could breathe now. "Let me go. Don't touch me."

My face was smothered back into the prickly cloth of the jacket.

His other arm braced across my back like a rigid iron bar and squeezed me tighter so that, crushed into silence, I could not move. I felt suffocated and dizzy.

"Now then, don't be frightened. We have a competition to win you see. How many girls we can seduce during our home leave. We are leading the count so far. You'll help us win. Isn't that a good thought?" He sniggered.

Seduce? If my face had been free, and I had air to breath, I would be screaming rape.

"Come, Perry, undo those buttons I've been eyeing all night. I much prefer this sister, riper breasts, more mature. More fun to see if we can make her react."

I heaved and strained to free myself, but both men sandwiched me between them. My head was held by a hand with grip like a blacksmith's, my face still smothered in the Dishonourable Francis's jacket, as the buttons were unfastened by a practised hand. No fumbling at all. Then my bodice was peeled over my shoulders and the Dishonourable Perry stepped back to pull it down to my hips. This gave me space to move my legs and I kicked out wildly but the men caught me by my legs. One lifted them, the other grasped my shoulders, and together, in a well-trained movement, I was raised and flung onto my bed face down. They even managed to slide my dress off completely and as one pressed me fiercely into the bed covers, forcing the corner of the turned back sheet into my mouth, the other untied petticoat strings and bundled them off with my drawers.

Terror? Anger? I think I would have expected that of myself. What I felt was acute embarrassment, mortification, shame that I could not protect myself and had to lie here almost naked, held down by these two animals. Revulsion made me shiver as I tried to sink the soft eiderdown round me.

They laughed. "A real missish middle class miss," one said as I was flipped over and forced to look at them. Gone were the polite gentlemen. These two animals leered and sneered, sniffing round me like feral beasts. Mouth dry, tongue scraped dry by the sheet I tried to speak. Fear had stolen my voice. Making an extreme effort I rolled to the bed edge, attempting to fall off and get under the bed. Dishonourable Peregrine grasped me, straddled me and lifted my head.

"Now then, which of us would you like first?"

He weighed me down like a mountain. I could smell his spice pomade and the starch on his collar. I hated the very smell of him.

As I opened my mouth to scream out he gagged me with his monogrammed handkerchief and then covered my face with horrible wet kisses. The Dishonourable Francis stroked his hands up and down my thighs, gently soothing and easing my legs apart.

He crooned. "Where's pussy, nice pussy?"

The Dishonourable Peregrine stopped slobbering over me. "See how nice we are? We don't bash or yank. We don't force you."

If looks killed he would have died. My muffled, pathetic sounds made him laugh. I wished to die.

"Look at this lovely pussy." Dishonourable Francis tickled my most private parts, invading my genitals with a delicate, soothing rubbing action. "We'll soon have her wet with desire." They snorted like pigs, holding down the volume of their laughter.

"We'll win that competition, Perry, my lad." They snorted again.

Anger chased away the fear. I heaved my body, trying to press my legs together.

"Tut, tut." The Dishonourable Peregrine began biting my ear and one hand slide down my throat and round it. "Oh she'll be good, or I might tighten my grip like this."

He squeezed until specks of light danced before my eyes and I couldn't breathe.

"You enjoy her first this time. I'll make her beg for it." He remained straddled over my torso, pinning me down, one hand round my throat, one massaging my breasts.

Nauseated and distraught I wept. I had dreamt of my first sexual experiences with my John on our wedding night, when we learned to love each other. What should be loving and caring was tainted now by this brutal travesty.

The Dishonourables laughed at me. "Don't cry. We don't rape, we seduce and you will beg for us to do this again. We'll be better than that lumbering cloddy you favour. Perhaps you can teach him?" They sneered openly now. The Dishonourable Francis continued his actions and the Dishonourable Peregrine continued to pet and stroke.

He eased his hand around my throat. "She's ready." He slid to one side of me on the bed, hand squeezing my throat. The Dishonourable Francis, with his trousers round his knees, slid over me, his member now rubbing against me.

I panicked, shuddering.

"Keep fighting, you slut, I enjoy it more."

I struggled not to react, but a spasm ran through my body as he thrust in and out, making my whole body arch and jerk in rhythm with his movements. The gag had dried my mouth and hurt, now I hurt even more.

"More" he said, moving in me until I collapsed.

He withdrew sniggering and rolled off me. "Not bad, these prudish doctors' daughters. Hurry up, Perry, I want another turn."

Weeping, I freed one hand, tried to remove the gag. but the Dishonourable Peregrine slapped it away and tightened his pinch grip round my throat.

He rolled over me, his fingers inside me teasing me as he began to rub and tickle. I twitched and jerked under his weight and he crowed.

"Hey ho, away we go." and pushed his way inside though I tried hard to keep my legs closed.

"Now, now, you wanton trull, don't play the coy maiden. We know you country girls." Too big and heavy for me to resist, the man simply shoved his way in. He nibbled my ears, hand on my throat. "Come, little fille de joie, ask nicely for release." And he held still, lifting me towards him so my body could not move.

A soft knock, Dishonourable Francis unlocked the door and Mister David slid his head round. "We've finished. Time to move on."

"Goddamit," the Dishonourable Peregrine swore, and pushing me down onto the bed, pumped vigorously so that he exploded wetly inside me. It felt revolting.

"Damn it to hell, this one's so easy to manipulate. I wanted another turn." The Dishonourable Francis tidied himself and looked like an innocent visitor again.

"Ours closed her eyes and cried all the time. We got her moving in the end. Not as much fun as this one looks."

Oh, my poor Dorothea.

Dishonourable Francis removed the gag. It was his handkerchief. They left me on the bed, tossed the exquisite yellow sari over me, and were through the door in a moment. The Dishonourables both turned, spoke softly. "No one will believe you if you say a word, and you will be the sufferer, for we are honourable gentlemen." They sniggered again. "No one saw us and you cannot speak, for you are nobodies and no one would believe you."

"My papa will hound your family…"

"And who will listen? An Earl bothered by some country nobody with a tale to cover his harlot of a daughter's disgrace? Poor country gentry accusing aristocracy? You and your family would be ruined socially."

They left with their bags and I crept over to the dresser and washed myself. Petticoats and dress were easy to pull on but I couldn't fasten my bodice buttons.

My sisters dashed in. "Which sari…? Oh allow me to help with the buttons," said Eugenie as Charlotte twirled round with the sari. I turned away from them, knowing I must reach Dorothea before she was discovered undressed. I had the sari as an excuse, She had none.

"Run and show Mama the sari," I managed to say. They darted out and I walked carefully to the guest room, my body sore and every muscle trembling. I couldn't decide what to do or say.

I tiptoed into the guest room and found Dorothea struggling into her clothes. "Dear Lord, Dorothea. Are you safe?" It was a stupid thing to say.

She looked at me through her tears. "I hate them, I hate that red headed Scot."

I helped her wash and dress and we held onto each other, too perturbed and dazed to find words for the degradation we felt.

"I can't wash off the scent of them," Dorothea sniffed and swallowed back more tears.

I too smelled them, the rank maleness, the raw sex. We would never be able to associate anything pleasant with those smells.

Their casual callousness, their belief that they had the right to behave like this with any female shattered us both. We had been reduced to nothingness, things to be used for a competition. There were no bruises, no marks of ill treatment. Nothing to show we had been raped, and this they counted on.

Imagining the distress, the shame, the disgrace facing us and our families if we made a complaint I looked at her and shook my head. "They've done this before, the evil monsters, and they know we can't say anything.

"I heard them counting how many since Christmas, for this competition. "

I wanted to retch, clutched my stomach, then grasped Dorothea's hand.

She flung her arms around me as we struggled for composure. "Pray God this is an end and we might warn our friends."

We never thought about the other consequence. God surely couldn't be so cruel.

Meet the Magistrate

India 1872

In my search for the villains I even went out to the army canton at Barrackpore to hunt down the elusive senior officers. I rode a hired hack which proved steady and reliable until a sacred cow lurched out from the ditch and jumped on the road in front of the animal. The horse, unable to bolt with my long legs wrapped round the ribs pushing it on, trembled, snorted and finished the journey in nervous fits and starts with much shaking of its head and suspicious looks in every ditch. No kind words would reassure the poor thing.

The senior officers I required were in town, the adjutant assured me.

"Indeed?" I walked through the adjutant, who gave way, protesting fiercely as I forced him into the main office. Two clerks, startled, raised heads revealing anxious faces.

"I intend to see the colonel and I will." I smiled that with-the-mouth-only-business smile at the clerks and bleating adjutant, and flung open the inner office door.

It was empty. I left a note, Sir Cuthbert's message and the M.P.'s card.

The ride back to town was dusty and tiresome. Locals carrying baskets and bundles, bullock carts, goats scurrying after small boys, people pushing handcarts and even an elephant among the sacred cows. The horse decided the elephant was tolerable, a cart of clattering tins bearable but an empty bicycle cart swishing past merited a quick side kick, fortunately missing the vehicle. Bird shrieks, raucous monkeys and the soldiers' racket whenever they marched past did nothing to help my gloomy thoughts. Another day wasted, but I'd have them in the morning, and I did.

God, I hated those regiment commanders. Their deep plummy voices, their arrogance, unthinking rudeness, that so called upper crust bray they called a whisper. Their absolute belief that they were in the right, in the know and the world belonged to them made me long to be as rude in return. It would have been a wasted effort, they wouldn't have noticed. The acrimony and lack of shame at what the young officers had done shocked me. I knew senior officers would want to protect their regiment, might even try to excuse their officers as 'Young men being young men'. I hadn't realised how much filth would be heaped on the victims. They were whores, sluts, loose, promiscuous, 'not of our class', rape was entirely due to their flawed immoral characters and position in life.

"They were strumpets who asked for it and enjoyed it." the Dishonourables had informed me. "We merely seduced them."

Even the statements from the victims about the competition, the invasion of their homes, the parents' anger at their homes being so abused, made little impression on the commanding officers. Knowing Aimée and her family, as well as several of the other victims, made hearing all the abuse unbearable. It left me full of fury at the injustice. I listened to two days' of such talk until my patience vanished, my contempt exploded all over the sniggering, excuse-making animals. I wanted vengeance now for Alice.

"Neither I nor these poor young girls have done anything to harm your hallowed regiment. Your officers and their bestial behaviour did the harm. Their actions in family homes to people with more government power than your antiquated ancestors can muster…"

The colonel in chief spluttered an interruption and rose up full of indignation. "How dare you, sir. We have listened to your speechifying. You have cost us two fine officers. That is enough."

"Not nearly enough. I want a list of names. I want that major named." I stopped snarling and shook my head at them, lowering my voice with an effort. "I am afraid that the members of parliament, lawyers and merchant bankers whose daughters your men have defiled are a powerful enough group to be demanding your heads. And the regiment to be reformed."

That wasn't strictly true but near enough to frighten the senior officers into staring at each other and muttering.

"I know too, which of you here need funds from banks like my family's and how your regimental mess is funded for its officers. You might well have difficulty raising money in future."

Silence followed that pronouncement.

"I have statements concerning named junior officers and I wish to confirm that they are in this regiment and took leave in England at certain dates. If you attempt to prevent me I'll bring in the magistrates to compel you."

Despite all that they balked and procrastinated, muttering amongst themselves.

"To hell with you all."

I fetched Sir Cuthbert Broadbent, whose weighty presence and special powers from Parliament allowed him to force compliance. Two more young officers were thrown out of the regiment and I hoped that Alice's mother would be a little comforted when she read my letter. Four bastards punished, six still to find and no news of the major I sought.

For the rest of the day I sat in a stuffy office reading records. Fortunately the office clerk, a babu I believe was his title, spoke English well and helped me considerably over files and dates.

Names and dates coincided. I had the correct officers. Now I had to located them physically. By the end of that humid and muggy afternoon I did not love my fellow men. And still no trace of the villain I hunted for my personal satisfaction, that be-damned major who remained nameless. I had to wait for further information, gathered by my mother and her friends, sent on after me by the next ship. There might be a name. The army hated to give up its men but I would have them, and force the administration to divulge those officers' names I needed.

Sir Cuthbert, who'd been reluctantly involved in the legal part of the solved cases, turned partisan. I think it was Alice's story which broke him.

"Your direct approach, young man, is too forthright. They'll never give up their major's name. We need my wife to do a bit of socialising and chatting over the tea cups. And perhaps my steward can catch some useful servants' gossip."

I wiped my sweating brow. "I'd rather squeeze the name out of them."

Sir Cuthbert grasped my upper arm and held me still. "Use the law. Violence would be immediately satisfying to you, but then come problems. How many do you hit? How often? How hard? Hit them with words and hurt them with the law. That will produce lasting results."

He reached up to pat my shoulder in a gentle fatherly way. He knew of my personal involvement but he didn't mention Aimée although I had forced myself to speak of her briefly as my fiancée when I went through the documents with him. I felt grateful for that.

"You're melting, young man, not used to this heat. Come up to the hills with us and wait for that information to arrive in a cooler place. The government will be moving to the hills shortly and everyone will be there, including your major."

I accepted with gratitude. He had been genuinely distressed, of real use, and his bungalow, up country in the cooler hills, sounded a perfect retreat. I wanted to obliterate the taint of evil from my soul and remember that humans were not all vile. For a little while, as I waited for the information and that name, I intended to forget the whole disgraceful affair, in a place distant from teeming cities, in a fecund green country with clean air, and less heat and stench than the capital city provided. Meanwhile I had another day to spend in that dusty office going through files.

Sir Cuthbert's wife, Ada Broadbent, sent a servant with an invitation asking me to tiffin, obviously intending a quick look-see in case I proved one of her husband's more disreputable acquaintances she was saddled with for a few weeks. I thought tiffin meant tea. Fortunately the babu corrected me when I asked what an Indian afternoon tea consisted of and sent me off in time for luncheon with a messenger boy to lead the way.

The Broadbents rented a rather splendid apartment in a very grandiose building not far from the government buildings. I paid off the boy and plodded up the stairs, pausing to catch my breath and enjoy the honey sweet scent from the creeper on the wall on the way. I had no chance to stand and mop my face or tidy my hair as the door opened when my foot grounded on the landing.

The door opener was a servant in white with a red turban. Mrs Broadbent stood in the doorway.

"Welcome, Mr Ackerman," she said and from behind her Sir Cuthbert bellowed.

"Come in Ackerman. It's cooler in here."

It was. The giant ceiling fans creaked gently to and fro as the punkah-wallah pulled the cords. Two magnificent Chinese jars, larger than the biggest wine coolers, sited beneath the punkas, held a block of ice and thus an almost cool breeze fanned its way towards us.

"Ingenious." I admired the clever idea. Mrs Broadbent inclined her head with a smile.

"Isn't it? My wife and the steward thought it up." Sir Cuthbert settled his wife at the table and gestured towards my chair.

Lunch, a mild curry with rice and a cooling cucumber and buttermilk drink, followed by a fruit dessert, was light enough to enjoy in the heat. Our conversation about why people came to India, now the buccaneering days of the John company, and opportunities to make a fortune, had been tamed and legislated by the British government, was perhaps a gentle way to enquire into my business.

Sir Cuthbert grinned at me. "She's quite safe, keeps a still tongue."

I shook my head. "I'm not here only for myself. I promised not to mention names or situations. I may not make free with other's stories." I looked at Ada Broadbent. "But I do seek to bring justice on a certain major you might be able to find for me."

She laughed, a very comfortable woman, she bore me no ill will for not telling her what I was doing in India when it obviously wasn't a banking concern. "My husband has already mentioned a major." She twinkled a flirtatious smile at me. "My spies are out seeking him."

I had to smile back. She was so good hearted, as sound as a ripe pippin, and looked like one with her plumped out pink cheeks and fat smile. "So tell me," I said "why people come to India if they are not government, trade or military people?"

She chuckled. "Did you notice certain types of passengers on your ship?"

No, I hadn't. I had been too busy composing the victims' judicial case and nursing my own private pain. I must have looked blank for Mrs Broadbent jogged my memory.

"All those single young ladies with their mamas or married female relatives?"

"Oh, yes?"

"Husband hunting, my dear. Weren't you a target?"

"Too busy working, Mrs Broadbent."

She tutted gently, her eyes dancing lights of amusement. If she'd held a fan she would have rapped my knuckles with it. "What an opportunity you missed."

Sir Cuthbert coughed that ahem, ahem warning husbands use and Mrs Broadbent pressed her lips together to hold back any indiscreet words.

Sir Cuthbert shook his head, but he smiled.

"If, Mr Ackerman, you are going to need to be social in the hills you will need a partner for balls and the Club dinners. The only young lady I know safe for you to escort is a charming young friend of mine. Bea will keep you on your toes." Ada Broadbent sent me a wicked glance. "I'll introduce you when we get to the hills."

I returned her glance. "I am not intending to be social, thank you. And I am not seeking a bride. Are you sure she is not husband hunting?"

Mrs Broadbent chuckled again. "Not our Bea. She has other plans."

I sighed, an exaggerated exhalation of relief, and we all laughed.

Beatrice's escape

Yorkshire 1870

Beatrice's Story

It began, for Beatrice, a month before the family's grand ball to celebrate her formal coming of age, as well as the dinner for her grandparents' wedding anniversary and her father's great business success. It was then that Aunt Alexandria swam into her ken.

"I am so sorry, my dear, but your father will explain." Beatrice's mother paused between strokes as she brushed Beatrice's hair. The maid, dismissed for privacy's sake, her mother had taken up the ornate tortoiseshell hairbrush and pampered Beatrice's hair with long slow strokes from the crown of her head to the ends above her waist. Beatrice, used to Ida's more staccato efforts, could have purred, and understood why her mother's Persian cat butted so insistently at her mother's hands until stroked.

"We can delay your birthday party and ball until the end of July. We must. Your father insists, and it is the only correct thing to do."

"I never knew, Mama, that I'd an aunt on father's side of the family, only uncles."

Beatrice's mother smiled at Beatrice's reflection and continued brushing.

Beatrice recognised the smile. She'd seen it frequently as a child, whenever she asked a question. "I suppose I don't, in truth, now have an aunt do I? But it is strange that I only learn about her when I must put off my party for her funeral."

"Your father will explain. I cannot. I never knew Alexandria."

There was a hint of more in her mother's voice. Beatrice tried coaxing, she'd learned to be good at coaxing. "But perhaps you might share what you heard? You know I'm old enough to hear family talk, and I can keep secrets."

Her mother laughed gently. "Well, you always were a good little mouse about not telling tales, I know I may trust you." She carefully placed the hairbrush, bristle side down, beside the matching looking glass and picked up Beatrice's carved ivory hair combs. "She went a little peculiar and broke off her engagement, a most respectable one your grandfather arranged. One of these women's nervous disorders, I believe your father called it." She deftly swept one comb through Beatrice's hair in a swift up and over stroke, lifting half of Beatrice's hair in a soft fold across her ear and to the top of her head. "I know she had the best of very expensive treatment, even those special operations, but she never really recovered, had to be kept quiet for the rest of her life. So sad."

Beatrice's mother repeated the hair gathering upsweep with the other comb, set it firmly in place, glanced in the mirror to check that the second comb sat level with the first. She adjusted the comb gently, her eyes scanning her daughter's face. "She lived with attendants near Ravenscar."

Beatrice's face sagged in amazement, her lips falling slightly apart. She saw her reflection in the mirror and hastily curved her mouth into a more becoming smile. "You mean she lived near our summer home and we never saw her?" She swivelled round on the dressing table stool to face her mother. Her mother turned away.

"Let your father explain, my dear. I cannot. Turn around so that I may fix your back hair. Thank you. Now, about your dress. We've decided against full mourning, we can do this because of your aunt's situation, so a dark pewter-grey would be becoming and permissible for you." She twisted the ribbons through Bea's hair. "Fortunate child to have such golden hair." She patted Bea's shoulder, raised a warning hand. "But we will have to be discreet. We can't give the gossips broth for scandal, you know, not now."

Beatrice bowed her head in acquiescence. She'd discover nothing more from her mother, but she would try to coax some answers from her father before dinner.

Her father, standing four square in his opulent study, smoking his cigarillos and flicking through the papers on his desk, was put out and terse.

"Your mother told you about your Aunt Alexandria. There is nothing else to say." He stopped moving papers to give her a most disconcerting look, even shook his finger at her. "But hear this. Alexandria refused to become engaged to a most suitable young man your grandfather chose for her and fell into a melancholic state. She had treatment and resided in an asylum for the rest of her life. That's what happens when a daughter is disobedient."

He glared at her once then returned to scanning his papers, lifting them from one pile, glancing at them, then sorting them left or right on to new piles as he continued to speak.

"Papa, why did we never meet her at Ravenscar?"

His answer, growled into his chest as he flung his papers aside, ostensibly looking for some special paper, she barely heard.

"I beg your pardon, Papa?" She moved to stand on his side of the desk, smiling up at him, using her specially cultivated, Papa-charming voice. Thank heavens for sisters, she thought as he checked and looked at her again. Watching them and Mama, copying them, actually heeding their advice for dealing with Papa, helped. Although she rather thought she had refined and polished her charm act to a greater perfection. "Papa?"

It failed. He strode to the fireplace, flung his cigarillo into the fire, strode back to her and stood so close she felt she must back away in order to breath. He towered above her, leaning into her face. "Because she was a damned disgrace." He didn't apologise for his language. "She was an overindulged child, a silly dreamy girl, a stupid disobedient young woman, and when our father found her a good match she refused it." He glared at Beatrice. "She refused a brilliant match for no reason at all. She had hysterics and wept herself into a melancholy, never to recover."

Beatrice quailed before his anger. Its intensity thrust at her, and she backed away. How could he? He really hated Alexandria, his own sister.

I'm sorry, Papa, so sorry," she stammered, catching at the back of the large leather wing chair.

"And so you should be, to question any decision I make on your behalf. I made that one to protect you. I have three daughters and I refused to allow any of you near the contaminating influence of my weak and silly sister." He flashed Beatrice one of his looks, the one used for dismissing unsatisfactory workers or servants, so full of scorn and vindictiveness that she felt flayed, only nerves left tingling over her bones. She had to grip the chair more tightly. She apologised again, with barely enough breath to stutter the words, but forcing herself to seem sweet and coaxing. "I'm so sorry, Papa, to awaken painful memories." She turned to flee, murmuring more apologetic words over her shoulder as she scurried to the door.

"You wait until I dismiss you, young lady."

Her feet halted. She willed them onwards without avail.

Her father advanced, grasped her shoulder.

She shuddered.

His grip on her shoulder, from which she flinched, was, in fact, firm, but not bruising. Bea quelled her instinct to tremble. It was Papa, he wouldn't hurt her. Would he?

"Painful?" her father articulated the word as though it was a mouthful of vile tasting medicine. "No, just expensive, needless expense, and me left to carry the burden, because I..." His voice stopped, he withheld the words, although they hovered in the small space between them.

Beatrice knew his favorite compliant, that of being the eldest and so held responsible. They heard it twice a day. She allowed two tears to fall, another accomplishment she had learned to deal with her father. She managed a quivering smile. "Oh, poor Papa."

"Hah!" he snorted, but seemed satisfied for he let her go, strode back to his desk and picked up another pile of papers.

Beatrice escaped and made her way to the old nursery, now being refurbished in preparation for the grandchildren her mother eagerly anticipated. She allowed herself a shiver and shake then tried to recover. Her father always had that effect on her. He did for her young brothers and still, so they said, her sisters. One obeyed Papa or...she didn't know what, but it would be terrible. One had to please Papa. She still felt shivery when the dinner gong bonged. Rather than face him again Beatrice joined her younger brothers in a school room supper, their old nurse welcoming her as a source of entertainment to keep the three boys quiet.

The following morning, Beatrice's young brothers, delighted with the delay to the adult celebrations, begged their mother to take them to Ravenscar for summer as usual. Bertie wheedled his mother shamelessly. "As I'm the only one away at school, Mama, and June is only exams and cricket, (which I'm still not allowed to play until my wrist heals,) you could take the tiddlers off to Ravenscar and I could come down after the exams." He smiled winningly. "I am top of the year, you know."

She did. They all did, Bertie's intelligence was a family boast. They called him the

professor already; his father had declared he would be, one day, at Cambridge. "It would be a pity to miss our holiday now the party and ball are postponed. The weather's so fine."

Whether Bertie put his brains to use furthering his wants, and planned his younger brothers' mischief or not, their prank stirred enough irritation for their father to wish them all away. They would never dare direct anything at him, but a little upsetting of the upper servants made enough ripples to reach him. The mud and mess annoyed their mother though, and she dealt severely with all the boys, a bread and butter tea and no supper. However she did broach, under Bertie's direction, the subject of an early departure to Ravenscar at a time when their father might consider them an irritation removed. To their joy he did. They were to leave the following day.

Beatrice, who had watched the building of the castle and moat in the servants' shrubbery, and even added a few useful design suggestions, allowed herself to be mildly amused and grateful to be removed from home. She discovered now that she was in two minds about her birthday ball and another London season. Frolicking on the beach, fossil hunting with the boys, sea bathing and fishing were pastimes she enjoyed, and she loved sculpting magnificent castles, giant dragons, and stout knights in the wet sand for them. There was so much scope for fluid forms when sand was wet.

"You, my dear," her mother said, "shall help me by leaving with them and allowing me a week to supervise this funeral and then our ball preparations without any other distractions." She patted Beatrice's cheek with soft plump fingers. "You've been a good girl and deserve a wonderful party. I want to make sure things are specially perfect for you." She hesitated, then closed her mouth firmly over any hovering words. Beatrice failed to coax more from her.

It was her father who gave it all away. Huffing over the bills at breakfast on the day of departure he humphed loudly, shot a look at his wife and addressed Beatrice. "Last time we'll be giving you a birthday ball, Beatrice. Thank the Lord. These bills are exorbitant."

Last time? Beatrice raised her head, porridge spoon suspended, and risked a look at her father.

He stared at her, then down the table at his wife. Beatrice's mother, two flashes of scarlet colouring her cheek bones, lowered her eyes to contemplate the muffin she was buttering.

Why was her mother flustered? Beatrice opened her mouth to speak, but her father forestalled her. "You haven't told her?" He almost snorted.

Beatrice carefully pressed her lips into a gentle smile. "A secret, Papa, and about me?" She coaxed a little more. "Would you be kind enough to tell me?"

"Certainly." Her father threw down his napkin, kicked back his chair and strode to the door. "In my study, immediately."

Her mother called out, "My dear, wouldn't it be..." then let her words die to a murmur when he aimed another glare at her as he closed the door with a definite click.

"Oh dear, your father is displeased, Beatrice. He has a birthday surprise for you. I wanted to prepare you as it is something you need to think about."

"Oh," Hope blossomed. She clattered her spoon into her porridge bowl and clutched her napkin, crumpling the starched damask. "Is it that

I may go to Anna's for the winter? Did you mention the university art classes?"

"No, my dear, certainly not. I have not been able to speak to your father about that and now…." She let the words vanish, and patted Beatrice's cheek. "Now hasten, your father is still apt to fret, your Aunt's funeral expenses have worried him."

Her father spared no words, softened nothing as her mother might. He looked her up and down and shook his head. "Women, my girl, need a firm hand if they're not to go hysterical on you. Started off with my daughters as I meant to go on. Your sisters were all pretty and pretty sensible. But I worry about you."

Beatrice opened her mouth to speak. Her father glowered.

"Let unstable ones like you have your heads and it'll be years of treatment and expensive care. I saw the same thing happening to your Aunt. And you," he scowled, "are too like your aunt in looks and ways."

Beatrice quailed. Unstable? Was she unstable?

"Your husband can have the making or treatment of you."

"Husband, Papa?"

But her father was in full flow, words rapidly fired, voice rising to a thundering shout. "How you've escaped I don't know. Where you've picked up these romantic notions I cannot tell. You always did read too much for a woman. Your brain can't stand it, how many times do I have to say that? I intend that you shall marry young Edlington. Refuse and I'll put you away like your aunt. That's your choice, Edlington or an asylum. There's an end to it. The engagement will be announced at your birthday party."

Beatrice gaped, unable to speak. Mr Edlington? Papa's young partner, and just like him. She'd only met him three or four times socially. He knew nothing of art apart from its value as an investment. He'd looked her up and down as though she were a thing, not a person, and said he was glad she did not prattle.

She stuttered a "But Papa…."

"Go and speak to your mother."

Beatrice fled.

Was this how it had been for her sisters? Surely not. There had been much socialising with neighbours and visitors and there had been a large group of young people of an age with her sisters. They had married young men they knew. She had no one in the area of her age and, to her Mama's surprise, she had not formed an attachment during her first or subsequent season.

"Too like Shakespeare's Beatrice," her brother-in-law, Anna's husband, had told her kindly. "If you want a husband, sweeten your remarks, Bea, or don't make them. You're too clever and you frighten young men."

She had laughed that off, but now she wept.

- · • - · - —

Leaving with her brothers the next day Beatrice managed not to panic or openly rebel. She told her Mama she felt confused. She told her Papa nothing, simply quaked as he roared. She told herself there must be an escape if only she could think of one.

Leaving her brothers, Nurse and the nursery maids to unpack and settle in, Beatrice took to the beach. The breeze blew off the sea, the sun shone fitfully and the day could not decide whether to be a brisk summer one or a mild spring day. Beatrice walked and walked. At the end of the bay, she decided. There was no choice. What her life might have been she knew. What it had become she felt with every particle of herself as unbearable. Marriage to a man she barely knew, who was a younger version of Papa? Never! No, she had hoped for escape, somewhere she could live without fear. Now there was no hope. Her life was not hers. Marriage to that man or her father would shut her away like he had his sister. She had no choices at all. There! Decision made.

She stood at waves' edge staring at the white froth which surged to chill her bare toes. The shriek of a lone gull hovering over the beach almost drowned out the voice of her brothers calling "Bea, Beatrice!" Should she or shouldn't she? Would she or wouldn't she?

She ran along the sea's edge, her toes in the froth, the gull gliding alongside, screaming for bread. Two more gulls slid into its slipstream, squawking. Now she couldn't possibly hear anyone else, no one could cry 'Stop.' What she'd dared to believe might happen had vanished under the avalanche of Papa's words, under his power to rule her life. Never the chance to be an artist, to travel, to see all those glorious paintings, to learn what she might do. A choice that was no choice. Either the foul Edlington or be shut up in some private Bedlam. She'd had twenty years of her father's rule, to leave it only for Edlington's regulations and restrictions was not to be borne.

"May God forgive you, Stanley Herbert Chayle, for your cruelty to my aunt Alexandria, your own sister, and to your own children. Nevermore will you be my father. May you rot in hell."

She cursed her father again, let her feet rush her into the waves, but her brothers arrived, yelling with excitement. They charged into the waves before Beatrice reached knee deep water. To them it was a game and they caught her arms to swing her around..

"Jump this one, Bea."

"Catch me, Bea."

"Hoo, hoo. Nurse will be cross. You've soaked your dress."

In a tangle of enthusiastic brothers, who hustled Beatrice and rushed her onto the beach and along the shore, she was prevented from dashing into the deeper water. Her brothers grasped her hands and dress and hopped or jumped her over the breaking crests with them as they headed back to the steep walkway and the house on the cliff tops. With more shouts, laughter and boyish noise they tugged her up the path.

Beatrice gave in, but Bertie packed his younger brothers off in a race to Nurse and delayed her by catching her elbow. "I have a letter for you from Mama."

Beatrice raised her eyebrows as she attempted to wring sea water from her petticoats and skirt. "Mama? Has Papa sanctioned it?"

Bertie punched her lightly on the arm. "Would Mama dare to write without his permission." He grinned. "I believe she did add a sentence or two after Papa had seen and approved. Are you still in a fuss about this engagement?"

Beatrice hoped she looked as bleak as she felt. "Yes. He's another Papa and I have no respectful or affectionate feelings for him."

Her brother grimaced. "You have to marry, you know, if you hope to escape."

"But not to him, never to him." Beatrice paused, breathed in the good sea air then shrugged. "My sisters found decent men. Why can't I?"

"From what I heard," Bertie grinned at her amazed expression. "From eavesdropping, naturally, you silly Bea, I learned you're safe for a year or more." He handed over an envelope, only slightly damp. "Papa dare not countermand this. You've been ordered to attend the Northrops, in particular, cousin Charis."

"But they are going to India."

"So are you."

Sailing on the Ganges

India 1872

Bryce Ackerman

For my delight and education, according to Mrs Broadbent, whose sense of humour I tickled, we travelled from Calcutta by steamship on the part of the great Ganges river called the Hoogli river and then onto the main Ganges river as far as a place called Kanpur. From there we travelled by what my companions called dak, the government travel stations. It would be a journey of some five weeks or more on the river and then several days' length on the road. Time for reflection, and the sorting out of some of the tangle of emotions raging within my head and heart. And, as Sir Cuthbert reminded me, I had to wait for that last packet of information arriving on the next ship.

"The train is faster but you, Mr Ackerman, need to learn to appreciate India." Ada Broadbent tutted and wagged a finger at me. "You cannot continue to blame this wonderful country for your personal distress."

I bloody well could, but remembered the rule about silence keeping friendships golden and smiled at her.

She slapped my hand. "I know that superior smile. We will explore mosques and temples, ancient ruins and stroll through villages and you will change your mind." She cocked her head like a little Jenny wren then she gently clasped my large hand between her small pudgy ones. "I do not know what drives you, but you are a rational young man. Do not forget to think rationally."

Ada Broadbent rightly called me troubled in spirit, gently inviting confidences I could not give. There were no public words to speak for what troubled me. I paced the ship's deck, or exercised vigorously, claiming that I hoped to make a place on our local cricket team when I returned.

I say ship. It was rather a flat bottomed river boat such as they use on the broad rivers in America. We had a well-trained native crew, good natured, smiling and obliging, but no other passengers apart from Sir Cuthbert's clerical staff. Apparently he had exercised his government powers and requisitioned the boat, legitimately I suppose, because whenever we stopped to refuel his clerks set up a table under a tree, usually in the middle of the village, and Sir Cuthbert dealt with all sorts of minor problems which had troubled the village population. Major ones were written down and their records sent back to Calcutta.

"For someone else to deal with," said he with a grin. "We need records to solve these."

India became real for me when I first stopped averting my eyes whenever we passed a ghat. These broad and wide steps down to the river could be stone, or concrete or hand dug out of the soil of the bank, and were used by the whole community as a bathing place, a laundry, a children's play area, a ceremonial place, and, it seemed, a meeting place. Their fishing boats were drawn up near the ghat, either in the water or on the river bank.

"Look at the women," Mrs Broadbent commanded one morning. "See how they wash so carefully, protecting their privacy behind their saris?" she nudged me with a dimpled elbow and chuckled at my blushes. "They are not indecent, they are modest."

They were beautiful too with all that long black hair and dark, almond shaped eyes. If they felt our boat was too near the shore they would retreat, hiding their faces behind their bright stoles or edge of their saris.

None of them appeared obese, rather lithe and slender like a graceful reed.

"All that laundry work," she added when I mentioned that. "And when do you ever see our British poor as clean in body or clothing?"

But this was not Great Britain and the climate was warmer. Still I was not going argue, her point had been made. The ghats made a fine picturesque scene when I allowed myself to view them with a traveller's curiosity. There were things to see and note and I should be less of a sore headed bear and more of an intelligent human taking in a traveller's experience many of my friends and colleagues envied me having. I could not give back to Aimée, Sylvia, Alice, all those other young ladies, what they had lost. I must stop feeling guilty for not protecting Aimée and concentrate on giving them what scraps of justice I could. I vowed to keep a diary from then on and note those peculiarly Indian sights which my family might enjoy. Mrs Broadbent knew some Indian history and her steward was an intelligent and educated Indian who liked to answer questions.

"Mrs Broadbent, I apologise for being a moody and morose guest." I bowed with my hand over my heart. "I promise to reform, immediately."

She burst out laughing and reached up to pat my cheek. "Good," she said.

Alice's Fate

Surrey 1870

Alice's Story

Alice, bewildered, found herself reclining on the dining room window seat, the raised pattern on the thick brocade curtain scratching her arm, a hint of dust filling her nose. Her mother sat beside her, weeping and stroking her hair. Alice tried to rest her head in her mother's lap, and think.

What had happened? Papa had insisted she come to breakfast although she didn't feel well. Her maid, Nell, had brought her downstairs, assisted her through the door. She'd felt her stomach heave at the sour smell of the kippered herrings her father so enjoyed. Papa came to escort her and…no, she couldn't remember what happened after that.

Why were her sisters ranked in front of her like a wall so that she could only see Papa's head and hear his anger? Alice couldn't see round them but she could see her sisters held hands secretly, behind their backs, clutching each other. They protected Alice like a barricade with their bodies and their voices.

"It was those officers."

"Papa, we found her, in the summer house, after they'd left us."

"They tricked us, strolled us round the garden leaving Alice asleep in one of the chairs."

Alice watched as her father grew tall, inflating himself with an indrawn breath and a scowl, his face flushing from neck to forehead. "Impossible, those young officers and gentlemen? Never! Families like theirs do not behave like animals."

Alice understood why he felt so strongly. He'd been pleased, almost excited, about the officers' visits. "Such politeness to me, such charm of manner," he'd said. He'd told mother and her sisters over breakfast that the visits were a sign of the family's acceptance into the county set, those distant aristocrats whose society he craved to be part of. He asked the visitors to return and they had, daily. Alice knew how important it was to her father. The boys were too young to understand what the visits meant but Alice did, as did her sisters. Father wanted so much to be part of the social set that existed in the community.

"It isn't enough to own the right house, have an impressive garden, the right sort of servants, and excellent horses we can have all that, but…" Papa would say. It was that but, Alice'd discovered, a large but…Papa was a lawyer, most highly qualified and with the best firm but…that but again…he was therefore a professional man thus not a true gentleman. Alice's sisters had carefully explained it to her.

"If you were with her how could these officers have touched her?" Papa's voice dripped with contempt and disdain. "You are hiding something. What is it?"

"Oh no, Papa." Three voices crisscrossing, even the usually scared-into-silence Letitia exclaimed "No, we can only tell you what we know." Alice saw her sisters' clasped hands tighten and whiten.

"They put something in her tea, Papa." That was Eleanor, she always had been brave enough to stand against their father in his furies if Alice needed protection.

"And where were you, Annabelle, their mother, their protector?"

Alice felt her mother struggle to stop her tears and speak. Poor Mama, her family owned a coastal shipping company carrying coal and wood. That, Alice's sisters carefully explained, was Trade and not to be mentioned, for, whilst her money made the family wealthy, it kept them not quite gentry, to father's annoyance, and definitely not aristocracy.

"We had problems in the nursery, my dear, ear ache. The boys needed special attention. The girls…"

"Young ladies," Papa corrected.

Alice felt her mother tremble. "Yes, yes…but our daughters were together in their own home and had Martha as chaperone as they always do when any young men call."

Father snarled something, twisted round and pounced on Nell. "Who did you let in to do this to my daughter?" He yanked Nell round so she had to face him. "Don't try running away. I'll have you wherever you go. Which of the village men paid you?"

Nell never lacked spunk. Alice, pushing herself into a sitting position, supported by her mother, watched as Nell tried to twist free. Her country accent reappeared and she began to cry. "I don't do nuthing bad. I've alway bin good to Miss Alice." She squirmed round to look at Alice. "I've tried to keep 'er safe. Tried to get shift of it afore she knew what'ud happened."

"Henry, Henry, please. Nell cannot have…."

What had Nell said? What did she mean? Alice frowned, trying to understand.

"Who then?" Papa snarled, shaking Nell. He flung her towards the door. "Out, you…you evil…shameless animal There'll be no references for you. I'll see no one will employ you again."

Alice heard her mother's gasp.

"As for you, you who were my most beautiful daughter…"

Mama stiffened and stifled her sobs. Alice felt her embrace become a clutch. She had warned Alice to be careful of young men because she was growing into a beauty. Papa, Mama said, dreamed of a county marriage for each of his daughters, but Alice knew she could be the one to achieve this. All the aunts and godmothers declared her a classic beauty. She'd been shy of her developed bosom at only fourteen, her sisters had been older, and, yes, young men gazed after her. Mama had cautioned her that she must never be without her sisters in the house or garden whenever visitors came, especially young men.

"Avoid the summer house and the swing seats," Mama cautioned and she did until a persistent young officer and his friends wanted to take tea in the summer house.

Father, bellowing, maddened, shoved her sisters aside, dragging poor Nell with him, towered over Alice, shaking Nell savagely. "Look what you've done to my daughter," he bawled.

Nell screamed and kicked out. "You ask her sisters," she cried. "They know all about it. And...and..." she was sobbing now, slid out of Father's grip to sink on her knees besides Alice, "my poor Miss Alice knows naught o' babies. 'Tweren't her fault."

Babies? Alice hid her head on her mother's shoulder, trying to remember what had happened, and wishing she didn't feel so sick. Meanwhile her father ranted and raged, raising his fists to heaven and actually swearing. "Damn you all. We have never been ostentatious. We have good taste and good manners. We did not push ourselves on others, nor presume. We spend summer here in Sussex and winter in London. All very proper, and just when we are proving acceptable, with visits from real society, my slut of a daughter ruins it by indecent behaviour."

Alice's sisters struggled to explain what had happened, words tumbled, spilling out in their distress. "It was those officers, Papa."

Alice listened to the words and heard again Martha rattling down the gravel path with the tea trolley, followed by a footman the heavy tea kettle and a stand. It was the summer house, she remembered and "Mama allows us," Caroline had whispered in her ear, "but we must not separate."

As Alice's sisters struggled to placate Papa a memory of handsome young men in the summer house returned. Honourables or something like.

"Splendid tea," the Honourable Francis had cried, and there were fellow officers too, four was it or five?

"It was Cook's best afternoon tea," Alice meant to reassure her mother, "with several sorts of little cakes, tiny biscuits and plates and plates of ribbon sandwiches, all in pretty colours."

Mama shushed her.

"Papa, Papa, oh please listen." That was Caroline again.

Alice moistened her lips and spoke. "Papa it was...The Honourables attended me. They brought my tea and added sugar, kept stirring in far too much."

"What is wrong with being polite, you stupid ignorant girl?"

Alice struggled to frame words. "It tasted...the tea tasted...."

He snorted again. "Rubbish!"

But Alice remembered how the Honourable Francis was most attentive, how her tea cup was filled, sugared and stirred each time by him alone.

Eleanor bravely tried to explain. "But Alice fell asleep, Papa. We were playing 'I Spy', and..."

Alice saw her sisters swop frightened glances. Eleanor moistened her lips and swallowed before continuing.

"The other officers persuaded us to leave Alice and stroll in the garden."

Alice shivered, Martha had gone. That was it, but of course we four girls – young ladies I mean – we could chaperone each other. And who was leaning over me? Smelling of Pears soap and Bay Rum hair oil. Him. Mister David St. John Worrell.

"Then how," roared Papa, "could any one of those gentlemen harm Alice?"

Alice heard Nell's voice crossing her sisters' voices in a jumble of words. Something about the way they clung to each other, the way Nell stood in front of them, and the fury in her father's face brought the summer house scene back to her mind. Her face'd felt heavy, her mouth hadn't worked. She'd tried to call to her sisters, raised her head a little to look for them. All she heard was men's low laughter and was it one of the puppies? There was whimpering and a sob?

Alice struggled to speak. If only she didn't feel so sick. Her mother clutched her tightly again.

"Alice could go to my sister, she would care for her and say nothing. The baby could be adopted by some family in the village. Or there are church charities would look after it in a city somewhere else."

"Baby?" Alice blurted out the word, her voice a squeak.

"Yes, you stupid little slut, you..."

"Henry, no...."

"But I'm not a married lady." Alice held her head, rubbing her temples to clear the confused thoughts. How could she have a baby? What had happened in the summer house?

She remembered her sisters sobbing. She knew they were crying for she'd felt drops on her cheeks.

"Three of them, the animals. At least we only had one abuse us."

"Shush, say nothing. Don't tell her. She might talk."

"No, she won't remember. They said they'd given her something to make her sleep." They'd pulled her clothes straight as they whispered to each other.

"We must sit with her until she can walk." Her hands were gently stroked.

"What can we say to Papa?"

"We cannot. They told us. Who will believe us when they deny it or call us sluts and whores who invited their attentions."

"God forgive them for I curse them. How could they harm Alice?"

Had those men given her a baby? How? "I'm not married," she repeated.

"No, you soiled baggage, nor will you be now," her father raged. "You have disgraced our family..."

Nell interrupted. "It weren't her fault, sir, you let me and Miss Alice go somewhere quiet and no one'll ever know. I'll help find the poor mite a home and I won't talk, sir."

"No you won't...."

"But I will, sir, if you don't support my poor Miss Alice and keep her hid away." Nell grasped her hand and smiled at Alice. "You'll be fine with me, Miss."

"You dare…you…you conniving…you think you'll get money out of me! An income from me to keep you and that slut and her bastard?"

"Henry please. Henry don't…."

"Out, both of you. I never want to see you again."

Alice found herself being dragged by one arm as her father also grasped Nell by the elbow. He hauled and pulled them into the hall and to the front door. Horrified servants watched as he commanded the door to be opened.

"Papa, please…don't…you're hurting me." Alice begged.

Her father snarled like some savage beast and thrust both of them through the door and onto the gravel drive.

"You're no longer my child. I never want to see you again. Get away from here and never return." He slammed the heavy door and the lock clicked closed.

Alice raised her face from the gravel and wept.

A retreat in the hills

India 1872

Sir Cuthbert, by virtue of his magistrate's position, was able to secure escorts for us of local police, and watchmen once we left the security of river travel. These barkandaz and chaukidars changed at each police station and, as government employees, need not be paid, although we did give them a few coins as a thank you. Using the government dak system with its secure bungalows for overnight rests, Sir Cuthbert and Mrs Broadbent, assured me, would ensure us a pleasant and safe journey. It did.

We travelled lightly by the usual government official standards. Apart from the police and watchmen, there were only two women servants, who were a general servant and a lady's maid for Mrs Broadbent, a man servant as a valet for Sir Cuthbert and one for me. Grooms, cooks, porters, any temporary servants, buddlis Ada Broadbent called them, we needed were hired on the way by their most efficient Indian sircar, a position which combined the duties of a butler and steward. He was also responsible for preventing the dak cooks serving us the eternal custel brun, a sort of Indian version of caramel custard. It was a standard of all the dak bobajis, resident cooks, according to Mrs Broadbent and very few could do it well.

Mrs Broadbent declared their steward, the sircar, to be exceptional. This proud gentleman could have outfaced any English butler in both demeanour and intelligence; his ability to organise native servants, no matter their cast or creed, was phenomenal. An unusual native, but then the Broadbents were not of the government pattern either. Mrs

Broadbent might look a regular memsahib, dumpy, rounded and smugly comfortable, but for all her expensive clothes she was a middle aged lady with no pretensions to beauty, and she didn't care. She rode well, remained unfussed about her garments and appearance, and travelled with enthusiasm. She had a fondness for elephants which I shared. Her husband despised manly pursuits, loathing sports, a thing unheard of in the Indian service. He slumped on his horse with all the skill and elegance of a sack of potatoes. I felt for the animal, but it was a stolid brute, unlike the lively part Arabs his wife and I rode.

There was cooler air, exotic scents and vivid greenery enough in the hills. Deep ravines full of rhododendron, oaks on the slopes and myriad brilliant wild flowers which Mrs Broadbent promised to name for me. Insects, butterflies, amazing birds, there was so much to see in this wilder part of India, and all so un-British, nor was there anywhere remotely like it in Europe. The scents and smells, the noises, the vibrant colours stridently demanded attention. It made my unaccustomed eyes ache, my head reel, but I forgot revenge and justice for a while to marvel at this so different world.

Our arrival in Dholpore, the town high in the hills, came as a shock. I hadn't realised how much of an army garrison it had become, cursed soldiers everywhere. I knew the government had built a hospital for the army sick but it seemed as though the military had taken over a good half of the town.

"We may well find your men here," Sir Cuthbert murmured as we left our horses at the livery stables.

I devoutly hoped so, and wouldn't they know it when I found them. I'd promised Aimée I would make them pay.

The air felt cold after Calcutta, despite the actual temperature being warmer than a British summer day, and the usual shoulder to shoulder crowds came in groups with spacious gaps between. That pleased me. No English gentleman liked to shoulder, shove or push his way through, especially when women formed part of the crowd. I wanted no social life, just quiet to sooth and calm my soul, and my hosts' bungalow suited me, sited as it was in a secluded valley away from the main township. The hills around were dotted with similar British retreats.

I sat out, that first night, on the verandah in the cool of the evening. Dusk lasted a short while then darkness wrapped round the hills like a thick velvet cloak. The orchestra of jackals yelping and insects stridulating in various keys made for an unusual musical background and I barely had time to reread Aimée's letter, wish for all that might have been, and try to be glad she was safe.

Aimée fights back

"Aimée, my dear. You cannot go into mourning because your fiancé is overseas. Come, your ring protects you from unwanted attentions. And these are distinguished guests."

My papa was nothing if not punctilious about our duties to society in our Yorkshire village, but I did not wish to be social. I wished for my beloved Bryce to be here. He'd gone to Vienna and then Venice. Three whole months without him, and he in Venice. I longed for Venice, the city in the sea. He'd promised me a honeymoon in Paris, but I begged for Venice.

"What, no shopping for extravagant hats or Worth gowns?" dear Bryce teased me. "No rushing to spend my annual bonus?" He grasped me round the waist, swung me about and most improperly kissed me on the mouth. Naturally, I most improperly kissed him back, and some more.

"Venice it shall be. Romantic evenings punting along the canals in a gondola and…" he pressed me close.

"Bryce…no." He was the best of men, but passionate. "Gently, my love. We have only to wait until June."

He gusted a hot emotional sigh in my face and stepped back. "You would bewitch any man. You have ensorcelled me. Let us go inside and find a sister or brother to chaperone and restrain us." He took my hand and we began to walk to the house. We had not managed even two steps before he stopped and snatched me into a hungry embrace. "It's hard to wait, my love."

Didn't I know it. My Papa and Mama had simply no notion of the hot torrent of desire Bryce stirred within me. I was their sensible poppet, Bryce Ackerman, a civil and gentle man. They allowed us free range in the gardens, with all its nooks and hideaways, and it took all my self-control, along with Bryce's self-discipline, to restrain from the ultimate act of love.

"We will allow you a few stolen kisses in the garden," my Mama said, but she didn't understand with what difficulty we controlled ourselves.

Bryce's touch brought up goose bumps. His large hand engulfing mine, his thumb secretly caressing my palm, melted my limbs so that I would turn and fall into his arms. His little nuzzling kisses around my neck and throat made me quiver. When his hands slid down to caress my 'little rump', as he fondly called my derrière, and he pressed me close so that I could feel him growing as he undid my buttons, with my help, to kiss my breasts, well, all was nearly lost. I wanted him as much as he wanted me.

As the eldest, with a season at a French finishing school, little brothers, a French companion, and a Papa and Mama who loved fine horses and bred them, I'd a better idea of matters sexual than many of my girl-friends, but I didn't understand the overwhelming physical feelings which swept one away as passionately as the spiritual feelings of love. And I thanked God that my Bryce was a good, Godly man who wanted a solemn ceremony and God's blessing on our union. We managed our physical passions with a shaky command that last evening, saying goodbye.

"In June," he said, sighing gustily, nibbling my ear. "And we will have three months of loving in Venice and years ever after."

"What about little ones?" I dared to ask. I was not sure about babies yet.

He laughed. "No children for at least two years. Only you and me, my love." And he promised he could prevent babies until I wanted them. Oh, I loved him so, and now I wouldn't see him for weeks.

"Come, my dear. You can control your young sisters and aid your Mama." Papa held the door open and I had to leave our snug morning room for the drawing room.

Our visitors came from the great house, as we locals called the family estate of Seamere. Held and run by an old lady, who was last of the old Anglo-Saxon Seamere family, she had never bothered to be social with us before. Lady Honoria's reputation for being an overbearing harridan she deserved. We knew.

She had coveted a racehorse my Mama and Papa had worked many years to breed, a thoroughbred foal of promise. She drove into our stable yard in her smart barouche with extra grooms in tow. Had them opening the stable doors before the frantic stable boy brought my Papa and Mama scrambling to the stables. She stood admiring the colt and spoke over her shoulder, words flung at my parents. "Yes, he is promising. I compliment you. My man of business will see you in the morning." She stood aside. "Lead him out," she ordered her grooms.

My father, always polite, gestured her grooms away and told our grooms to hold the colt. "He is not for sale. We are racing him ourselves." He did not roar nor did he quaver.

He was ignored.

There might well have been a fight between the grooms if I had not led my brothers and sisters into the colt's box and we made a fuss of petting him and thus moved between the foal and her ladyship's grooms.

Our men stood firm and Mama and Papa asked her ladyship to leave. She finally removed herself in a fury, declaring she would have the colt.

Papa and the grooms organised a security watch and new gates and doors with locks. We needed them, but had no proof of the wrong doer. Eventually her ladyship sent her man of business, who made a miserly offer for the horse. He left without a sale, having been told a vastly inflated price Papa might possibly accept.

Since then there had been ice between us, a frigid silence in the street and no acknowledgement whenever Lady Seamere attended our village church. So why these visits?

"I don't understand why they come, but suspect mischief, Papa."

"It is not our wish to be behind in welcoming the officers of such a fine regiment, especially as they are welcomed by our neighbours. After all, my dear, young Somerville is perhaps here on a peace making visit on behalf of his Aunt."

"Oh, Papa!"

Sometimes I wished for Bryce's parents who were people one could talk to and discuss important things with. One was even permitted to disagree. I needed to talk out my fears of these visitors. I believed their visits might be leading to some form of payback, a retaliation for refusing to let her ladyship have our thoroughbred.

As if he could read my thoughts Papa stopped my leaving the room by resting his hand on my shoulder. He smiled down at me. "I have thought of our horses and they are protected with extra men from the farm."

And so Monday proceeded to Tuesday and on to Thursday with regular morning calls and yes, the young officers did have horses in mind, but only to purchase two good hacks and arrange the breeding of a special thoroughbred mare to Papa's best stallion.

Once that was in the open we relaxed, became comfortable again. The officers bade us farewell on the Thursday visit, arranged for their grooms to fetch the horses the following week and send the mare when it was her time. Life could return to normal.

Mama celebrated Friday's freedom by taking the carriage to town and freed me by including my younger sisters for a day of pleasure, shopping for new summer gowns and hats. My brothers and father rode off to a luncheon and archery contest in a neighbouring village. I rejoiced and took Bryce's letters, Shakespeare's sonnets and a picnic luncheon to the morning room where a fire burned and crackled, making the pale February sun seem almost warm. Curled up in the cushioned winged armchair, feet tucked up under my skirts, I thought of toasting crumpets and roasting chestnuts, but Bryce's letter of yesterday claimed my attention. He wrote so well of the coffee houses, the incredible cakes, Viennese music, art museums, and his hope of seeing the famous white stallions at the Spanish Riding School, if his aristocratic host could inveigle an invitation.

The door opened. I looked up, no one had knocked, the servants would be enjoying a quiet lunch. Perhaps Mama had returned early.

In strolled the two young officers, the plain misters, Ian Somerville and John Fitzgerald, along with an officer, an older man I had not met before. They wore mufti not their dress uniforms.

"They're not here, Major," Somerville said.

I hastily untucked my feet, slid them to the floor and rose. "Pardon me, sirs?"

The major, quite at ease, scanned the room carefully. "Where are your sisters?"

I felt a prickling of unease. "Please excuse me, and I'll find my Mama and sisters." I made for the door but Mister Somerville, standing beside the door, leant across me and barred the door with his arm.

"Please allow me to pass."

His smile looked more an ogle, a smutty demeaning expression. "Where are your sisters?"

I turned and faced the major. "This is my home. How dare you allow your men to behave with such manners."

"We know," he replied, strolling towards me," that your Mother goes into town most Fridays. We watched the carriage leave this morning."

"Then you will know where my sisters are." I darted forward and grabbed the door handle. I turned it but tugged in vain. Mister Fitzgerald propped his back against the door.

"How dare you, sir! Back off and permit me to leave the room."

He sneered, looking down at me from his lanky height.

Giving way to fear was useless. I doubted that screams and hysterics would be heard beyond the baize door that led down the long passage to the kitchens, instead I dashed for the bell pull.

The major was there before me. "Oh no, my pretty bird." He grasped my wrists and yanked me towards the sofa. "Come, sit, I need you." He thrust me down so hard I bounced on the cushions and nearly fell.

"Lock the door, Fitz."

Fitz leapt to obey. Both young officers advanced and stared down at me.

"We have a little time," the major announced. "I had hoped to show you some methods of obtaining the best results with these middle class, school room misses, these nobodies who claim to be gentry. The young sisters are not here, but as we have this ripe wench, this nobody's daughter, I shall show you how to subjugate a young woman and make her react as you want."

I sat bolt upright and my mouth opened in amazement. Then offended disgust gave way to bewildered terror. This was my home, how could anything happen to me in my Mama's snug morning room?

"How dare you, sir. This is my home. I want nothing to do with you or these men. Leave immediately."

It was as if I had never spoken.

"If you, Fitz and you, Vill, hold her arms I will show you how to proceed. Try always to be where you need not forcibly silence the trollop. Here we safe. The servants are far enough off, taking it easy with the family out, and won't hear cries or screams."

The officers moved behind the sofa and grabbed my upper arms.

"Don't touch me." I tried to wriggle free but their hands gripped like manacles and I found myself lifted onto my feet. Kicking out hurt me more than the major for he blocked me in against the sofa. I opened my mouth to yell and a large hand slapped across it.

"Removing clothes should be done without damaging them." The Major began to unbutton my bodice. "Note how you make it a sexual act, caressing and stroking as you slowly unfasten each button."

I bit the hand covering my mouth. "Sutton!" I shrieked in the hope that our manservant might be in the main house. One officer pressed his hands across my mouth, the other grasped me by the throat.

"Quiet, you strumpet. Shut her mouth with this."

Vill bent over me, tied on the handkerchief as a gag all the time scowling into my face. Then he squeezed my throat with his hand and choked me until daylight became dancing lights, then blackness.

Closing in

India 1872

Dholpore

The military headquarters – the sadar

No home leave this year. The major swore again, his babu, out fetching messages, was not present to be shocked by sahib's language, not that the sahib cared. His office smelled musty, the air he breathed was stale, second hand. He felt choked; he wanted to go home. He strolled to the window and tried to open it. A fierce yank and up it came. A breath of a breeze touched his cheek. Below a rickshaw boy was screeching "Bajke bajao, khabadar" at the people in his way. The breeze brought the scents of India when he wanted the scents of England, of the lime trees in the avenue on the family estate now his. He might sell out, reap some useful cash for his commission. Yet he could not, not in the situation he found himself.

He cursed again. *Why did I marry an Anglo-Indian, knowing what the reaction would be at home? Oh yes, I did know, but that meant nothing to a younger brother. My family connections would make all right. Now I am the last male Wulfsige and we are the aristocracy who rule our county.*

He scowled, remembering. *All should have acknowledged my wife, the princess. I forced my parents into accepting my wife.* He laughed out loud. He'd thought he'd been so clever. *By making our wedding a great Indian affair, a Christian church wedding reported in all the newspapers at home. My family's acceptance of my wife should have meant all recognised her.*

He swore again, threatening further vengeance on those who'd opposed him by refusing to accept his wife. *How dared they, those county*

~ 71 ~

gentry, those middle class upstarts, lawyers, doctors and merchants. They had spoken as one.

'Anglo-Indian?' *Always the question.*

'A Princess.'

'But Anglo-Indian.' *Their condemnation.*

'Wealthy and a maharajah's daughter.'

'But Anglo-Indian. Mixed blood of the worst sort.' *Their decision.*

And so my wife was shunned in England.

I should have chosen a lesser Indian woman, one I could marry by their Indian laws and leave behind when I returned home with the regiment, but Kalindi had money, a fortune in jewels and gold, and Indian ways. She knew how to please a husband sexually. She fed my appetite. The thought of sex with some scared, inexperienced English girl, trying to teach her to enjoy what I wanted plenty of every day, is repugnant. My Kalindi is a warm blooded, sensual girl eager to please. Or she was until we spent that leave in England and she felt their contempt and heard what the family planned to do with our sons. And there is the rub. I cannot have half breed sons brought up here or at home.

He slammed his fist into the window frame, rattling the panes. *Damn them all to hell. I want to go home.*

The clerk returned, bowed. "Message, sahib," he bowed again. "From the visiting government man, sahib."

"Well?" He extended his hand for the note.

"Mr Northrop, he comes tomorrow morning." The clerk bowed again, cautiously handing over the sealed note.

The major took it briskly in his right hand and indicated, with his left, the pile of files on his desk. "Deliver these, and return with requisition files. When that's done you can clear off for tiffin."

"Sahib." A deep bow and the clerk scuttled away.

Bloody Northrop. Blasted man, sent to inspect by the government. He'd expect a decent luncheon in the mess. Well, he could go to the Club. We can't let him see too much and the officer's mess at mealtimes will bring on his parliamentary puritanism. He'd even brought his wife and son. Nice piece of pussy, that one, oozed sexuality, but she'd spurned him when he'd moved in on her. Told her husband too, the bitch, the wheedling whining bitch. She'd outshone my princess, my jewel of a wife, put her in the shade by her perfect Englishness. My wife is a person of beauty, of grace and light, yet that commonplace little English whore took her high place in precedence at the Club. Why isn't she down in Calcutta or Chandrapore, amongst the common throng where she belongs?

The major stalked back to the window and shut out the street noises with a bang that vibrated the glass. Why had the Northrops come to the hills and spoilt all his plans?

Perfect mother, perfect English lady, all charm and sweetness, beloved of all. How dare she come here? How dare she bring her son?

Oh, yes, she would have a son. A son, when I have none. We have no child yet, four years married and no child. My family call for an heir. I need an heir. We must have a son. Her son is such a perfect little specimen of English manhood, blond hair, blue eyes, fair white skin. His pet name is Felix, his father's Latin joke. How superior they think they are. How they shun the social round as though they are above our norms of society. Yet my family has a far better pedigree. We are of ancient lineage not they. And she is a no-one, a doctor's daughter. I watch her. If I see just one curl of a lip, one flip or swish away of skirts from me and mine then she will regret it for the rest of her life.

The major opened the note and snorted. He straightened his spine and marched out. *So Northrop wanted to use the officers' mess for a private meeting with all officers did he? Hah!*

"I'm out to lunch," he announced to the air as he clattered down the stairs.

Trouble at the military headquarters

Dholpore 1872

The military headquarters – the sadar

The office door burst open. "For God's sake, what have you done?"

The major, readying himself to leave the office early for a bout with the foils at the gymnasium, looked his surprise, even quirked an eyebrow. "Now what are you doing here?"

Trust Richard to spoil the day. He does fly into a pelter for no good reason.

"What did you set your young officers to do when home on leave?" The captain slapped the flat of his palms upon the desk. "I know you and your wife stayed with your family on your estate, but there is talk of a major involved in the scandal. What the bloody hell have you done this time?"

"Well, thankfully my office is empty. My babu is out and the other clerks dare not come near me, but lower your voice please and address your superior officer correctly." The major settled himself back in his chair.

"Yes, sir."

"I don't like that tone either, Richard."

The captain leaned over the desk, looming into the major's face. "My apologies, sir! I am concerned for us all." He hissed the words. "They've not only arrested them. They've been cashiered. It's all over the officers' mess. Cricklehurst brought the news back with him from Calcutta."

"What? Who? Ah, that's impossible."

Richard shook his head. "What have you done?"

The major began to have an inkling of what set Richard in such a stew. *Good Lord. The man was sweating in fear.* "Who and why?"

"The junior officers in our sister regiment. They've been drummed out and actually sent home."

"Who? On what grounds? Who dares speak out?"

"There's a man from England brought legal documents. He's official, with government backing. Several families sent him. He's had two junior officers disgraced, there's talk of trials in England, and now he's hunting officers in our regiment. There's a list of names and reports of rape, rape of school room misses, young girls drugged for God's sake, and respectable young ladies violated." The captain pounded the desk again. "What in God's name did you get up to? The top brass are appalled but cannot stop him. It's all to be hushed up here, but two have been taken to London for trial. The disgrace to our regiment will ruin us all. Our lads might also have to stand trial in England." He paused and heaved a great breath. "What have you done?"

"And who is this man?"

"Is that all you can say? I don't know…not an officer…some middle class moralist possibly. Bloody missionary or Quaker most like. He has evidence, documents, statements and intends to extract revenge. They say his own fiancée was involved."

"He won't get far if he comes here. No under-bred moralist can touch us."

"For God's sake, man. Your arrogance will undo us all. It might already have done so. He's coming here with the magistrate empowered to act on their behalf. They must have some reason for arriving in Dholpore so early in the season. They must have learned that our detachment is here. One of the officers must have talked."

"We shall see. We can defend our own. Dates and times can be obscured."

"And that is not traceable? We keep records of where our men go."

"And records can disappear. I have access. I will manage the affair."

"Why, Aubrey? Why these respectable females? Seducing a few servants, that's nothing, but according to Cricklehurst these are middle class girls raped in their own homes."

Richard leaned his face until it hovered mere inches from the major's, his shoulders set squared and rigid, his hands clenched so tightly he might be about to swing at the major. His whole body shouted outrage.

The major sneered and looked down his nose. "Sit down, Richard. So the magistrate who examined those officers and the Englishman who insisted they be cashiered have arrived in Dholpore. What can they do? Precious little without regiment support and you know they will not have it."

He really is panicked. Why can't he see that I can protect us all? The regiment values my name and lineage.

Richard straightened, strode up and down in front of the desk. "You did not hear me. The magistrate insists on justice. He cannot be turned. Cricklehurst is to be part of the investigation and has spoken to him." Richard fidgeted with his sword, tugged at his jacket.

" Be calm, Richard." *But the poor fool can't, if anything he grows more agitated.*

"For God's sake Aubrey, Cricklehurst knows of that last competition you organised, here in Calcutta. Why do you suppose he spoke to me?" He made a fist and thumped the desk so that the ink well rattled and the paper knife jumped. "He wants those involved to quietly resign, save the regiment."

"Hah! The regiment is safe. I'm surprised that the families dared appoint any person to seek justice, or speak of what happened." The major sniggered. "I wonder how many have had little bastards introduced into their worthy families?"

"Aubrey! What did you dare those young officers to do?" Richard grasped the major's arm. "You may be my friend, and you are my commanding officer. Your junior officers may adore you and follow your commands, but it behoves me to tell you that enough is enough. Do you want to be cashiered yourself?"

"Behoves? Really, Richard. Aren't we being military?"

Richard stiffened as the major grasped both his wrists and not gently.

"Do not forget I am your commanding officer. Be calm, Richard, your major has a plan and has been waiting for an opportunity to carry it out."

"How outrageous is this plan?"

"It will tie the hands of both the magistrate and this officious do-gooder. Any further action against us will harm them more than us."

Richard stared at the major. "What on God's good earth…? You cannot be seriously contemplating some such action?"

The major smiled again and nodded, releasing Richard's wrists and patting his shoulder.

The captain flung up his hands, swore, and left, slamming the door.

The major laughed.

The captain discovers the truth

Dholpore

Bryce Ackerman

For the first two days the Broadbents avoided all social contacts, being resolutely Not At Home, which in truth we were not. As I planned revenge and waited for the legal documents and other information, Sir Cuthbert did a walk round the town on the first morning, leaving our cards.

"We won't be socially recognised if we don't leave cards," Mrs Broadbent explained. "But it's a peculiar system. One doesn't need to see anyone, just deliver the cards." She smiled, and her plump cheeks rounded up like two pink crab apples. "That is why Sir Cuthbert goes. He won't stop to chatter."

"Part of the regiment we want is coming," Sir Cuthbert assured me on his return. "Indeed some officers are settled in already."

"But for the first few days we'll run away. Tomorrow we will abscond, avoiding our social duties." Ada Broadbent said with a mischievous twinkle. "Show you some of unspoiled India."

We rode out on the little local ponies. Rough and rugged, they had clever feet, and their hooves never slipped on the narrow tracks. Just as well for the paths skirted ravines, breath stopping drops full of jagged rocks or sharp-spined thickets. My feet might dangle near the floor as I sat aboard my pony, but I felt safe. The solitude allowed me to gradually feel more charitably inclined towards the human race and mankind in particular.

Mrs Broadbent chaffed me for being churlish and lacking social conversation. "You had promised, Mr Ackerman, to be less morose. Are you really trying?"

I didn't argue, without knowledge of why I was in India she could not understand the deep melancholy that occasionally swallowed me, or the force of rage and need for revenge which gripped me in a vice. I meekly agreed, renewed my promise, made efforts, thus thwarting her teasing.

The first day we visited a picturesque place, a waterfall falling into a valley full of flowers and birds, a beautiful place that soothed the spirit. Even I relaxed, simply thinking. The Broadbents relaxed, Sir Cuthbert sketching and Mrs Broadbent collecting flowers, leaves and dead insects. The magistrate drew neat line drawings in a large notebook he used as a diary, which went everywhere with him. Mrs Broadbent particularly enjoyed collecting, pressing and drying flowers and leaves, intending to use them for making pictures and cards. The dead insects she collected had glossy wing cases. I mentally arranged the conversation I would be having with that major and followed Ada Broadbent, partially listening to her informative chatter.

Our manservants carried and served a simple al fresco meal, an interesting mix of Indian and English foods. I grew to enjoy the different spicy tastes, the sweet and sour, the tongue curling bitterness and the throat scalding hotness. The quality of the fruit, particularly the mangoes and grapes, far exceeded home grown versions for flavour.

On the third day, over breakfast, Mrs Broadbent ended our solitude. "We cannot remain 'Not at Home' forever," she announced, pulling a mournful face at her husband and myself, as she sorted a pile of visiting cards. "Sad though that is."

Sir Cuthbert noted my expression. "We must wait. We can do nothing without the statements and summons, and whatever other information your family have gathered. The ship will arrive within days and the important mail, the government post, will come through immediately."

Breakfast is not the place to swear, thump the table, or jump up to kick the wall. I wanted to do all three.

Mrs Broadbent raised eyebrows but did not enquire. A well trained government wife, she merely inclined her head and patted the stack of cards to the left of her plate. "We only need to meet all these people at the Club." She fanned out the few remaining cards. "And I do not have to entertain to meet these persons." She smiled. "My dear, we are spared a grand dinner party. Julius and Charis have sent us an invitation to a welcome back informal supper at their home and promise that only our particular friends will be there."

And that was how I first heard of the Northrops.

Meeting the Northrops

Dholpore 1872

Bryce Ackerman

What constantly puzzled me was the behaviour of the young officers. Sir Cuthbert and I held several late night discussions trying to find some rational reason for their behaviour, and what irrational reasoning lay behind the competition.

I constantly ran my head against their parentage. "These officers come from good families, the so-called cream of their counties in some cases. Why would they do such a thing?"

"Arrogance. Some of the so-called old families, the aristocracy they call themselves, believe that they are the law, they have power and abuse it." Sir Cuthbert sighed. He was 'old family' himself, but of the paternal, 'I protect my people' squire breed. I'd be willing to bet his tenants had sound roofs, support when old or ill, and basic schooling.

"Trouble is," he continued, "that these regiments considers themselves above common man and above our regular laws." He grinned, a feral baring of teeth that did not bode well for any such man who came his way in court.

"I blame this Indian culture offering so much temptation...."

"You're prejudiced. Open your eyes to India, the real India, which had a civilised population before Greece or Rome." Sir Cuthbert chided me. "What a country. But it is, for young men who cannot marry or mix with suitable young women, a place devoid of lawful sex."

"Those officers were home on leave," I retorted. "There were plenty of brothels for them if they couldn't control themselves."

"Yes, yes, but the problems start here. India's not easy for young men with the absence of English women and many pretty Anglo-Indian girls around."

"Not a sufficient excuse." But I remembered, with reluctance, how I felt when separated from Aimée.

"The soldiers, both officers and men, may not marry unless they fulfilled certain difficult criteria, and they needed to obtain permission. It is made as tough as possible for them to marry."

"I understand all this, Sir Cuthbert. What I cannot understand how those so-called gentlemen should make a sport of good Englishmen's daughters. Have they no respect for the fair sex, no respect for their mothers?"

"The men have access to clean army brothels," Sir Cuthbert frowned. "But they do little to help healthy young men. That's why all the fuss about physical activities and b…" He looked over towards the chair where his wife had been sitting and amended his language even though she'd long been abed "… blessed sports."

I smiled. Rotund, roly-poly Sir Cuthbert had never been a sportsman and he could respect his wife even when she wasn't sitting with him. He was a good man.

"What was wrong with those young men that they could regard rape as a kind of sport, make a competition of it?"

He huffed his moustache at me. "I do not know, but there are extenuating…."

"No, Sir Cuthbert. Knowing all this does not excuse their behaviour. Where was their self-discipline, restraint and sense of honour?"

He shrugged.

"One needs a strong will to stay morally sane in this sexually bewitching and enticing country. Where were their consciences?"

It was what I found the hardest to understand. After all I was a normal young man with a healthy sexual appetite, but I believed my will strong enough to control myself. My beloved Aimée and I had been sorely tempted, impelled by our love, its passion and physical desires, yet we had controlled and disciplined ourselves and lust never had its way. I believed myself well able to control those desires, despite the erotica surrounding us. Or I did until I met Mrs Northrop. She drove away all melancholy thoughts about the major and made me have a little fellow feeling – against my inclinations – for those tempted. And it was all my attraction to her, in no way was she responsible for my temporary infatuation.

The journey to the Northrops' bungalow had shaken me physically, unable to obtain ponies we travelled in a form of transport called a palkee – a kind of palanquin. It allowed one to be carried on a sort of portable string bed with a hood, the wooden frame supported by four skinny men who did not appear to have any muscles yet trotted us up the hills and down the valleys without discomfort. The paths were narrow and I pondered on the difficulty of passing other travellers.

"Pray we meet no one wishing to go in the opposite direction," Mrs Broadbent called out on a particularly steep curve.

Sir Cuthbert snorted. "She hates being lifted high over the other travellers, makes a dreadful fuss. I get off and walk."

I vowed I would do the same. I am not a small man, being tall, broad and of big bones, indeed my fiancée once called me a hulking great bear of a fellow – well, compared to her dainty tininess I was - and I feared to be pitched out and down those appalling slopes. Happily we travelled undisturbed, although much jostled and tumbled about. But that discomfort was physical. The Northrops – Mrs Northrop – destroyed my mental state, shattered protected memories and brought me back to callow youth and those years of intense infatuations, and the stir of male lust. She made me remember again the pain of rejection and the ardour of a youth's burning passion. In light of my present task she made me feel ashamed that we men seemed so easily roused to lustful thoughts.

The Northrops were an attractive couple. Mister was of the lean and handsome English gentleman type, dark brown hair, fair skin, a good nose and chin, very Anglo-Saxon.

But his wife!

I had never seen a more desirable woman. Such a waterfall of emotion poured over me as Julius Northrop introduced us. This was not at all what I felt for my fiancée, yet I loved her with heart stopping intensity. How to explain this more physical than spiritual reaction? It could only be lechery. It was not that Mrs Northrop was outstanding as a beauty. The blonde standing beind her was the story book beauty, golden hair, blue eyes, and a delightful profile, with features fine drawn and in perfect proportion. No, Mrs Northrop held something more for me, a definite sexual allure. Some accident of birth gave her eyes, face and body the colours and proportions to turn her into a magnet of sexual attraction. Although I preferred not to name it as such, it was sheer carnal desire which struck me down. I noticed Sir Cuthbert held her hand a little longer than necessary, with softened face and smile. Was he too affected, or was it friendship? Yet her innocent eyes and gentle manner showed her to be unconscious of the power of that sexual force within her.

Unaware she may have been, but I was thrust back into the guise of my clumsy, elbows-and-knees, gangling, fifteen year old self in the throes of passionate shameless longings for the most unsuitable females. My feet felt overlarge and heavy. My skin heated with awkward embarrassment. As sweat broke out on my brow and my palms grew clammy I fought the emotions and damned India's eroticism as the cause of my lack of control. Bryce Ackerman succumb to lust? Never, I was not one of those immoderate intemperate men I hunted.

The reawakened sixteen year old me wanted to grasp Charis Northrop, desiring to touch the soft fuzz on the curve of her cheek, kiss the fine hair at the nape of her neck. Filled with self-disgust and extreme mortification I tried to concentrate during the introductions, barely touched hands. For God's sake, this woman was Mrs Northrop. A married woman. Not one to think licentious thoughts about. Yet I was. My body reacted in a purely sexual, and extremely physical manner. Once more I cursed India for its overblown erotic atmosphere stimulating sane rational gentlemen like me into uncontrollable upsurges of sexual feelings, though I knew it was myself I needed to control. I bowed my head to the lady. How could I, who had seen what unrestrained, undisciplined, seekers of the pleasures of the flesh could do, suffer myself from the same urges? It must not be.

Shame made me turn to the blonde beauty left standing a few paces behind the Northrops. They took Sir Cuthbert and Mrs Broadbent towards the house. I bowed again to the young woman as I offered her my arm, embarrassed because I had been so overwhelmed by Mrs Northrop that I had not even noted her name, despite Mr Northrop's careful introduction. I fell back on social trivialities.

"I know nothing of Indian gardens or the native flowers. Would you be kind enough to escort me round this charming garden and show me the outstanding Indian flowers?" I covered the lack of her name with an admiring smile rather than a "Miss…?" which, in the face of her notable beauty, seemed boorish beyond belief.

My hostess saved me from further problems. "Beatrice," she called. "Bea, my dear, come inside and bring our newest guest in with you."

Beatrice took my proffered arm, gave me the remote suggestion of a smile, and led me to the front door. The house the Northrops hired for the summer season perched high on the slope with a well-established garden, a pleasure of flowers and shrubs, vivid colours calmed by greenery, some familiar, some exotic, which sheltered the house. It faced north-east as most of the Indian houses did. Took some getting used to, facing a home to the cooler aspect instead of the sunny south, but made sense in India's furnace of a climate. There was a lack of the usual ostentatious twiddles and flourishes the British deemed necessary in India. The Northrop house was as simple as a Dak bungalow though larger, with the usual servants' quarters and kitchens to the rear. Steps wide enough to sit on were roofed over by a broad verandah.

Beatrice looked up at me. "There are cool drinks inside and a more comfortable seat than you found in those body-battering palanquins." Her voice was as attractive as her face, soft toned, with musical cadences. I wondered if she had been taught by a good singing master because of those cadences. Mrs Northrop's voice lilted too.

"Are you a singer?" I asked. "Your voice has a pleasant rhythm. Perhaps you and Mrs Northrop would sing for us this evening. I have missed my own family's musical evenings."

In reply I received a quizzical glance. "Perhaps, Mr Ackerman, now please come in."

We trod up the wide steps together, Miss Beatrice asking the usual polite questions about my journey and was it my first visit to India? Such trivial social politeness allowed me to steady myself in order to face Mrs Northrop again.

"This is my first and hopefully last visit," I informed her.

A tilt of her pretty head, and she skewered me with her response. "Indeed and so India has fallen short of your expectations? It is not easy for India to fulfil the expectations of some people, I know. But I love this country." Her tone was cool, even contemptuous.

Interest aroused, for this Beatrice was no empty headed, husband hunting visitor then, I began to question her. She hardly had time to begin an answer when the servant advanced to offer drinks.

Wanting to know more, I provoked her as I accepted a cold concoction of some minted non-alcoholic drink. "India is too hot, too exotic and too full of people afflicted by a mysterious hysteria caused by over-respect for the ancient cultures," I told her.

She flushed, frowned, and began a terse response, but Mrs Northrop arrived beside her. Sliding her arm around Beatrice's waist, and laughing up at me, Mrs Northrop stopped my breath. She smelt of lavender and starched muslin, so English, like the warm apricot tea roses in our garden in Surrey. Neither lady wore stiff silk. Their gowns were loose, their hair softly arranged up and off their faces, for coolness I suppose. They looked delightful together, and I felt strangely overwhelmed and tongue tied.

Mrs Northrop took pity on my awkwardness. "Did I hear you sparring with Miss Chayle, my sweet cousin, Beatrice, about India? You will never overset her opinion. I believe she would stay here forever if she could."

Beatrice's answering smile held a wry touch of agreement. I wondered what a pretty young miss could prefer in India to her English home, but I now felt physically uncomfortable near Mrs Northrop. Of course one cannot adjust one's dress in public. I cursed the whole situation and concentrated on asking questions about the notable Indian temples, mosques and palaces the ladies had visited. That filled in the conversational gap until I could sit in a deep armchair, fussily hitching my trouser knees to camouflage my attempts to ease another part of myself into some more comfortable position. It was a damnable situation.

The servant offered another drink and the ladies took seats opposite me. Thwarted sexual desire turned to frustration and then disgust. How could I be so afflicted? I was not that major, or those junior officers. I restrained, barely, my need to leave, to walk away until I could settle my body.

I began to understand what the commanding officer had said back in Calcutta, his excuse for his men's behaviour. 'The erotic hysteria which seems to hang in the air in India is aggravated for my men by severe continence. There are no women other than the Anglo Indians sluts or Indian whores. No decent British women to temper their lusts.'

I had had no truck with his excuses. I still didn't, but as I shifted in the chair to reorganise my physical comfort I cursed the power of the urges which his men had not resisted and I must.

Mrs Broadbent joined the ladies on the long sofa, gave me a swift smile and turned to Mrs Northrop. "And will Felix be joining us soon?"

"Oh yes." The smile on Mrs Northrop's face was of pure delight. Her cousin's face reflected similar pleasure.

As Sir Cuthbert and Mr Northrop, business talk completed, walked over to sit on the other sofa, an Indian servant entered with a small boy clutching her hand and chattering away in childish treble. He wore a soldier's cap.

Mrs Broadbent clapped her hands. "Felix, I do declare you've grown again."

The boy released his ayah's hand and marched to the sofa. "See how tall I am now."

He held himself straight-spined like a soldier, halted beside us, and backed to the wall, measuring himself against the line of black marks made there.

The ladies made the appropriate admiring comments.

"So tall for a four year old," Ada Broadbent said and handed him a small gift, a wooden soldier.

Felix responded with a smart salute, knocking his overlarge cap skew-whiff. "Thank you." He spoke well, sounded like a much older child.

"A soldier are you?" his father asked. "Where did that cap come from?"

The ayah said something in her language which made Mr Northrop frown, but Felix now saluted his father, a pretty good attempt too. His father returned the salute.

"That gives me an idea," Mrs Northrop said. Her expressive face and eyes spoke of pleasure. "For the Club competition."

Miss Chayle laughed. "Wonderful, and we have enough people now Mr Ackerman has joined us." She turned to me. "You will help us win the competition won't you? We need a group of six people for this competition. It's only a little acting which I'm sure you'd enjoy. We've not had enough people to enter before."

Her smile would have won any other man's head and heart, mine kept yearning for a smile from Charis Northrop. When Mrs Northrop begged my aid I was lost. I found myself cajoled into playing a part in the Club competition with a woman I had much better avoid.

Bryce finds the major

Dholpore 1872

Each day I rode or walked to the government buildings seeking my packet of information from home, but 'Any day now' turned into a week. The exercise helped me think of things more important than my ridiculous and demeaning infatuation with Mrs Northrop. The irrational craving had eased a little. I needed that information from home so that I could finish my unpleasant task and return to my work for the bank. Work eased the pain of my loss, for I still thought of Aimée and what could have been but for that as yet unnamed be-damned major.

Acknowledging my folly, giving way to Mrs Northrop's plea, I allowed myself to become part of the Northrops' circle and their acting group. I had to force myself not to stand close or touch Mrs Northrop. I controlled my constant efforts to let my gaze follow her with difficulty. I accepted my small part in the play thankful that Sir Cuthbert and Ada Broadbent worked with me and it was Miss Chayle I had to make eyes at. As my hunt for justice had to wait, I could concentrated on the play.

Charis Northrop wrote the piece. It was a simple, heart touching story about a boy soldier, and Felix was the star. Julius Northrop played the villain with gusto, his wife played the boy's mother, which was clever writing as this gave young Felix a known base to lean upon. The Broadbents made a convincing country Squire and his wife, ('Playing ourselves,' Sir Cuthbert whispered when the parts were allocated.) Beatrice Chayle was their daughter, whilst I became a Mr Bumble of a vicar. When I didn't have Charis Northrop in my line of sight I played a pompous, puffed up bumbling fool. It nettled me that I still found my eyes wandering to gaze after her despite my efforts. This fixation was demeaning, its physical effects embarrassing. I suppressed them firmly, exercised vigorously, and worked hard every night making sure the case against each officer was watertight.

The night before the performance the Northrops relaxed quietly at home, allowing young Felix to rest and recover some energy. I visited the Club to see where we would perform. The Broadbents dined out with a fellow magistrate and did not wish to come to the Club.

"All that simpering and fuss." Mrs Broadbent said. "All those people I avoid will be there."

"Unfortunately they are not people you should avoid, my dear." Sir Cuthbert's tone chided.

She gave a little shrug and pulled a face. "In Calcutta perhaps. Here we can relax the social round somewhat."

Sir Cuthbert turned to me. "We British are forced to stick together, Bryce. Remember that in India, we may rule the country, but there are few of us and we are obliged to work together. I am, by nature of my peculiar position, able to avoid some things, but it is our duty to follow accepted patterns of behaviour, despite my wife's antipathy." His voice quivered, he glanced at Mrs Broadbent.

Ada Broadbent's mouth quirked upwards with suppressed laughter even though she stilled her face and lowered her gaze.

The couple were an oddity in British India, would have appeared eccentric even back home. I found them comfortable to be with and was grateful for their kindness and easy company. I needed Sir Cuthbert's power and authority to snare those miscreants when their superior officers and their regiment tried to protect them.

Picture the Club on a warm spring evening. Even this far from Calcutta it was a slice of Great Britain, and could have been any British Club for the officers and gentlemen anywhere in India. Gentlemen being military officers, district officers and British advisors, Sir Cuthbert told me, one eyebrow quirked, his moustache quivering. Families meaning respectable white wives and offspring, of course. No Indians. The building, emphatically British and rather at odds with its surroundings, had pillars and a portico, a grand entrance drive and red turbaned servants waiting by the doors. Naturally evening dress was de rigeur and I had dressed accordingly, but my dinner jacket was a lightweight one from Poole of Saville Row, the outfitters for the Indian Raj, and it was, thank God, cooler than the standard woollen jacket.

The Club, as the only place for the British to socialise, vibrated like a wasp colony, the bar well filled, the dining room also. But I'd come for the theatre. Her Majesty's employees were not so numerous this early in the season in this small hill resort that they could put on big shows like musicals or plays with a large cast, but there was a weekly charade competition, and these were not schoolroom Charades.

"Brilliant small plays," Mrs Broadbent told me. "Worth watching if one could stand the audience."

Her disregard for the niceties of society now she was free from her dutiful rounds in Calcutta amazed me. "Go and see some, let us know what the competition is like."

I went willing for I hoped to gain an impression of how well the Northrops' play compared. I feared our performance would appear to a disadvantage despite all our preparation.

As a visitor I signed in, Sir Cuthbert having already done the introductory honours when we first arrived, but before I could proceed there was a swirl of activity in the doorway. A draft of mild air touched my cheek as the doors swung open. The red turbaned servants bowed then elevated to attention, and a well-dressed man strolled in with an Indian woman on his arm. He threw some comment over his shoulder to a younger man, also escorting an Indian woman. Four juniors, starched and ironed and giving off a military air, via haircuts and straight spines, completed the party.

What caught my eye was the native escort of four handsome men, well-armed and well-dressed in some form of uniform. Obviously private guards, they settled down outside on either side of the shallow steps. These Indian women then were important in their native world. Both wore vivid silk saris, heavily embroidered, gold flashed at wrist and waist, and diamonds shattered the light, making rainbows in the sheen of their lustrous black hair. I knew it was not polite to look overlong at an Indian woman, but they were lovely and I did wonder what they were doing in the Club.

The senior man, definitely a bit of a grandee, looked down his nose as he cast a glance around the foyer. He fixed his gaze on me. He viewed me as if I were a carriage horse he might purchase. I kept a polite expression but promised myself a chat with Mrs Broadbent. She would know who Mister Arrogant was with his Indian…wife?…mistress?

His arrogant lordship disregarded me and swept his party towards the dining room, escorted by the abdar, the head servant, and a fussy British gentleman, the senior secretary. The other secretary caught me up in the whirl of their passing.

"Sir Cuthbert asked me to introduce you to certain people," he said. "Now he is here, may I introduce you to Major, Lord Aubrey Wulfsige?"

I had no chance to protest for he gripped my elbow and pushed me after the party. I did not wish to make social conversation with any major except the one I planned to kill. I expostulated but was ignored.

The fussy secretary saw us approaching and murmured to Major. The Major turned his head and looked down at me over his shoulder. He didn't even bother to copy the secretary's hushed whisper. "One of those merchant bankers? Hah! A Jew boy eh?" he brayed in that peculiar voice men of his ilk considered a discreet aside.

My own secretary smirked, then pretended not to, and although he must have felt my arm stiffen. He continued with an introduction. "Major, allow me to introduce Mr Bryce Ackerman, of London. Mr Ackerman this is Major, Lord Aubrey Wulfsige, of the Darkshire regiment."

That was an unexpected surname, an old much respected family, indeed. And the Darkshire regiment was the regiment I sought. Sir Cuthbert's information about that stood firm. Could this be the major I sought? Surely not, he seemed to have his…wife?…woman from his harem?…mistress? there to settle his sexual needs. He was older too than I understood was the major I sought.

We shook hands. He had a firm shake, but not the dominating officer's grip I expected. He looked over his nose which seemed more of Roman shape than Saxon. A bred-in arrogance and superiority flowed from him, but I couldn't place his family estates. We bankers always knew the old families; they needed the most money from us. I'd ask Mrs Broadbent which county they assumed they graced.

Now he introduced me to the Indian woman as his wife. I found myself floundering for she was royalty, "The Maharani, Kumari Kalindi." As I was unsure of correct protocols especially as she was his Hindu wife I assumed the air of a comfortable English country gentleman, one more familiar with a country estate than international banking, and gave her an Englishman's stiff bow.

His companion came forward to be introduced, Captain Richard Rankin and his Hindu wife, Sevitri who was cousin to the Maharani. The usual minutiae of weather, heat, and my stay took but a moment's casual chat. We men shook hands again and they proceeded to their table. I gripped the secretary's elbow and trundled him out to the entrance hall.

"Bibi from the bibi khana or wife?" His horrified face made me want to laugh.

"Those gentlemen brought their wives." He spluttered and struggled to express his

outrage. "No one, not even Major, Lord Aubrey Wulfsige would bring his…his…mistress here," he hissed.

"Really? Please tell me how the Indian women are allowed in this Club." I could be an outraged and bureaucratically proper Englishman if need be.

The secretary wrenched his elbow free. "By special permission. Major, Lord Aubrey Wulfsige is a man of considerable influence and prestige." He stalked away like one of the Adjutant storks I'd seen on the river, a gawky figure, like him, his 'feathers' awry in the discomposing wind of my words.

The fussy secretary pattered back, gave me an apologetic look and escorted me to the Club theatre. "What's upset young Mathers?" His voice told me he was a lowland Scot.

"I expressed amazement at Indian women in the Club."

"Ah, yes…" he murmured, but said no more. He showed me into a good seat, central to the stage. "Mrs Broadbent likes to sit here." He then kindly introduced me to the men on my right. "Visitors also, from New Zealand. Enjoy the performance, gentlemen."

So I sat on a well cushioned wooden seat, inclined my head to my neighbours and listened to them explain about the settlement plan they had brought with them, hoping to persuade retiring officers to take up land and opportunities in New Zealand. They tried hard to persuade me that our family should start banking in their settlement area and mentioned gold mining. I stored the information, murmured polite nothings, and fortunately the opening curtains quietened them, allowing me to settle back and watch the performance.

Kidnapped?

Dholpore 1872

Our play came last. It was a warm night and I sweated a little under thick greasy stage make-up as we waited in the square box of a green room, which was indeed an oppressive shade of dark fir tree green. Young Felix had slept at home all through the other performances; his mother brought him to the Club in time for ours. He enjoyed being out at night, relished not being in bed guarded by his ayah, and dressed himself in his soldier's costume, with Miss Chayle's help, whilst making cheerful talk to any who would listen. His attitude I envied. I feared to make a fool of myself.

The Broadbents sat, Sir Cuthbert uneasy and his wife pretending not to be, both muttering their lines. Miss Chayle now read a book about Africa.

"We cannot let Charis down," Mrs Broadbent repeated. "We mustn't spoil her play. Don't you agree, Beatrice?"

Beatrice Chayle raised her head, smiled faintly under her face paint, returned her gaze to her book.

Julius Northrop twirled his villain's moustache and grinned. His wife applied stage makeup on to Felix's eager face, and her husband called across the small space to her.

"She has a point to prove to certain people about little boys and their place in this society, haven't you, my dear?"

The bewitching woman hesitated, a pot of scarlet face paint cupped in her hand like a clot of blood. "That wretched military"...mutter, mumble..."military junta...rude men..." her voice diminished to nothing. She smiled down at Felix. "Are you ready to be the brave soldier boy?"

Felix saluted. "My face feels funny," he complained, but his mother caught his hand before he could rub at it.

"So does mine," his father told him. "My villain's moustache tickles," and he waggled his lips to make it wobble.

Felix chuckled and patted at the moustache. His father caught him up straight armed, holding him away from his body, looked into his face. "Be brave in front of all those people, little man. Let's do this well for Mama." He lowered the boy with care and gently pushed him towards the door. "Lead us on, soldier boy."

He did. Taking his mother's hand he marched resolutely to the door, and his father, opening the door for us all, saluted him, then tenderly cupped his wife's cheek. How I envied Julius Northrop that right and swore at myself for twitching at the nearness of her. Such an infatuation was infantile.

Felix behaved impeccably. He made one error of movement, going to Beatrice Chayle before he should, but she managed to make a pretty tableau out of it by kneeling and holding him in her arms until he had to move again. And he did call his father 'A bad man,' where he did not have to speak, which fitted so perfectly within the framework of the story that no one in the audience would have noticed. I managed to bumble well enough to raise laughter and felt better for that. Our ending tableau brought much applause and Felix merited a special bow on his own, his parents proudly behind him.

Sir Cuthbert huffed and puffed with relief. "Not a bad effort," he murmured in my ear as we left the stage.

The aftermath of the competition, the judges' results, took place in the Club meeting room. This room opened directly into the foyer and the double doors between the two had been flung wide open. The servants by the outer doors were commanded to open them also and they briskly complied. A trickle of cooler air ribboned its way through the cloying mix of stage face paint, clashing perfumes, and stale air.

Having been the final performance of the night and then needing to remove all the messy face muck and tidy ourselves made us last to arrive, so we were actually just outside the meeting room doorway, standing in the foyer. There was a crowd of the audience and well-wishers jostling together in the room, making it difficult to hear the speeches. We pressed close in the doorway.

Young Felix backed away and settled down on the foyer floor under a spindly legged table to the left of the doors, not three feet away. He had been given a present by Mrs Broadbent as a reward for his performance, a remarkable sort of wooden puzzle in a tray. She had designed it herself and the coloured pieces could make various mathematical patterns and shapes. Their multi-talented steward had organised the making of it and Felix was delighted and fascinated.

"It is most educational," Mrs Broadbent assured the Northrops so they allowed him to play with it quietly as we waited for the results.

The judges, a panel of five men and women, awarded the marks in reverse order, the lowest first. They made polite and appreciative comments about each performance. When they announced the fourth group's place we knew we were first or second.

I had not seen the fifth play as we had to put on our costumes and make up during it so it was with some surprise that I noticed Captain Rankin and his Indian wife had performed in it and stood with a group of military people, including the prejudiced Major Arrogant. The judges awarded them second place and Miss Chayle, beside me, gave a whispered cheer.

"We have succeeded then. Previously that group placed first in every competition."

The Northrops, in front of me, touched hands briefly. The Broadbents smiled and in the midst of remarks about charming performances, well written speeches and remarkable acting from a splendid young man we heard that we had won.

After the applause faded a press of people swirled round us, congratulating us. Drinks were offered, trays of delicious mouthfuls of savoury somethings appeared. Mrs Northrop brushed past me, making me jerk back a little. That was too close a contact for my still lusting body. She smiled, uttering a soft apology as she moved on. "I must congratulate Felix" she said, walking towards the table.

Still besotted, my eyes followed her automatically, and as I looked after her I saw only an empty space under the table, the wooden tray upside down, and the puzzle pieces spilled over the tiled floor. Charis Northrop blanched as white as her shawl, dropped to her knees. Her lips moved, but I could not hear the words above the voices round me. I knew though. I reached round Miss Chayle to grasp Julius Northrop's shoulder.

Beatrice Chayle turned within my arm, looked up, about to make a sharp comment, but saw my face and cried "What is it?

"Where is Felix?"

Julius Northrop heard and barged past me. His glance took in the upset puzzle, the absence of his son, and he faltered, his expression stricken. Then he straightened, stiffened his spine and hastened to support his wife. He raised her. She leant against him. Their heads touched, expressions matching. I had never seen such anguish. It struck me like a blow and I needed to do something.

"Come, let us look. He can't be far," I turned to Miss Chayle.

Ada Broadbent now joined us. "He will be outside, on the step, talking to the men servants."

Beatrice Chayle hurried to the outer doors, looked, looked back, shaking her head.

Sir Cuthbert suggested we divided up and thoroughly search the foyer and then the meeting rooms. We began our search, Charis Northrop leading the way with renewed vigour.

I scoured the foyer and then joined Miss Chayle outside. She stood on the broad steps, addressing the doormen and two of those bodyguards I'd seen with the Wulfsige party. The servants stood, heads bowed, as she addressed them in their own language. They listened politely as she picked out the words in a slow and faltering fashion. Her distress was visible and the bodyguards leaned towards her to listen, eyes moving in darting sideways glances to see her face.

I left her to it and walked round the entry way, checking the side of the steps and the flower borders of the gravel driveway. It was all open space and nowhere for Felix to hide, but I called his name despite that.

The news had spread. People leaving the Club, and latecomers arriving, denied having seen Felix. Expressing concern, many of them peered around, barked questions at the servants and promised to look for him. I judged the time between seeing him and not seeing him and wondered how far he could have walked. I returned to Miss Chayle and expressed doubt that Felix could have gone farther than the gateway.

"The doormen say he did not walk out. But we have to try, we must look," she said. "We cannot be sure. We cannot truly know that." She actually grasped my arm in her effort to persuade me.

"He knows you well, Miss Chayle. Would you please come with me along the road and call him?" I had barely finished speaking before she led off, pulling me along, in her anxiety, like a dog on a leash.

We paced for five minutes asking all those we saw if they had noticed a fair haired English boy. There were stalls and little shops open, places which might attract a small boy, but no one had seen Felix, and he would have been noticeable among the dark skins and darker hair.

"We must return, Miss Chayle." I did not add that we should hope the boy was found. The situation was too strange for that.

"People have been so kind," Beatrice Chayle told me. "They promise to look. Do you think the offer of a reward would help motivate more searchers?"

"There is a problem in offering a reward." She looked to argue, opened her mouth. "No, please pause and reflect. What if the boy has been abducted, kidnapped for money?"

She stopped, stunned by the idea. "But why take Felix? The Northrops aren't wealthy."

"They are wealthy when you compare them to most people in India." I caught her hand in mine, tucked it under my elbow and urged her onwards.

She jibbed like a balky horse. "Why would you think that?" Her voice sagged, her body drooping in desperation. "Surely Felix went to find a drink or followed a servant with a tray of food." Her face told me how much she longed for that assurance.

What to say, what to do when a high spirited young lady asked for an answer but wanted comfort? How much speculation or reasonable guessing could she bear? And what was the truth? I could only pat her hand and urge her on.

She was taking none of that. "Mr Ackerman, what is it that you fear?"

The Club entrance was in view. We stopped and looked all round, called the boy's name. As we waited for a reply I said, "Felix had a new toy. He found it fascinating..." I paused.

"Well, and so he did."

"Did you note it spilled over the floor and the tray upside down?"

She nodded and her face, under the door lights, turned as pale as Charis Northrop's had been.

"If Felix had left to seek a drink or food would he have tipped up the tray and spilt the pieces of his precious new toy in that manner?"

Comprehension lit her face. She hurried up the steps; I followed closely, and Sir Cuthbert met us. We all exclaimed "Did you find…?" then shook our heads.

The secretaries were now involved and the Club had become a place of anxious scurrying servants and people issuing commands. Sir Cuthbert headed for the kitchens, Beatrice Chayle ran after him, urging him to set up a search of the food stores.

"Look at them," hissed Ada Broadbent in my ear. "Some of them are enjoying this."

Charis Northrop stood encircled by silk encased, corset-stiffened backs. Well reinforced matrons of the community murmured and commiserated. She, poor girl, drooped like a frost snapped birch sapling.

"And some are shocked," I retorted. But one face gloated. "If guilt gave itself an expression would that be it?" I asked Ada Broadbent.

Mrs Broadbent turned back to look. "The colonel's wife." Her facial expression hardened, set into glacial smoothness. "We must…."

"Get my wife home." The order came rough and abrupt, and too late.

A party swept into the foyer. One clear voice, raised to carry. "But little children should not be left alone should they? Nor be in the Club, especially at night."

And another carefully pitched voice. "Why wasn't she watching over him?"

"Careless wasn't it?"

The voices faded away as the group descended the steps. The remnants of that military group who had lost their usual first position, full of spite and venom, drifted home without even helping in our search.

Julius Northrop, haggard yet vibrating with a furious rage, repeated his order. "For the love of God, take her away."

Beatrice Chayle ran to Charis Northrop. Sir Cuthbert aided her, forcing a passage through the matrons, touching and moving aside the bodies blocking their way. Beatrice Chayle grasped Charis, telling her repeatedly not to heed such slanderous comments.

The secretaries took over Sir Cuthbert's task and the society matrons moved off with backwards, head over shoulder glances. The groups and small parties of people who lingered were encouraged to head homewards as we were shepherded into the bar and the doors closed.

Julius and Charis Northrop held each other up. Ada Broadbent and Sir Cuthbert gently inserted them into one large winged armchair.

I watched Beatrice Chayle sink into another chair as though her joints had collapsed and turned to secretary Mathers. "Could we all have some brandy, with a good medicinal draft for the Northrops?" Leaning towards the fussy secretary I indicated with my head the two half fainting women. "Is there sal volatile available?"

"Yes, of course we have such a thing in..." he broke off, started again. "This is impossible." He sounded horrified. "How could the boy disappear?"

Mathers, having directed a servant to bring brandy, turned sharply back to us." It's nonsense, the boy must have...."

I growled, grasped his arm, and shoved him towards the doors. "Come here," I ordered the other. He came with reluctance. "Stand in this doorway both of you." I hauled the protesting men with me, kicked open the doors, and shoved them rudely into place. "Use your eyes. I will show you."

I stalked to the meeting room doorway. "We stood here. You know. You saw us."

They mumbled and inclined heads.

"Young Felix sat under here." I lifted the table into the air, shook it at them and plonked it down again. "How far is that from the doorway?" I bore down on the two men. "How far is it?"

"Arm's length." Mathers grew bolder. "That's why it is impossible...."

"It should be," I snarled "but it happened. We all saw him there. Others saw him there. But he is gone. Where? His father is devastated, his mother collapsing, and you bleat of impossibility?" I could have throttled the fool.

"Mr Ackerman, shouting won't help." That was Ada Broadbent. "Mr Mathers, don't obfuscate. The situation is unbelievable, yet it happened."

Sir Cuthbert joined us. "The stewards have found nothing. We have searched every possible place within the Club. The child is not here." He addressed the secretaries. "Where else can we look?"

They raised hands, shook heads, expressed completed bafflement.

"Can we question the servants again?" I turned to the secretaries. "Those doormen must have seen something for all they deny it."

Beatrice Chayle lifted her head. "No, they did not deny it. They said they had not seen him walk out."

I held out my hand to her. "Come, we will tackle them again."

Julius Northrop arrived in time to hear me. "We can't. If it is an abduction, for money, they may well be part of it. We need to examine them again carefully tomorrow, after the ransom demand has been made."

"But do we know it is a ransom?" Secretary Mathers was hushed by his colleague.

"What else can it be?" Julius Northrop, voice ragged, hands shaking, sounded desperate.

"Enough," Sir Cuthbert grasped his friend's arm. "We must all return to our homes and wait for the morning and what news comes with it."

It was sound advice, but difficult to follow with a frantic mother crying out to us to hunt through the Club again and again, and a father silently wishing the same. In the end Ada Broadbent rallied them with thoughts of a message waiting at home and she escorted the Northrops and Beatrice Chayle to their carriage. She told Sir Cuthbert and myself she would accompany them home.

Sir Cuthbert and I returned to the bungalow and took ourselves to bed without much conversation. We too were exhausted.

The hunt is up

Sleep came swiftly, full of uneasy dreams and threads of ideas which drifted into nothingness when I woke enough to try and capture them. In the morning I only remembered Charis Northrop's agony and prayed wholeheartedly to be able to wipe away the memory of it by finding her son.

At breakfast Sir Cuthbert looked as wan as I did. He too had slept little and scarcely ate the excellent meal. The waiting came hard.

"Ada has not returned, therefore there is no news." Sir Cuthbert tugged at his ear, thinking. He looked across the table at me. "Surely a message must come today."

I brooded on that. "Can't we organise soldiers to search for Felix? Could we persuade his ayah to enquire for him in the places around the Club? Might he not have become trapped, shut in somewhere and fallen asleep?"

"Yes, we will do all that." He huffed out his moustache, still thinking. I fretted over our inaction, but felt it too, this not-rightness about the boy's disappearance. It required more thought. Eventually Sir Cuthbert called for his steward.

"Amal, where are you? I need you."

The man eased quietly into the room and padded over to the breakfast table. "Sir Cuthbert?" He knew about Felix, we'd told him last night.

"Sit, man, sit. We must reason this event through. It makes little sense to me."

The steward remained standing. "It is better for the other servants if I stand, sahib."

Sir Cuthbert humphed but said no more. He returned to massaging his ear lobe, frowning in his attempt to puzzle out the whys and hows of the boy's disappearance

"Amal?"

The steward regarded me steadily. I trusted his loyalty to the Broadbents and thus his willingness to help, but how could I phrase my questions without insulting his dignity, which was great. "Amal, have you heard of such a snatch before?

He remained silent, his face placid, his eyes dark.

I tried again. "Amal, from what you understand of such rogues, men who would abduct a sahib's child, do you think these men would dare to enter the British Club to seize a child?"

"They would have to plan, sir. They could not enter the Club."

"That," said Sir Cuthbert, "is the sticking place. Natives couldn't hang around the Club, they'd be kicked out. They had to know Felix was there and then they'd have to have help from the doormen to get in and out."

Amal inclined his head in a stately bow. "I do not think, sahib, that even then they would try such an abduction without a definite promise of a fabulous sum of money and the knowledge that they had safe access and exit."

I looked at Sir Cuthbert. "We must tackle those doormen before they can disappear."

He shook his head. "It might put Felix at risk if we start an enquiry before we have had a ransom demand."

"I didn't mean ourselves or with soldiers." I stopped. "I apologise for snapping, Sir Charles." He flapped a hand. "I meant is there some quiet discreet way we can make enquiries?"

Amal bowed deeply from the waist. "I beg to be allowed to do this for you, sahib. I can find out without alarming them. I too am anxious for the small one."

He and Sir Cuthbert settled the details. Sir Cuthbert wished to overhear the proposed conversations and it took some time before they worked out that the best place for the interview would be in the Club servants' quarters.

Meanwhile I thought about what I could do. That one facial expression hovered on the edge of my mind, to be recalled whenever I sought a reason for the boy's disappearance. If it was not abduction what reason was there for removing the boy? I reflected on why I was here in India and prayed it had nothing to do with that. How could it? Now was not the time for irrational thinking. How to find Felix? The Club might be a good place for me to start as well.

Amal left ahead of us, to avoid any suspicion of collusion. Half an hour later Sir Cuthbert and I rode the little native ponies into town, stabling them at the livery beside the Club. We strolled into the building past two doormen. With difficulty I refrained from staring. It would have been of little use as I would not have recognised the men, but Sir Cuthbert, before he wandered off to the kitchens, told me they were not those on duty the previous evening.

I searched for the secretaries. It was the fussy one who found me.

"Desmond Jury," he introduced himself properly this time, holding out
his hand. "Is there any news?"

"None."

He looked upset.

I took his arm "I need you to help me." I led him back into the foyer. "If Felix did not scamper out by himself how was he removed? That we must solve."

I trusted this fussy man to be the decent, honest, committee man he appeared to be.

Sir Cuthbert thought him adequate though a dour chap. Ada Broadbent said he was the mainstay of the Club. I did not think he had any foreknowledge of the abduction.

"How many people gathered round us during that rush of food and congratulations?"

He paused before answering. Looking round with eyes shut, and his head nodding as though counting, he obviously tried to put himself back into the scene of the previous night. "I would say," and he sounded cautious, "nineteen people, possibly one or two more or less." He opened his eyes frowning. "I am sorry. I cannot be accurate. I wish I could. There were people arriving and leaving. My work here can be very demanding and the play competition…" his voice faded, his hands spread out in a gesture of hopelessness.

I understood. Humanity being what it was I could imagine he had egos to soothe and tender feelings to tiptoe around, especially with the matrons in this closed society. Women, like hens, could be so cruel to each other.

"Can you name the people so that we can talk to them? Surely not one of them would object to helping find a lost child?"

"Yes, I believe I can remember most of the people who were there." He paused.

I knew what he would say and smiled. "You would prefer not to give the names but make a general request for all those present to speak to the Northrops."

He agreed.

"Make a list." It came out as an order. "This is not the time for polite niceties."

He winced but nodded.

I indicated the table with a wave of my arm. "How could someone take Felix from there? And with us standing nearby."

Desmond Jury surprised me. He turned, almost ran into the bar and returned, struggling with an unruly bundle which was a partially rolled up rug. He rerolled it tightly and placed it under the table. "It is about the little boy's size."

We spent a considerable time trying to move the rug from under the table and out through the entrance. It was not something done rapidly.

"How could the child be hidden? Under what garment?"

Desmond Jury shook his head. "I don't think any of the ladies wore an evening cloak, but it would need to be some such loose garment."

I had a vision of a possible way. I did not dare voice the whole thought, only part of it. "Suppose someone swept down on the lad, scooped him up and swung him around as his father would do. He could whirl him out through the doors and into…into a carriage or waiting arms." And that way, I thought, Felix would not yell, scream or cry out in alarum.

Jury nodded his head unhappily and gave me a sideways glance. "You do realise that…"

I interrupt him, my voice soft, for him alone. "Yes, I do realise what it means. No native could enter the Club and remove Felix without someone noticing, even if the doormen were complicit. Therefore…." I left the rest of the sentence unfinished, raised my eyebrows at him.

The secretary almost stuttered in his disbelief. "No gentleman here would stoop to such a…such a despicable act."

I knew better than that but had no wish to start rumours. I did not think Jury a man with a loose tongue, yet I did not know that. Felix's safety came before all else. "When the ransom demand comes we will know more."

He murmured agreement.

I swooped down on the rug once more, swung it out from under the table, up into the air and around to the doorway. It was feasible, explained the tipped out puzzle, and solved my problem of the lack of outcry from the child.

"Hah!" Sir Cuthbert had arrived. "I see." He turned to Jury. "Well, Desmond this is a fine how-de-do for the Club. Bear up man, and know there is no blame attached to you." He clapped the secretary on the shoulder. "Just help us find the boy. Turn the Club upside down again for the Northrops' sake. Search every chest and cupboard."

He had me out of the doors as he spoke and down the steps as Desmond Jury promised.

"Come, Ackerman. We have news to pass on to the Northrops and I hope we are about to find out that a message has arrived." He sounded as frustrated as I felt. "If not…" his voice trailed away. He looked grim. "If not," he repeated, "God help us."

I wondered if it were too late for that.

Search parties

Dholpore 1872

We rode swiftly to the Northrops. Sir Cuthbert wanted to tell his tale once and urged his poor pony on, swaying in his usual careless slouch.

I heard nothing of those strange shrieking birds, gibbering langur monkeys or the clatter and chatter of humanity when we rode through the town. My thoughts clamoured in my mind in dreadful cacophony. A native could not have entered the Club, not without help from the doormen and even then he would have been noticed. All the amorphous unease I felt about this abduction fretted at me. The only obvious solution was that one of Club members, a non-native, was responsible. But why? What blackguard would rob such a beautiful woman and devoted mother as Charis Northrop? What member of the British society here could stoop to such behaviour? My banker's mind answered that. Many men had debts so might one be desperate enough to try a kidnap? Or could it be an effort to stop the government enquiry? Or was it some spite because of the plays and Felix would turn up tomorrow? I couldn't decide but kept weighing up one solution and then another until my head complained.

We arrived at the Northrops and the servants scurried out behind a pale and worn Ada Broadbent who greeted us first with "Have you found…?" which crossed with our "Is there any news?"

"I have some information," Sir Cuthbert said. "And Ackerman did some useful research. Should we speak to Julius on his own?"

Mrs Broadbent halted on the top verandah step. "Julius has just returned. He is exhausted. Charis is beside herself. Beatrice is holding the house together." She reached out a pleading hand. "Can you modify what you say? Please make the truth palatable to two desperate women and a heart-sore father." She included me in the plea.

Sir Cuthbert humphed.

I spoke. "My research will not, I believe, cause distress, Mrs Broadbent. It might give them some hope."

Ada Broadbent gave me a 'thank the good Lord' look. "Come along then, Mr Ackerman, but trim your words to encouragement not just plain facts." Her governessy tone suggested a pat on the head. Sir Cuthbert grimaced at me, pulling such a face that I might have laughed in other circumstances.

If Beatrice Chayle appeared pale and wan, Charis Northrop was bleached a deathly white. The ayah knelt before Miss Chayle weeping at her feet as Beatrice spoke to her in her own language. Julius Northrop crouched beside his wife's chair, holding her hands between his. His face had lost flesh, appeared all bones and angles, as if his skull pushed through. But my first shameful thoughts were not of pity, but that I wished I knelt in his place, holding her hands. I quashed them, full of self-disgust and appalled at my lack of control.

"No messengers, or news or note?" I murmured in Ada Broadbent's ear.

"Nothing."

Sir Cuthbert cleared his throat, demanding attention. The ayah made to rise and was restrained by Beatrice Chayle. Her face reflected the fear in Beatrice's face, and she cringed away from us. Sir Cuthbert beckoned me to speak but I hesitated. Into my confused thoughts came the memory of a soldier's cap, the cap which Felix wore. I reordered my mind and addressed Beatrice Chayle.

"Would you ask Felix's ayah about that soldier's cap? It may lead us to someone who knows something. Would this ayah talk to other ayahs? Could she ask about gossip and rumours of a plan to take a sahib's child? Could she ask if any of them saw Felix near the Club yesterday night?"

Beatrice's face lightened. Her whole body kindled with purpose and renewed energy. "Oh yes. We'll go now. There is a good portion of the day left and we might hear something." She rose. "I'll ask about the cap later when the ayah is calmer and not fearing blame." She embraced the Northrops and whisked herself and the ayah away. The ayah, with much jangling of ankle and arm bracelets, turned in the doorway to bow. She looked desolate and genuinely concerned for Felix.

The Northrops, wrapped in their own bleak imaginings, gave no indication of heeding the departure. Ada Broadbent gently replaced Julius Northrop and gripped Charis Northrop's hands. That gave Sir Cuthbert the opportunity to touch Northrop's shoulders and draw him to his feet.

"Come man, take heart. We have much to tell you. We need your attention and your intelligence. Listen to what we have uncovered. Ackerman, explain how you think Felix might have left the Club."

I made a succinct account, and demonstrated using Mrs Broadbent's shawl. Charis Northrop watched, a little colour touching her skin. Her husband frowned. He began to see the complexities of the affair. Before he could comment Sir Cuthbert forestalled him with the description of his morning's work.

"The servants on the door last night were the regular men. They have a sound record of good work and of being as honest as these servants usually are. Mr Jury claims they have never given him cause to consider their dismissal. Amal has watched and listened and all reports are of honest men, yet these honest men have disappeared. He could not find them."

"Ah," cried Charis Northrop, "they have him then, and have hidden themselves and my poor brave lad."

I held my tongue with difficulty. Ada Broadbent opened, then closed her mouth, her chubby face blank. She paused to look across the fair head to her husband, showing him a questioning expression.

Julius Northrop tried to accept this hopeful idea, and I wondered how much he would shield his wife when the truth became obvious.

"I want to search the town tomorrow," he said.

Sir Cuthbert' hands and facial expression urgently negated the idea. He chose his words carefully, one eye on Mrs Northrop. "I would wait another day. You may well receive information, a message, or even a note, tomorrow. It could take time for the kidnappers to find a way to send information without being discovered. They will want to remain unknown."

Julius checked, nodded his head, glanced at his wife and noted the anticipation. "I concur. I will wait. My men are keen and ready."

Ada Broadbent, clearly used to her husband's silent messages, raised Charis Northrop. "Come along, my dear, you need to rest and be strong for Felix." Supporting Mrs Northrop round the waist, and letting her lean against her ample shoulders, Ada Broadbent persuaded the distraught mother to leave us.

The door closed behind them. I walked across to check that it was soundly shut, that no servants hovered near.

"What…?" began Julius Northrop, but he was hushed by Sir Cuthbert.

"Keep your voice low. Do not disturb your wife nor let the servants overhear." Sir Cuthbert gestured towards me. "Listen to Ackerman, he has some disturbing ideas which might alter what you do."

"This is all speculation and conjecture, Northrop. I think you begin to understand that no native could have taken Felix from the Club. Any open inquiry we make will be soon discovered by the British community and thus is fraught with the possibility of causing danger to Felix."

Northrop's legs gave way. He plumped down in the chair his wife had vacated.

"We must continue to work as though we believe it to be a native kidnapping, but you and Sir Cuthbert need to find out who is heavily in debt in our community or even the Anglo-Indian community."

"I can do that with ease for the government men," Northrop agreed," but not for the military. For me to do so there would raise questions."

I turned to Sir Cuthbert. "What military contacts have you? Enough to do this?"

He nodded. There was another task I had for Sir Cuthbert, but that I would not mention in front of the boy's father. Later, tomorrow would do for that task. Meanwhile there was the soldier's cap.

"Northrop, you questioned your ayah about a soldier's cap. I wonder if the soldier might have been making friends with a purpose."

He thought carefully before speaking. "She said a kind soldier gave it to Felix."

"Did you ask where?

He shook his head. "I didn't see the need to."

"Could the soldier have been visiting her here?"

Sir Cuthbert, shocked, began to expostulate. I held up my hand. "What do you think, Northrop?"

"She has been a good nurse, devoted to Felix….She is trained, you know, came with us from the city. She has family there and she is promised to a man…." Julius Northrop leant his head against his hand and sighed. "I don't know."

"We cannot know. We need to find out…." I stopped as footsteps sounded down the hallway. The door opened and Mrs Broadbent entered.

"Julius, my dear, I think Charis would sleep if you reassure her once more with details of tomorrow's plans to find Felix." Her voice wobbled, but she bravely continued. "I've told her again that not receiving a note today, or a message, is not important as it would take time for such men to get a note written or message composed and delivered. Your repeating this might soothe her into sleep."

He clutched her hands in a convulsive grasp, she squeezed in return, and guided him towards the door. Muttering thanks he left the room.

Ada Broadbent sighed, turned and faced us. "What is it you men are hiding?" She moved across the room to me and looked up into my face, searching my features, my eyes. "What is it you fear?"

I could not tell her, dared not.

She turned round, faced her husband. "What is it? I gather this is no ordinary kidnapping."

"Hush now, Ada."

"Not here, please, Mrs Broadbent."

She gave us a look which said clearly what she thought of our silences. "I must stay until we hear about this abduction. Charis is in need of sleep and a time to weep; as yet she can do neither." She reached out, touched her husband's arm. "Amal will take care of you both. At least you may be searching actively, out there doing something to find that beloved boy." Tears left a silvery trace over her reddened cheeks.

Sir Cuthbert huffed his moustaches and slid his arm round her waist. I turned away so that their emotional moment might have the privacy they needed. On the wall I saw the measuring marks which Felix had stood against and my own eyes prickled. I closed them and prayed, prayed I was wrong. Tomorrow would show us, please God.

In the brothel

Dholpore 1872

Ada Broadbent had phrased it well. We men could get out and search. It did ease the pain of waiting and allowed us a fair night's sleep. Amal organised the household, issued orders for the day, and departed to search again for the doorkeepers. Sir Cuthbert headed into town to chase up his secure and top of the ladder military contacts.

"A bit of a boozy gossip with one," he said, "and a sober magisterial warning to a commanding officer with the other." He rode off, as slouching and slack reined as ever, his pony shuffling along in resignation, his syce trotting behind with a similar expression.

I sat in the shade pondering. It was no use hankering after Charis Northrop, wishing myself over there to hold her, to comfort her in her own home. Such thoughts were merely a sign of my infatuation and not a jot useful. We must find Felix. It was the why of why had he been removed which seemed so important. Why did I feel it was an act of revenge? Was I so enveloped in my own efforts to bring justice to the devils who'd hurt my family and those other families that I could only see any terrible actions in the same vengeful light?

Who would want to harm a boy? Who would want a handsome little chap like....I remembered my thought of the previous day, Surely not. Pray God not that. I had wondered if Felix had been taken to be sold as a slave to some discontented Maharajah who felt a white page boy might be one in the eye to the British community and a way of paying back the British for their Indian page boys. Now, thinking about my own problems led me to a more dreadful conclusion. I needed someone who would know the white community intimately and yet not feel outraged by my questions. Perhaps I could start with Desmond Jury. He could be the man to verify my fears and he might know someone who could help me on my quest. I also needed to speak with the despised military. Soldiers would be able to make that sort of contact and know who would pay for a spunky boy like Felix.

My pony, a shaggy brown fellow, watched his feet, leaving me to watch my thoughts. My attendant, the syce who cared for my pony, followed behind, grasping the animal's tail on the steepest parts. Both came willingly to town and vanished swiftly towards the stables as I entered the Club.

Desmond Jury's office door stood ajar, and arguing reached my ears. Jury's voice rang out loudly, an aggravated pitch, the other fell into a fierce low tone.

"No, I may not do that, and nor will you." Jury thrust the younger secretary out of the door, almost into my face. "If I learn, Archibald Mathers, that you have as much as…." He broke off, seeing me. "Any news? Is the boy safely home?"

I shook my head. "No message yet."

"Mathers here thinks the boy is with one of the military families. He believes the child accidently slipped out with one of the young officers, who might not realise who he is."

Mathers shook off Jury's hand and looked at me. "It is possible, you know."

I doubted the accident part of the idea, but any guess ought to be explored. "Then go and find out. Send messages to the families, or better yet go yourself."

He went, casting a look at Desmond Jury who sighed.

"The young idiot has a head full of bees and pretentions. This gives him the opportunity to socialise with Major, the Honourable Aubrey Wulfsige and those of his ilk." Jury twiddled his collar stud, distracted and annoyed.

Here was my opening. "If it's soldiers who have their hands on Felix they might well need to hide him until our hunt and search is over. I thought of brothels being a place they would know, with women who would care for the lad and keep him hidden. Do you know where such places are in town?"

"A bawdy house? Not I." Jury sounded mildly insulted. He pondered. "Yes, I can understand that is a possibility if soldiers have the child. But why do such a thing?"

"For a senior officer, to pay off debts. For themselves to sell the boy to some wealthy native family who have a fancy for a white page or slave."

"Good God!"

"Indeed. Yet it is possible and explains the ease with which the lad was whisked out of the Club." I gave him a narrow eyed glare. "You yourself considered that."

Jury made assent with his head and body, then coughed. "How is Mrs Northrop? She must be desolate."

He didn't blush, but I recognised the tone. He was another smitten by Charis Northrop.

"She will be well when her son returns." I leaned over him. "Brothels, man. Who can tell me?"

He shook himself out of his contemplation of Charis Northrop. "Come with me. Captain Rankin is in the theatre, collecting properties, I believe. He's a good officer. He'll know what his men get up to and where they go."

Desmond Jury had to leave me outside the dressing rooms, called away to deal with some culinary supplies disaster. Inside the middle one of the row I heard the captain directing the removal of the properties. Boxes were being passed by a sergeant through the doorway into the arms of two soldiers who blocked the passage. The soldiers muttered at me, but I frowned them down and called to the captain.

Captain Rankin's head appeared round the door post. He made an effort to remember who I was.

"Mr Bryce Ackerman, I'm with Sir Cuthbert Broadbent."

He recollected and made one of those assenting, half word, half noises.

"I need to speak to you."

"Come inside then." He addressed his men. "Be off with you and don't damage or lose anything."

The tone was savage but the men grinned. An officer liked by his men then. Captain Richard Rankin must have some redeeming features. I entered the cramped room and we looked at each other. His head reached my shoulder, his lean body was half my breadth. I think he resented this so I took care to part sit on the dressing table so that we were both at eye level.

I had to be careful. Any suggestion, without concrete proof, of his men being responsible for kidnapping Felix he would deny. "There is a possibility that the Northrop child is being hidden in town." True. Now for a partial truth. "There is a link between those door servants last night and a brothel. We cannot discover which one but hope to find out and make a discreet search. Could you help us by telling us which your men favour, or which they might suggest would be best to search?"

"Hasn't the boy been returned?" The captain sounded astonished.

Why would he think that? "No." I refrained from adding that this was the reason we wanted to search a brothel. "We are waiting for a message from his kidnappers, but hope to trace the child and rescue him."

The captain remained silent, frowned, appeared worried.

"His parents are nearly out of their minds with anxiety."

Captain Rankin looked as if he did not mind the Northrops fretting and frightened. Perhaps last night's loss still rankled.

"I can't help. The regiment has an official brothel to prevent disease and loss of morale. My men…."

I didn't let him finish. Prig he might be, but avoid this he would not. "Men will sneak off. Where will they go? What is this town's equivalent of the French House of Madame Clotilde?"

His response surprised me. "How would I know," he snapped and thrust past me. He was out of the door before I could grasp his arm and stop him.

I made after him, calling his name loudly.

"The boy will be returned safely, I'm sure," he flung over his shoulder as he disappeared, following where his sergeant had gone.

I flung up my hands, clenched them into fists and thumped the wall. The door of the next dressing room cracked open. Ready to apologise for my outburst I stopped as a hand reached out to me. As the rest of the arm was clad in army uniform I had no qualms about easing through the narrow gap and into the dressing room. Both of the privates waited there.

"What…?" I began but was hushed.

"Sarge'll be waiting outside, we can't be long." This from the chubby, sandy haired private.

"So it's true? About Northrops' wee laddie?" The lanky private was clearly a Scot.

I didn't know what these soldiers wanted but they seemed agitated, inclined to help, and might be my source of information about brothels. "Yes, he's been kidnapped, snatched from the Club last night."

"That Mrs Northrop, she's a bit of all right." The chubby man blew out his cheeks. "Nice lady but. She'll be half mad wi' worry."

"Aye, that she will." The Scot nodded sagely. "Did us a grand Christmas party for our regiment's nippers and lassies. We heard you. We could help. Can't reckon why Captain'll not, he knows where his men go."

Eavesdropping, but I had to be careful not to accuse them. I encouraged them with a nod.

"We're trusties, keep our ears open, our mouths shut and don't get into trouble with natives or booze. Heard a few things yesterday, but not enough to understand. We've got a better idea now." Chubby patted his mate's shoulder. "I'll take the things and shut Sarge up. You take him," he tilted his head at me, "and show him. I'll cover for you, mate. Out with ye."

We edged into the corridor and I led off. "Follow me as if you've a task to do for me," I told the Scot. "And don't look pleased about it."

He grinned. "Aye, sir." He pulled a sad face, but winked. "Know where we're going then, sir?"

I didn't, but I ignored his cheek and headed for the foyer and outside. Once on the top step outside I played the arrogant Englishman. "Don't drag behind, soldier, step out before me. We've a long way to go."

"Aye, sir." Another wink and brief salute and we strode off with me behind his shoulder.

Once clear of the Club we headed downhill and took the route through the market. We shouldered our way through the crowd, trying not to jostle the women and children, avoiding the beggars, and ignoring beseeching shopkeepers. All those voices crying out in a babble of unmusical tones cut across the more musical wails of the snake charmer's bheen, that peculiar hybrid flute affair they used. The Scot, ignoring everyone and everything, marched on. He turned left into a smaller street. The smells in this much narrower way were all of food, a sharp, spicy and heady mixture, but he ignored the stalls, making for the large building half way down on the left. He did not stop there, merely indicating with his chin as we passed the double entrance doors.

Two stalls further down the Scot began bartering with the owner for fresh cooked

chaat. This variety of chaat included some eye watering, nose prickling, well spiced fruit pickles with cooked vegetables folded into thin crispy flat bread.

"Try some, sir? Old Pranit here makes the best."

I leaned over the smiling stall holder who appeared clean though a little hot from being near his brazier. "What is this?" I pointed to the cooked vegetable mixture.

The man smiled and bobbed his head. "Sahib?

"Doesn't speak English, sir. Can't repeat what we say." The Scot jerked his head in the direction of the grand double doors. "That's the brothel officers and some soldiers use. It's the only one where the little nipper might be hid. T'other places are mainly native places, sir, and the lad'd stick out like a sore thumb 'cos they aint fancy houses, more like cots or hovels."

I paid for the soldier's food and pondered my approach to this brothel. "What's the brothel keeper like?" My hope was for a real French style brothel with a 'respectable' (if that is what you can call a procuress) middle aged woman who valued being seen as 'clean' and 'discreet' in authority's eyes.

"Why thank you, sir." He took the mess of food and began to eat.

"Well?" I was a bit sharp. He nodded and swallowed.

"Got to look at ease, sir. She's a stout woman, a brummie, talks posh though."

"From Birmingham? Good Lord. Well, thank you, soldier." I hesitated to slide money into his hand because he struck me as one who would take offence. I clapped him on the shoulder instead.

Before I could turn away the Scot indicated, with his eyes, that there was more. He leaned towards me and whispered. "Captain knows something, we heard him at our mad major this morning and he sent his young officers out to find someone. Asking about bodies he were. Something's not right, sir. " He flung me a salute and clattered off. "Best of British, sir," he called over his shoulder. "M' mate'll be in trouble if I don't move at the double."

Bodies? I dare not call after the soldier, but I would have to find out or get Sir Cuthbert to enquire. The mad major knew something? Would that be Major Arrogant Aubrey? More things to contemplate. Meanwhile I had to disobey my mother and enter a brothel. Not for the first time. The memory caused a rueful smile.

A group of us during our first Trinity term at university made a trip to Paris. Naturally a visit to a highly recommended bawdy house had been our aim. We knew nothing of sex and wanted to learn from the best. It was an accepted way among the upper crust to learn how to cope on the wedding night and I was foolish enough to be pleased to be included. There were some notable Parisian places. Alas, it was a spring crossing and the boat's frolics left most of us in no fit condition for totty hunting. All I remembered of the famous place was a lot of dingy white and stuffy, dusty gold plush with rooms too hot for comfort. I clung to a chair and drank watered wine. The girls I could barely remember. I wondered at my younger self and sighed inwardly. At least this was a morning visit and the 'girls' would be abed.

The door bells made a melodious jingle. The servant opening the door was the equivalent of our parlour maid at home, dressed in similar fashion, but she was a native girl. I gave her my card and asked to see the person in charge. She gave me a peculiar look but bade me wait in a reception room any respectable house would have been proud of.

Madame whatever-her-name-was-from-Birmingham was stout, but well encased without in a sober dress of tobacco brown, and within by some kind of fierce corsetry which creaked a little as she sat and beckoned me to sit.

"Mr. Ackerman?" She looked at my card carefully. She did not give me her name but regarded me with a steady stare, off putting even to me. That, I presumed, was her intention. I did not allow her rudeness to nettle me.

Now how did one appeal to this veritable dragon who appeared to have a mind as rigid as her corsets? I smiled down at her and sat in the wing chair she indicated, crossing my legs as if I felt completely at ease in her formidable presence. "Have you heard of the kidnapping of the Northrop's son from the Club?"

"I heard some such tale." Her cautious reply gave me hope.

"The magistrates assure me you are discreet."

Her eyelids flickered at the mention of magistrates. I hoped the word might carry a powerful reminder to her. "Sir Cuthbert Broadbent assures me that you might well prefer a visit from myself rather than the police making a full search."

Her face became more expressionless, her spine more rigid.

"It has been whispered in Sir Cuthbert's ear that a soldier is involved and that he has brought the boy here." I forestalled her indignant reply. "Without your foreknowledge we are certain."

Even with the oblique compliment I expected an explosion of wrath. Instead Madam regarded me with an almost pitying look.

She rose and beckoned. "We have no such child here. Follow me Mr…Ackerman isn't it?"

She knew very well it was, but had the spirit to try to suppress my status and depress my hope. I raised my brows and followed Madam from Birmingham in a slow march through every room.

She did it well, flinging doors open and standing outside whilst I inspected the interiors. I swear she smirked as we reached the second floor because these rooms were where the girls lived. Most of them were in bed, or worse, dressing. I maintained an icy politeness but the sight of a bevy of bare ankles and pretty feet, uncovered shoulders and flowing tresses did discompose me physically. Damn that Indian erotic atmosphere and damn all sluts who tempted good men. All honour to the girls though in that they made no flirtatious approaches and wore dressing gowns, although the robes, gauzy lacy affairs, were practically diaphanous. They were charming bits of nonsense I would like to have bought my wife in Paris on our honeymoon. Anger flickered and tore at that still raw wound.

I sighed. "I have seen that no one has a child here, thank you, madam….?" I waited for her name. She did not give it. "Is there anywhere else a child might be hidden?"

"No, Mr Ackerman. Indeed not." She tripped off down the stairs and I followed. We had not been in the servants' quarters or near the kitchens, but I had every intention of seeing every part of this establishment.

We descended to the more opulent first floor with its silk hangings and patterned rugs and half way down the grand curving staircase leading to the ground floor I heard a sound like a cry. Madam coughed, but I heard it again. A faint wail.

The moment my feet hit the ground floor tiles I grasped Madam rudely round the waist, lifted her and firmly put her to one side. I strode out towards the rear of the entrance hall, almost running. The wailing was clearly the sound of a child's distress.

"Felix," I roared. "Felix, where are you?"

Behind me Madam was bleating something in shrill angry tones, very much Birmingham inspired.

Dear God. If only I had found the child. All that pain and anguish put to rest. Please God, let this be Felix.

I charged down steps into the kitchen area and swerved left, following the cries. I burst into an open area, a kind of verandah leading into a garden.

Where was…? A little girl child sat in the lap of a native woman, a nursemaid or ayah. Behind her, clinging to her sari was a small boy with brown curls. He wailed as he tugged, demanding a share of the sweetmeats the little girl enjoyed.

Not Felix.

The disappointment hit like a well-placed boxer's glove. I even staggered backwards a step. Before I could regain any semblance of control or mental balance Madam was upon me, berating me and ordering me to leave.

I exploded. "You unfeeling infamous wretch. Two nights that little boy has been missing. His mother is heartbroken, his father distraught. The crime of kidnapping is not a joke, but you, you think it amusing to lead me through this bawdy house and not tell me of these children." I waved a hand in the direction of the ayah and children who huddled together their mouths open, shocked into momentary silence.

"Soldiers told me this was a likely place to hide a child. That tale must surely have grown out of the sight of these children. It raised my hopes. I ought to report you to Sir Cuthbert. English children are not permitted in a bawdy house." I tried to lower my voice as the children now cowered, sobbing in their fearful ayah's arms.

Madam from Birmingham ventured to touch my arm. "Mr Ackerman, please. I can explain. There is no need to shout and frighten everyone."

I heaved in a great breath, and inhaled again, trying for control. I glowered at her, looking down my nose from my full height. "Where is Felix Northrop?"

"Believe me, Mr Ackerman, if I knew I would have restored him to his mother."

I did. Her voice told me, the accents of Birmingham touching her vowels, and I glimpsed the woman she once had been, hidden behind the brothel madam front.

"I lost a child through illness." She spoke softly; I leaned down to hear. "That was a terrible experience. To have a child snatched away by a stranger stops my heart, it is a terror beyond thought."

I am nearly sure she meant exactly that, or perhaps she thought she ought to feel that. Whatever it was motivated her she had altered her attitude. Meanwhile servants peered at us from their doorway, and the girls were coming, judging by the sound of pattering footsteps hurrying nearer.

I felt shame yet again. Mortified by my lack of control I apologised. "We are desperate."

Again she touched my arm. "I understand. Come I will see you safely on your way."

She led the way, gathering up the girls in front of her until they all spilled out into the foyer.

A handsome redhead upbraided me for upsetting her child. The other girls added noisy reproaches. It could have been a cat fight. I drew myself up to full height, about to respond, but Madam Brummie interceded.

"Enough, ladies, Mr Ackerman acted under a misapprehension. He was told the stolen boy might be hidden here."

A shocked outcry burst from all present; vigorous denials followed.

"Do any of you know where the boy might be hidden?"

Pauses, head shakes, a chorus of negation, and the girls drifted away. If I'd been a man for cursing I would have used some of those marvellous Jewish curses my father's family occasionally indulged in. Instead I remembered my question. "What are those children doing in a brothel?"

Madam ushered me to the front doors. "Mr Ackerman, sometimes one of my girls finds herself with a problem. Sometimes we cannot make that problem disappear and so those problems become our family, our children."

I felt incredibly foolish. I had never thought about the possibility of prostitutes bearing children. I had assumed they protected themselves. I shifted from foot to foot, looking into Madam Birmingham's face. Madam Birmingham looked back.

"Those children are safer here. I promise you."

I believed her. India was no place for unprotected half breed bastards, the adha seer as the British soldiers called the Anglo-Indians. Most British people believed that it was bad to interbreed with Indians, a cross, according to them, which created bad blood, and inferior mentally unstable people.

"Mr Ackerman, I give you my word," she said, as I trod down the steps, "that we will listen and let you know of anything which might be of significance."

"Thank you," I said as the doors closed. I strode off down the street wondering how I could return to the Northrops with so little to give them hope. I waded my way through the crowd and saw Amal coming towards me.

"Any news?" I called.

He inclined his head in a regal nod. Heart and hope both leapt.

Now it's murder

Dholpore 1872

We could hardly stand in the middle of the street and discuss the news even if the crowds would have allowed us to do so.

I managed to stutter, "Has a message arrived?"

Amal's face told me not. I swallowed down every curse I knew and tried to find some reason for this delay. I assured myself that the more terrifying ideas which whispered in my ear and drifted through my head were the result of the last two depressing years searching and seeking information to bring villains to justice. I chided myself mentally for indulging such morbid thoughts and took note of the direction Amal led me.

"Where are we going?"

"To the police station, sahib."

Asking why would be a waste of our time. Amal might not know or be forbidden to speak. And here we were. At least I presumed this building, with uniformed barkandaz, each man with his baton at the ready, was an official building. It certainly looked like a government building, and there stood Sir Cuthbert, at his magisterial best, talking to one of his government colleagues, obviously the senior police officer.

"The superintendent, sahib," Amal hissed in my ear.

A portly man, the superintendent was one of those petty bureaucrats overfull of self-importance. I wished we'd found another Desmond Jury.

Sir Cuthbert saw me. "Ah, good, now Mr Ackerman is here you can take us to these bodies."

Bodies? The soldier had mentioned bodies. The same ones? I would have to find out.

The superintendent pulled a wry face, frowning at me. Sir Cuthbert did not introduce me but waved the man on. This did not please him, but Sir Cuthbert prevented any protest by talking to me. I quirked an eyebrow at him to ask why the incivility and what were we doing? Sir Cuthbert turned his face towards me, waggled his eyebrows and surreptitiously raised a finger to his lips. He then continued blethering about the need to be sure and could I help?

I had no notion of what he meant.

"You don't mind dead bodies do you?" he finished.

"All this fuss over a couple of stinking natives. Soldiers brought them in early this morning, but you had better cover your nose." The superintendent, with a sardonic smile, handed us over to a native officer who led us through the back of the building to a stairway leading down to cellars. The reek grew as we descended. It became a stench of decay and rotting which reminded me of the dead horse I saw long ago, killed in an accident and lying in the street with its leg bones visible and guts spilling out of its belly. Despite the ice the bodies in this mortuary stank of old blood and slit guts.

"Here, Ackerman, look." Sir Cuthbert pointed to a stone slab where two bodies lay.

I was not afraid of dead bodies but unused to seeing them. I reminded myself they would be mere empty shells, their souls departed, and steeled myself to look. I saw two naked men, similar height, bodies bruised and beaten, and their faces smashed and cut so that it would be difficult to tell who they were.

Sir Cuthbert indicated the back of each head. The pulpy mess made my already uneasy stomach, the result of the smell and the sight of those wrecked faces, lurch and heave. A powerful blow had stove in each skull.

"Do you recognise the men?"

"Good God, man," my roiling stomach made me testy, "how could I when they look like that?"

"Amal had the families in. These are the doorkeepers from that night at the Club."

"The poor devils. How could the families know, with faces like that?"

"The families are sure and according to Desmond Jury, one of the men had a right hand with a slightly withered little finger. One of these bodies has a right hand with a withered finger."

I nodded, holding my handkerchief to my nose, and bending forward to examine the hand Sir Cuthbert indicated.

When I straightened I looked for the native officer. He waited by the far wall. His face crinkled in distress, he would not look in our direction.

Keeping my voice low I murmured in Sir Cuthbert's ear. "If these are the doorkeepers from the Club then my thoughts are travelling in a direction I do not like."

Sir Cuthbert nodded. "They were involved."

"Perhaps not, perhaps silenced for what they saw. Come, sir, I need a drink. Can we be private at the Club?"

"The committee room, I'll commandeer that."

He did, with Secretary Jury's assistance "And send us some whisky, there's a good chap." Desmond Jury examined our faces and nodded.

We sank into round-backed, barrel shaped leather chairs, typical of committee rooms the Empire over. I stretched out my legs, patted my stomach. "Make mine brandy if you please, I need a restorative."

Jury fussed away and returned himself with a drinks tray and the requisite bottles and glasses. "No news then?" he asked, hovering as we poured generous dollops of the spirits.

He was no fool and inferred from our glum faces that the news was, alas, no news. I hesitated to fill his head with other fancies. Perhaps we should inform him of the death of his doormen. That might send him off on other concerns. It wasn't that I did not trust him…but it was wasn't it? I feared to trust anyone outside our circle because it was becoming steadily more certain that Felix's disappearance was not a kidnap by natives for a ransom.

Sir Cuthbert exhaled sharply and made his moustache leap. He poured himself another generous drink. "No news," he said and buried his face in his glass.

Jury sighed. "That poor mother."

I made up my mind, leant towards him, lowered my voice. "But your doormen are dead, battered to death."

The man stared. "Did you say battered to death? Murdered?"

"Yes." I finished the brandy in one gulp. My throat flamed but my stomach settled.

Jury sank into the chair beside me. "But this is terrible."

"We know."

"I had better arrange to hire others." But he remained seated. He blinked and fiddled with his cuffs as he thought some more. "This means…."

"Don't say it. Not now or to anyone until Sir Cuthbert and I have untangled the affair."

Jury frowned.

"Think of the child's safety. If a rumour reaches the culprits that we suspect soldiers' involvement, he is dead."

Sir Cuthbert protested. "Ah no. They will hold off."

"Not," I retorted sharply "if they think a dead boy tells no tales."

Desmond Jury's frown deepened. "Very well. I agree to say nothing other than that I know nothing."

"Thank you." I leaned forward to grasp his hand and shook it heartily. "For the Northrops' sake, we both thank you."

"Yes…yes…quite." In a haze of embarrassment Desmond Jury left us.

I looked at Sir Cuthbert. "Come with me to the brothel. I would like you to talk to Madam from Brum. I need you to lean on her."

He sat up. "She knows something?"

"I hope she has some information we might need, but which she will be reluctant to part with." I rose, paced, trying to grasp all the nebulous ideas afloat in my head. I shook my head to clear it. Was it time to share my fears? Perhaps.

"And better that we ask her, whom we can compel to silence, than try Jury, Mathers or your colleagues, Sir Cuthbert."

"What is it? What do you fear?" Sir Cuthbert pushed himself out of his chair and walked over to me.

"The damnable military, so we must trace this possible explanation to its end."

He gave me the wise-old-uncle-to-foolish-young-man stare. "Are you sure that's not your prejudice talking?"

"No note, no message. Just silence. That's not native work." I paced round the table, nudging each chair with my foot.

Sir Cuthbert returned to his chair, reached for the whisky. "Go on," he said, sounding most reluctant to hear me.

"Is there a small group of soldiers here base enough to do the deed?" I held up my hand to stop an interruption. "Or an officer with men rogue enough to obey an such an order, especially if they receive payment in gold or in favours like silence over what they did in England on their last leave?"

"Ah no, surely your business does not reach here?" Sir Cuthbert waved the brandy decanter in my direction.

I shook my head, paced some more. "I do not want to believe it but think, man think. It is, God forbid, a possible explanation. The danger is that Felix is a clever boy. He will know his captors. My only hope is they mean to move him away rather than be found out. I wonder if they mean to sell him."

"Ah, no. Not that. You can't mean…" Sir Cuthbert stared, his glass poised half way to his mouth.

"It is possible. Do you know where they would sell the boy? He would have to be moved across the country for them to be able to lose him so completely that we would never find him or trace him to them."

"Too risky, Ackerman." Sir Cuthbert swallowed a mouthful of whisky. "There is no train to move the child from this place. Ordinary soldiers would not be able to take leave for several days without permission and others knowing about their leave."

"Which would involve officers."

"Damn you, yes."

"You know it has to be so. I had conjectured that the losers, that group of military who lost to us in the play competition, they might have taken the boy overnight to punish us."

Sir Cuthbert spluttered into his drink. "Impossible. How could they return him without scandal and much talk?"

"That arrogant major could do it easily. Suppose he claimed that the boy must have slipped into their carriage and fallen asleep under the rugs?

No one could nay-say him or deny his tale because no one could prove it.”

“But the boy would…ah.”

“Precisely. Imagine an angry group sweeping up the boy from under the table. They then find that Felix is not stupid, will remember who has taken him, and cannot be silenced.”

“Oh dear God. No, I won’t believe it. Do not continue, Ackerman. This is…is utterly damnable. None of Her Majesty’s officers would behave like this.”

“And isn’t that what you told me when I first came to you in Calcutta with my story?”

He dropped his head into his hands and groaned.

“I had proof then and letters and documents with permissions and introductions. I have none now, but dare you tell me that British officers are incapable of such bestial action?”

“Damn you, Ackerman. No.” He knuckled his temples and grunted in pain.

“I also have a suspicion. When that information finally arrives I believe that Major Arrogant Aubrey will be the major I seek. Can you find out how many of his junior officers have been home on leave in the past two years? I could, by God’s grace, be in the right place to find the villains I want. And they might well be capable of taking a little boy if their major demanded it.”

“Beware, Bryce Ackerman. Be wary. Don’t whisper any accusation without solid truth, backed up by a multiplicity of proofs.” He hauled himself to his feet and wagged a finger at me. “I will find out for you, but remember, the honourable major is of impeccable lineage and social standing. You would do well to think about his power and influence.”

I thought of the power we merchant bankers had when these landed gentry wished to expand their business interests or cover their debts and borrow our money to do so.

"There are many sorts of power, Sir Cuthbert." I gave him a knowing look and took his arm to hurry him along. "What will Mrs Broadbent say when you tell her you've been to a brothel?"

"Shan't mention it." He winked.

I nearly laughed out loud. Ada Broadbent would winkle it out of him in two brief seconds, catching us unawares with a sly question or two. "To the brothel then sir, and please intimidate this woman. She won't want to tell us what we need to know and we have to have this information." I pulled a wry face. "It's our last possible explanation, apart from the military one, to unravel what happened to Felix." We rose and headed for the door.

Fun and games in the brothel

Dholpore 1872

Desmond Jury stopped us and invited us to a Club luncheon, he wanted to talk. We delayed our visit and ate an early lunch with him. The food was unimaginative and stodgily British. Not even a curry or an interesting dish of vegetables. There was an excellent selection of fruit though, the melons being particularly delicious. Sir Cuthbert, for all his stocky form, ate sparingly. I had more bulk to fill. Conversation was of a religious festival the Broadbents had observed at a small shrine, but with elephants playing a major role. We leaned our heads together as though conferring in confidence, which put off those who wanted to talk about the Northrops. We did have a quick drink with the men from New Zealand, who entertained us with tales of the colony. They painted a realistic picture, did not try to make the place a paradise, and were most persuasive. I tucked the idea away as worth mentioning to my family as a banking possibility.

We managed an escape from the majority of the lunchtime crowd for as they questioned poor Jury we slipped out behind them. The streets were busy. Natives bought the cooked food which every other stall sold and enjoyed the entertainment. The snake charmer sat in his corner and wailed upon his flute. A group of tumblers danced around beating drums. Unlike Calcutta, where everyone slept at mid-day, the heat was pleasant here, and the shopkeepers actively sold and shouted their wares as the market stalls and shops remained open. I usually stood taller than my fellows. Sir Cuthbert was only an inch or two above average height, but h e still towered over these hill tribe natives. The noise and smells outraged my unaccustomed ears and nose. The whirling coloured mass startled my eyes, I tried to look everywhere at once, but Sir Cuthbert strode on, accustomed.

"Don't dawdle, Ackerman. You can see all this any day."

At the brothel the parlour maid opened one door, saw me, bobbed, told us the mistress was not at home, and swiftly began to close the door.

I pushed my shoulder into it and Sir Cuthbert proffered his card. "This," he announced clearly for the whole hallway to hear, "is a Magistrate's Inspection."

A huge white man, perhaps their bodyguard or evening doorkeeper, loomed behind the parlour maid. "We're not due no inspection," he announced and slapped spade sized hands on the door.

"Ex-soldier are you?" Sir Cuthbert asked. "Then you should know I can go where I like, when I like."

"Not here you can't," the mammoth replied, filling the doorway to prevent our access. "We've got a bit o' officers' privilege." He began to force the door closed against my opposite efforts.

Oh no, he would not. My sharp knee jerk caught him exactly where no man ever wants to be kicked. He howled in outraged pain as he doubled up, blocking the doorway. I shoved the door against him to clear the entry. Sir Cuthbert squeezed through the gap, hooking the moaning lout's left foot as he did so. The doorkeeper collapsed on to the floor still clutching his crown jewels. I hadn't meant to hit so hard and almost winced for his agony.

Sir Cuthbert hurried across the hallway. I followed, pushing down on the back of the mammoth's head as he stirred. The poor fellow flattened out with a thump onto the parquet floor.

I indicated the reception room and Sir Cuthbert shot in, leaving the door open. I braced myself by the door. The diminutive parlour maid had fled, wailing. We'd have the whole house after us.

We did. I heard them first.

"What is making that infernal noise?" Sir Cuthbert turned in amazement.

They came in, a furious buzzing hoard. All, it appeared, of the 'girls', armed with short polished sticks, batons similar to those the local police carried. Into the room they swept to surround us.

I know my mouth fell open.

Sir Cuthbert's eyes tried to pop out of his head. "What is the meaning of this?" he roared, taking in the bevy of girls all dressed for afternoon tea, a flurry of frills and frou-frou with those menacing raised arms.

I did not laugh. These young women knew how to swing a baton.

"Visitors are not welcome. Please leave us." Madam from Birmingham had arrived.

"You have disturbed our household. You have no right here." She stepped through the door and indicated with her arm that we should leave that way.

Sir Cuthbert's chest expanded as he drew breath and he raised himself up to full height. He pulled some internal lever and radiated righteous power and authority. An impressive display. "I am here for information," he said, "and we will not leave without it."

I stopped leaning against the architrave, stretched out and caught Madam by her upper arms, lifting her round to face me. "Tell your girls we may stay. We must talk. They can remain if they wish." I set her down firmly on her feet, retaining my grip on her arms.

"I apologise for all this unmannerly behaviour," Sir Cuthbert said "but we are frantic to rescue the Northrop child."

Batons lowered, the girls hummed and muttered amongst themselves, still half wary, glances cast in our direction frequently.

"Very well." Madam was all gracious and condescending, erect in my hold. "Girls, you may go." She shrugged, trying to free her arms.

Most of the young women departed in an elegant wave of rustling indignation. A knot of three gathered across the room, heads inclined as they conferred. A treacherous breath of hope touched me. Did they know something?

I released Madam and went to them. "What do you know? Please, please help us."

They backed away to gather round Madam from Birmingham who was firmly denying any knowledge of Felix.

Impatience directed my manners. "We know that, Madam, but you are the most likely person to know where that particular group of men go, those who don't like your 'girls'."

Sir Cuthbert's eyebrows vanished into his hair line, but he kept a still tongue.

"Madam, you must know where those other men take their pleasure." I sighed into her silence and firm pressed lips. "The men who…who prefer men."

Sir Cuthbert banished an expression of distaste and spoke with authority. "There is no danger to them from me. I have no wish to close their…their club. We just need to know about the boy. If he has been offered to them." He stopped speaking and looked at me.

"Would they take Felix as a catamite?" It was as though I had stilled time. Silence, no movement, then a universally drawn, shocked breath. All stared at me.

"Come, Madam you would know this. There are men who…play both fields…shall we say?" I examined her face. It revealed nothing but disapproval.

"Mr. Ackerman, those particular men, in that group, are not pederasts. They do not bugger little boys."

I stared.

Sir Cuthbert blinked at her. "By heavens, madam, you are forthright. That is not an expression for a lady to use."

"I am, thank God, not bound by your ladies' rules."

Sir Cuthbert seethed, unable swiftly to politely return the repartee. He was bound by those rules.

"How do you know?" I challenge Madam's statement and she looked up at me and sneered in my face.

"You know very little, young man of those men who…play both fields as you call it. I know more."

The trio moved forward. "Indeed gentlemen, those poor men you refer to would not harm a boy. In this case I am sure they'd have him sent home." The speaker was one of the 'girls'.

I turned to them. "Do you know where such men have their club?"

Lips closed into tight lines.

"If they are as you say I mean them no harm. If they do not, then I hope that they might know who would take a little boy to train as his catamite."

"Madam?" The obviously Anglo-Indian 'girl' spoke, reached out and touched Madam's hands. "Please." but Madam remained obdurate.

"How do we know they are not going to arrest the men?" she asked the young woman, and turned back to me.

Sir Cuthbert raised his eyes and hands to heaven. "Madam, I give you my word."

The handsome redhead, she who was one of the mothers, put her arm round Madam's waist. They presented a united front. "We protect our children, Mr Ackerman. We would not allow a pederast into this house. Believe me, we would know one. Those men you wish to question, they would warn us. There is no such in this community."

Madam silenced her. "Thank you, girls. We have said enough. Away you go."

The girls gracefully bowed their heads and drifted away, all light charm and prettiness, a distinct contrast against the darkness our conversation had wrought.

I paced and thought. Relief that my dreadful imaginings were just that, warred with a fury that I would have to sort out the military connection to Felix when I desperately needed to finish the task I came to India to do. A second thought arrived. I would have no way to ease the pain tearing Charis Northrop apart. Julius might survive this but his fragile wife surely could not.

During the past two years I had seen mothers shatter, minds splintered beyond repair, and yet others recover, but so changed, bitter and bitterly afraid. I had revenge and action, pursuit and the bringing to justice to keep me sane and soothe the ever-present pain. What would Charis Northrop have to aid her?

"Come, Ackerman, bear up man. It was a good idea." Sir Cuthbert came up behind me and clouted my shoulder blades. "Thank God it is wrong. Madam, I apologise for our unmannerly behaviour, we are desperate, but that is no excuse for the damage we inflicted upon your door keeper."

Madam flung up her hands. "You are forgiven. I understand. I would help. Gossip has it that Mrs Northrop is like to sink into a decline." She shook her head. "When I heard the child had gone from the Club I knew it could not be for ransom." She clasped her hands against her breast and allowed herself the luxury of sadness. "The boy was noted for his fair prettiness and liveliness. There is a maharajah comes to the hills to his summer place. He is father to the Anglo-Indian wife of a major here in town. He brings all his family and one of his brothers is 'famous' for his boys, his catamites. He would pay well for the Northrop child."

A truly vile curse escaped Sir Cuthbert. It shocked even me, used to like comments occasionally made against my father and his people. Sir Cuthbert clapped a hand to his mouth, apologising, but Madam made as if she had not heard him.

"The Maharajah has access to the British Club," she continued.

"How do we tell that to the Northrops?" The words wrenched out from some place tucked down in my heart. I had spent the last two years surrounded by others' suffering and hurt. Was there to be no end to it? My hands made fists of themselves and I longed to use them.

Sir Cuthbert ceased pacing and, pulling himself into polite mode, made an effort to thank Madam from Birmingham.

She waved off his thanks, and attempted to offer some comfort. "The boy would be well treated. He's young yet for…." her words sank into silence.

"Yes, yes, and thank you for your help. We will remember." I managed a half bow, caught Sir Cuthbert by his elbow and propelled him out of the room and to the front door.

I pictured Charis Northrop's face as we attempted to explain to her husband what we had found and he told her what a catamite was. "We say nothing. I believe these women. There is just a remote chance that Felix is with the Maharajah's brother Even if we know this is the truth of it we say nothing."

"Gently, Ackerman, I feel as you do."

"Do you? Well then, how do we storm this maharaja's palace?"

Sir Cuthbert halted and pounded my shoulder with a hard fist. "We cannot, you young fool. We must do this diplomatically. We cannot have another Indian uprising. There are not enough soldiers in India to contain another."

The muttering door keeper slammed the heavy doors right on our heels and we walked back to the Club, heads bent, thinking furiously. After some quick decisions Sir Cuthbert rode to the Northrops to collect his wife, escort her home and carry a severely censored report of our findings to the Northrops and Miss Chayle. I suggested using the murders as a way of giving the Northrops hope. Something along the lines of thieves falling out and so not contacting them until all disputes were settled. Sir Cuthbert grumbled disagreement, said he'd find something to say, and shambled off on his pony. I mounted mine and rode back to the bungalow to do some further thinking.

The message arrives, further villainy's afoot

On the journey to the bungalow I distracted my tired brain watching the birds as I rode. There were swallows so like the swallows back home in England. I'd proposed to Aimée at dusk in the church meadow with swallows skimming past, dipping over the scarlet poppies and blue corncockles in the wheat field beyond the stone wall. Aimée. I missed her so, a physical ache like a nagging toothache. The last two years had been truly a hell upon the earth for so many, not just myself. Now here were the Northrops, another family beset with grief, and I would wager my soul on the cause of all our pain being this regiment here in Dholpore. How I loathed the army.

Bulbuls called and an Indian cuckoo replied or challenged. I gave up on the birds and sought a little calming solace in the clouds. The sky always wore fantastic shades of blue in India, deeper hues than home. And home was where I was not needed. I sighed and found myself outside the Broadbent's bungalow. The syce took my pony and Amal himself opened the door.

I shook my head at him. "No, no news."

Amal bowed, his gravity and concern affecting. "A letter has arrived for you, sahib. I think it is the one you waited for." He handed me the large official envelope, clearly government stationary, franked and stamped and sealed.

"Thank you, Amal."

At last. I went to my room to read the missive and think. The seals cracked open, the envelope flap lifted, and I removed a wad of paper, blank paper. "What the…?" I turned the envelope upside down and shook it over the bed. Nothing fell out. I examined the envelope carefully. It had been used before, the flap was not sticky and there were signs of another seal under the top ones. It had been resealed and sent to me.

Dropping the envelope I grabbed the paper and checked every piece. Each was blank on both sides. I sat on the edge of the bed and picked up the envelope again. This time I put my hand inside to widen it and peered inside. Jammed in the fold at the bottom was a white square of card. I prised it out and stared at it.

The boy is safe and well. If you wish him to remain so remove yourself from here within two days. Leave India and meddle no more in matters military. No more officers are to be accused. No more men are to be cashiered. You will place all documentary evidence in a government envelope and leave it in the Club messages box before 6 p.m. tomorrow evening. Leave nothing with the Magistrate and you will not speak of this to anyone. If you do, Felix will spend the rest of his short life with men who appreciate little boys.

I read the note at least five times, trying to make the words say something different. I now knew what being pole-axed felt like. I could neither speak nor move. Indeed breathing came hard. Eleven families relied on me to extract some form of justice, private justice, which they fully deserved. Now if I pursued their cause another family would be devastated. And I knew Charis Northrop and young Felix far better than many of the other families. Who had the most value? One small boy or the eleven families I knew of, and certainly more uncovered by now. Let those officers escape scot-free and it would happen again.

I struggled to my feet weighted down by the whole mess. Pent up breath escaped in a roar I could not contain. God help that major. Action,

I needed action to release this frustration and rage. I had two days, less really but I could surely….

Amal entered without knocking. "Sahib?"

I shook my head. "My apologies, Amal. I am overwhelmed by this situation."

As he turned and left he scanned the room, the bed, the scattered papers, and nodded.

What should I do? Think. I needed to think carefully and some of this thinking involved making assumptions, guesses really. God help me if I made the wrong assumption.

I could be like Hamlet and reason all the ways I should not do anything or I could risk all on my assumptions. Well intended guesses in truth they were.

I sat at the small desk and wrote out a list of my guesses.

1.   *We knew the major or one of that party took Felix from the Club.*

2.   *We could be fairly sure the boy was not hidden in the town.*

3.   *The major would surely involve his wife and use the maharajah's palace as a safe place to hide Felix. He could hide the child from the maharajah in the women's quarters and his Indian wife would obey him. He counted on the British government's reluctance to visit its wrath on the maharajah.*

4.   *We had a time limit.*

5.   *We needed a rescue party now to get to the boy before that time limit expired.*

It was amazing how clear my mind became once I had written out that list. As Sir Cuthbert said, we could not enter the maharajah's place without an invitation. I was too big and visibly non-Indian to play at some army scout's adventure and disguise myself as army scouts had done before. We would have to invite ourselves and that right quickly. How could I manage that and not endanger Felix? I did not need to speak to the Northrops as I could allow them to read the note. A little specious and certainly devious but I could truthfully say I had spoken to no one . Truth mattered even more in a mess like this.

Another thing mattered. Julius Northrop needed to know what had happened and how I intended to circumnavigate the problem. He had a right to know and to approve or add to the decision. If I caught him at home in the morning we could be at the maharajah's palace in the afternoon, a perfectly polite time for making calls. I tucked the note into my pocket and called Amal. I had no time to waste and needed to be sure of rising early.

Mid-morning the following day I set off. Despite my notes nagging me from my   pocket I found the ride to Northrops pleasant. I knew much more and had a plan to do something about the situation. The day had warmed but it was not outrageously hot and my syce trotted behind whistling softly. He was young to be a sahib's syce but Amal had chosen him, and the young man worked hard. My pony might still be a shaggy little native beast, but his coat shone and his harness was clean and supple. I was wondering if I could find him another post as syce after I left when he slipped in front of the pony and halted him. He pointed. We were at the foot of the slope, where the road met the driveway which led to the Northrops' house.

I could see nothing. "What is it?"

"Horses, sahib, horses."

This time I leant down and made my head and eyes follow his arm's direction more carefully. Indeed, in the shade of a group of wild apricot trees I saw the bulk and swishing tail of one, yes, two horses. Large ponies by their size. What were they doing there? The Northrop stables had been built to the side of the house, just at the top of this driveway, so why had the two horses been left down here?

I dismounted, and we walked slowly forwards. Call me suspicious of mind, but with Felix stolen away and the work I had been about for the last two years, I needed to be distrustful and wary. "Now whose horses can they be? Do you know?" I did not expect the syce to be able to answer.

He barely looked them over. "Soldiers," he said, his hand over my pony's muzzle. "Amal-ji warned us." His voice hissed the words. "Amal-ji said to watch for soldiers."

We advanced cautiously, but the animals were tethered and without a groom. That troubled me. They moved their heads to observe us but did not snort or whicker for my pony had not greeted them.

"Sahib, I know…these soldiers' horses. The soldiers…." My syce did not have the English to express himself clearly. He struggled. "The Club…the door man…mens…." He tried again. "Soldiers…we know…Soldiers kill my cousin…my cousin, the doorman."

His face convinced me he believed this. Earnest truth shone in his brown eyes; he might be mistaken, but he believed he was not.

I shook my head, trying to clear the fuzz of complicated thoughts and puzzlements stuffing my brain so that it was full of questions but no answers. Killed? To silence them? After all the usual military attitude to natives was deplorable, killing a native meant nothing, Sir Cuthbert informed me. We halted beside the horses and I checked the animals, then their saddlery. Under the saddle flap I saw a stamp and number. Definitely government issue.

My syce watched. "Soldiers' horses," he said again. He nodded his head fiercely in emphasis. "I know horses."

He did too, and had spoken out. I must find him a decent place when I left.

"Good man." I paused to think. To dither is not my way. Yet now I did. It was logical to believe Felix stolen away by the officers and hidden at the Maharaja's place. But had I made the wrong decision? Were these soldiers the kidnappers, the villains with a message? Or had they some better news from a commanding officer who had uncovered some soldiers' plot and knew where Felix was? Should I be alarmed or hopeful?

But, but…but why leave the horses hidden under the trees? And why, oh why, were they left without syce or any servant?

"Tie up my pony with these two. We had better see what is happening." I laid a finger to my lips in that universal sign for silence and my syce bowed his head in acquiescence.

He put my pony on the far side of the others, loosened the girth, eased the bit and began to fix a nose bag of feed.

I waved at him. "Hurry, man, I might need you." He stared, then ducked his head again, acknowledging me. I beckoned. "Come quietly."

He followed two paces behind me as I cautiously approached the house. The garden offered shadow and leafy shelter and I made the verandah without disturbing anyone or thing. I felt a fool sneaking around under the rhododendrons, acting like a burglar. Any of the servants might observe, wonder at my behaviour, and tell their mistress. But the house was still. No noise came from servants in the garden. There were none out working. That was odd. Even more peculiar was the lack of babble and chatter from the servants' quarters behind the house.

A hand touched my shoulder. I swear I leapt sideways six inches.

"Sorry, sahib." My syce tucked himself behind me, waiting his orders.

I could see that one of the set of French windows was open. This gave me quiet access into the house. I crept to the door, and, crouching to stay below the normal line of eyesight, peered round the open edge. Two young officers stood in the centre of the room facing Mrs Northrop. If my ears could have flapped they would have done so for I could not hear the words the soldiers said, just a murmur of voices. I sneaked back, beside the door, out of sight, waiting for understanding, waiting for more speech.

Then Charis Northrop sobbed. Horrified I peered through the slit between the door and the frame. Mrs Northrop wept, fell to her knees before them, hands clasped, begging.

"Give me back my son," she cried, voice rising in anguish. "Let me have my son back." The words came in spurts and gasps as she sobbed.

Transfixed was a word I knew, but I had never experienced the feeling. I did then. Stunned immobile by her agony and desperation I allowed the unpardonable to happen.

Those fine officers and gentlemen grasped Charis Northrop by the arms and hoisted her up. I could hear them now, voices near laughter. "Come, come, Mrs Northrop, our major wants you, and if you give us what we want, and you might have what you want. We know where the boy is."

The shorter of the two helped her stand. He stood behind her, and as she straightened he slipped his arms round her, wrapping them tightly so that he bound her to him, his hands cupping her breasts.

Charis cried out. Both men jeered.

"You spurned our major. Now you must entertain us. Give us what we want first. After that, we shall see."

I wasted just enough time to turn and hiss at the syce. "Go to the servants' quarters. Rouse them to help their mistress. Then run, take all the horses, take them all, and ride for the magistrate, ride for Sir Cuthbert." He slithered off, a snake on legs.

I turned back. The young lieutenant holding her from behind was rubbing his groin against her. Charis Northrop, slender and frail as a dandelion seed, struggled hopelessly, but she fought.

The dark bearded lieutenant in front of her was yanking her skirts and petticoats up crooning. "Puss, puss, pussy."

Charis screamed and kicked.

His comrade laughed and began to push himself harder against the panicking woman. "Front and back eh, Dom?" he said.

I was not a trained fighter, but I was a big man and strong. I could not hope to enter without being noticed, but I could leap in, roaring and bellowing instructions as though to servants following me. Surprise them, and I would have enough time to grab them before they could go into some soldier-trained action.

I surged across the room, snarling like a tiger. Unleashing my anger and disgust gave me all the impetus I needed. The rage and fury I had been controlling so firmly roiled in my head. I did indeed see red. The dark haired man, startled, froze. His companion reacted more quickly and turned, thrusting Charis Northrop at me. I anticipated that move and dodged to the right, hurdling the falling woman. I hammered my right fist down onto his shoulder, felling him to his knees. At the same time I grasped the other by his tunic then flung him at his stunned companion. They went down in a pile of flailing arms and legs, but bounced back, pushing each other up to kneeling. I pounced.

"You verminous scum." I hauled them up by their scruffs and smashed their heads together. "You vicious devil's spawn." I shook them so that they crashed into each other and tangled their legs. "You lascivious fiends." There weren't words filthy enough to describe them and I wasn't soiling my mouth with them. I slid my arms round each neck, bent my elbows, raised both men and began to squeeze. "You…you…filthy lecherous disgraces to your regiment."

I would have killed them I think; the rage had taken over completely, but Charis Northrop began to stir, calling out. I kneed Dark Hair in the arse and flung him into the wall, head first. He hit the floor in a limp heap. Shorty, I kneed under the chin, with enough force to almost break his neck. I had the satisfaction of knocking him out. I threw him after his filthy pal, and let them lie.

The red rage faltered. I forced myself to stand and breathe slowly in and out to control it, stop the trembling, stop the desire to kill.

Charis Northrop pushed herself up until she was sitting. Rage nearly under control I went to assist her. She moved her head from side to side, her eyes unfocussed, her expression confused. Her dress was torn at the waist and hem, thoroughly disarrayed elsewhere. She began to shake and whimper, soft utterances of distress.

I looked around for a lap rug or coverlet. Nothing. I crossed the room and yanked one of the Indian rugs from the back of the sofa. I dragged it to Charis Northrop and draped it round her. She trembled, raised one hand to her head, then focussed on me. She didn't know me and panic filled her face.

I knelt down, making soothing noises and shushing her. "You're safe now, Mrs Northrop. Your husband will be here soon." I devoutly hoped he would be. "Let me call your maid. Shall I do that?"

She managed a faint whispered "Yes." She shook violently and dropped her head into her hands, weeping.

I didn't resist the temptation and scooped her up, wrapping the rug round her so that she was decent and warm. "There, snug as a bug in a rug," I told her as one would tell a child. She sobbed, turned her face into my chest and her tears poured, soaking my shirt front.

Inside my head that watchful voice, my conscience, told me I'd wanted to hold Charis Northrop in my arms. Was my lust satisfied? I smiled wryly at myself and called for Mrs Northrop's maid.

No response.

Where the hell were the servants? Hadn't my syce found them? And typically the dark haired lieutenant stirred.

I bellowed for help. Charis Northrop shuddered in my arms. The French windows crashed back as Julius Northrop led a group of people into the room.

"What...? he began.

"Seize those soldiers." I ordered, holding his wife closer for I felt her go limp in a faint. "They attacked your wife."

He blenched and whirled to stare at the two bodies. Sir Cuthbert, appearing behind him, turned and called through the doorway. His syce appeared with another servant.

"Tie those soldiers up."

"Sahib?"

"Yes, my orders are to tie them up. They are evil men."

The servants bundled the two recovering men outside, with Sir Cuthbert behind them, urging the servants to bind the ropes tightly. Both lieutenants could be heard protesting.

"How dared the natives touch us..."and "There would be trouble...." Sir Cuthbert's shouted orders drowned out the rest.

Julius unfroze. He did not anxiously ask what happened or rush to wrench his wife from my arms. He stood, face whiter than goose feathers, and began berating her. "Charis, what have you done? I have warned you never to let men in the house without your servants near. See what can happen, you foolish woman. You..."

"Enough." I could stand no more. "Those vermin claimed to have knowledge of Felix. That's how they gained entrance."

Other voices sounded, women's voices, raised in horror, demanding to know what had happened. There was a noisy babble outside, people entered the room.

Julius began shouting, Charis, now stirring in my arms, quaked. I fell back into the past. It wasn't Charis Northrop I held but my fiancée, my beloved Aimée, my dearest petite Ami. It was her father reproaching me in a thunderous volume, her brother yelling, her mother weeping.

I no longer smelled the sharp demanding scents of India. It was late May, an English summer beginning, and the breeze carried a hint of a warm day to come. The scents were of sappy growing grass and Queen Anne's lace, the honeysuckle and wisteria around the house windows and the last of the lilacs. The train arrived early, I had walked from the station, casually entered my fiancée's home, and found chaos in the drawing room.

My Ami's father saw me. "You blackguard, you…you…how dare you show your face," he cried.

His wife looked shocked and sobbed. "How could you, Mr Ackerman? You must leave, take a continental tour and be married on the continent."

Her young brother advanced, fists raised, spluttering threats.

Aimée clung to her maid, both of them cowering in the bay window. Seeing me she straightened. "Bryce will listen," she cried, turning sideways to squeeze past her maid and run to me.

With the light behind her I saw her body's profile in sharp clarity. I faltered, shocked. Her brother rushed me. I batted away pugnacious young David as if he were a cobweb. Opening my arms I caught ma petite, my Ami, in a fierce embrace.

"Who did this to you? I'll kill him. Let me seek him out for you so that I can kill him." The pain I felt made me out-bellow even her father.

Silence fell. My dear one broke into sobs, shivering. "They won't listen. They want to blame you." She spoke between her sobs, looking over at her father and mother. I swung her up, cradling her in my arms and holding her close to my chest. She buried her face beneath my jacket and wept down my shirt. I carried her to the sofa and snarled at the rest of the family, those upset and bewildered Huntingdens. "How dare you think such a thing of me. Go away. I'll speak to you later."

I clutched ma petite Ami closer and a voice broke into my anger. "Mr Ackerman…. Bryce Ackerman…Bryce! Let Julius take his wife."

I blinked and blinked to clear my vision and found myself back in India. Charis Northrop lay in my arms, face against my shirt, her breathe coming in uneven gasps. Ada Broadbent stood in front of me looking up anxiously and tugging at my elbow.

I carefully carried Charis to her husband. "You don't deserve her. How dare you scold her. Your wife fought bravely against two strong soldiers." I lowered her into his arms. "Now comfort her. They hurt her. If I had not arrived it would have been far worse."

Julius Northrop cradled her tenderly. "I love her, you see," he said.

The simple statement told me all.

"I feared the worst. I couldn't bear it." He pressed his forehead against his wife's. "Forgive me, my dear." He carried her away, murmuring gentle words into her hair as she sighed and nestled close, content in the safety of his arms.

"No doubt about it, Ackerman," Sir Cuthbert strode up to me and slapped my shoulder. "We've found some more of your miscreants. Two of them anyway."

Ada Broadbent looked at her husband then at me. "Could you tell us what has happened? Is it about Felix? The syce talked of soldiers."

Us? A quick glance showed it was us. Miss Chayle, the Northrop's ayah and Amal gathered round. They all appeared bewildered. Where to start and what to say? I tried to think. Sir Cuthbert coughed and directed a quick glance at Amal.

Amal inclined his head. "I will discover what has happened to these useless, so invisible servants, sahib." He gathered up the ayah before him, and they departed, heading for the kitchens.

"Are those soldiers secure? I asked.

"Safe enough," Sir Cuthbert replied, "tied up and barred inside a storage hut."

"Before I rode here I sent your syce on to town," Mrs Broadbent said. "He's a good boy, ran into town to save the ponies in case we needed them. He is to bring back some of Julius Northrop's men and the police. And he asked me to say that the Northrop servants are locked in and he could not undo the locks."

"The despicable bastards." Sir Cuthbert sounded furious. "I'll have these blackguards in the magistrate's lock up."

I nodded. "But we have to be cautious. The regiment will be displeased with us and try to take over. We have to be clear, and say publically that these men are arrested because they attacked Mrs Northrop in her home. No hint of the kidnapping or my affairs."

Sir Cuthbert tapped his chest. "I was here. I have the details. I will make sure the reason is clearly recorded. Why are you so overly concerned?"

I tried to explain. "There is a problem…."

"What has happened? Please, please explain." Beatrice Chayle caught my sleeve. "Does my cousin need my aid?"

Before I could tell my tale, Charis Northrop, leaning on her husband's arm, came back into the room. She was wrapped up in her dressing gown, an elaborate concoction of embroidered satin and velvet, Indian made judging by the glorious colours. It covered her decorously from head to toe, most unlike those worn by the bordello girls, yet was, to me as sexually alluring. I swore at myself in my head.

"I cannot settle until I have thanked you properly, Mr Ackerman." She paused, took a steadying breath, "thank you for rescuing me from those men." She spoke with her chin slightly raised, holding her head so bravely. She looked for all the world like ma petite Ami did when she had faced me.

It was too much. I began to speak, to dismiss my part, to praise Charis Northrop and found I saw again Aimée facing me, saying "No." Breaking my heart.

"No…." To my extreme mortification my throat blocked, my eyes filled and I had to turn away. I found my way to the French windows, stepped on to the verandah and leant against a verandah post, struggling to control the tears. I fought my shoulders into stillness as I sucked in uneven breaths, striving to control the passionate outpouring which threatened.

Sir Cuthbert raised his voice so that I could hear him. "I think it is time to explain why you are in India, Mr Ackerman. I think the Northrops need to know what it is you do and who you seek, especially as your affairs might be connected to Felix's disappearance."

Still unable to speak, or turn to face them, I rested my hot head and flushed face on the cooler wood and waved an arm in acquiescence.

"Each of you must swear before God that you will not repeat what you learn here today." This was the magistrate at work, all dry voiced efficiency and power. "Ada, my dear, Miss Chayle, Bea, you are bound by this oath to secrecy too."

Murmurs of agreement, of promises, reached me.

Sir Cuthbert began, telling them of how he met me and what I had come to do. I could feel their listening in the silence, hear their shock in the hissed indrawn breaths.

I fought with myself, seeking control over my rage and pain. It was not passion which would bring those men to justice or save Felix. It was the rational elimination of the facts and logical thought-out action. Justice, not revenge.

When I knew I had command again I walked slowly back inside, reluctant to speak but knowing there were explanations to be made. I tried to keep to the simple unadorned facts, frugal with my words.

"Two and a half years ago I returned from a three month business trip to Vienna, and found my fiancée's family in an appalling uproar. My fiancée was disgraced, with child. Her father and mother accused me. Her father threatened legal action. Her mother insisted on a wedding on the continent and a year's travel after the birth."

"My dear fellow…." That was Julius Northrop, murmurs from the others.

I would not retain my composure if I saw their pity. I gazed over their heads, avoiding catching anyone's eyes by looking at some well executed sketches pinned up on the far wall.

"My fiancée trusted me and told me what had happened." I exhaled. "Even then I did not know the full story. It was her younger sisters and friends, coaxed by my mother, who revealed details of other families in the county so sordid they sickened us."

I strode the length of the room and back again. "I could not believe it. Two regiments competed, you see. It was a game. Selected groups of their young officers held a competition to see how many school room misses or young debutantes they could deflower and rape whilst they were home on leave. There was a prize for the winner."

Beatrice Chayle spoke for the others as they stared at me. "Two regiments …? Mr Ackerman are you telling us this truly? Two regiments? Groups of officers? Selected officers? Gentlemen?" Her voice rose in the highest pitch of amazement.

The faces in front of me showed varying shades of shock, embarrassment and horror. I nodded and paced across to the French windows and back again.

"Yes. I came to India to find justice for the young women and girls so harmed and disgraced and to punish those officers, in particular the officers who cost me my wife. But now we have an additional and terrible problem. My seeking justice has caused your pain."

I took the note from my pocket. "You must read it. Read it I say, and do not speak or quote from it." I unfolded the card and gave it to Julius. "Say nothing. Hand it on. Above all do not speak. You all must read it then let me explain. We must obey the words, but I believe we can avoid the consequences. I have a plan."

Charis Northrop read the note with her husband. Their two heads drooped, touched, and Julius groaned. Charis looked ready to faint. They both turned their anguished eyes in my direction and did not need to speak. I felt their pain.

Ada Broadbent almost snatched the note. Sir Cuthbert made her share it with him. They read it twice then both stared at me, mouths opened, but tongues still. Sir Cuthbert grasped his wife's hand, she clutched at his.

Beatrice Chayle whisked the note from Sir Cuthbert's fingers. She scanned it rapidly, became outraged, furious and then her face paled in fear. Her mouth opened.

"No," I warned her.

"Beatrice, wait. Please, for me, for Felix. Listen to what Mr Ackerman plans," Charis Northrop pleaded.

"Patience and listen, Miss Chayle, let me tell you my way round this." I begged.

She tossed the note at me, tossed her head, glared at me, but hurried to sit on the arm of the sofa Julius and Charis Northrop shared. "Well then, Mr Ackerman, explain this master plan."

It was the Northrops I must convince and their suffering I wished to end. I went to them, knelt and took hold of Charis's hands. "I cannot and will not disappoint those families in England. There are girls of fourteen and fifteen violated and two with child. My own fiancée makes three."

Beatrice Chayle spluttered and might have spoken, but Julius whipped his hand over her mouth.

"But I cannot and will not allow Felix to be harmed."

Charis squeezed my fingers. Julius exhaled sharply.

"We must strike first."

"How?"

"Tomorrow morning, before nine, I will take an envelope of documents and leave them at the Club. I will not give them any documents with personal details and addresses of the families involved, but I will leave enough. There will be lists of officers I hunt and a letter explaining that I came here to the hills for a rest and the documents with the full details are coming via the government postal system."

"That is known," Sir Cuthbert nodded. "My staff and the officials here have that information and all of them know you and I await documents from Britain. What they know others will know."

I focussed on Charis Northrop again. "Tomorrow after I deliver that letter Ada and Sir Cuthbert will join me." I looked up at Beatrice Chayle. "And you, Miss Chayle, if you will." I tucked Charis's hands between mine and pressed them gently. "You and your husband must be brave and wait, but we are going out to the maharajah's summer palace to pay a morning call actually in the morning, by ten o'clock."

That joke brought weak smiles.

"I expect you to manage an official group of police or some other official group to form an escort, Sir Cuthbert. But not soldiers. We need two of the government carriages, those used in the parades, and you must have papers with seals and signatures which might be taken to be London documents."

I released Charis's hands and rose. I looked each person in the eyes and found agreement. "I want us there by ten. I want us to sweep in as if we were an official party with permission to demand and inspect."

Sir Cuthbert tutted. I gave him a look. He returned it.

"Ada, you told me about women's quarters…"

"Zenana," she corrected.

"Very well, zenana. You and Miss Chayle are to go straight there. You can find it? I will…no, Sir Cuthbert will demand you are escorted there when we arrive. If fortune smiles we can order a servant to take you there before we have to outface the maharajah."

"Why?" Trust Beatrice Chayle to challenge.

"Where will the major hide Felix, where will the boy be cared for and kept safe?"

She thought and nodded. "I see."

"Yes, and we must hurry because we don't have time. If we can swoop tomorrow morning and take Felix away we will have beaten the kidnappers."

Charis Northrop gazed at her husband. We all could see how hope and fear warred within her. Julius bent and whispered in her ear then spoke to me. "Are you sure Felix is there?"

I recounted the reasons. Sir Cuthbert supported my statements. "And those two blackguards we have just routed said they knew where the boy was. I will shake it out of them before we leave, but knowing who took Felix makes the zenana the most likely place."

"Then God speed your search and bring our child home."

We all cried "Amen."

A plan of attack

Dholpore 1872

Personal revelations amongst a collection of people who have a common cause and must work together, can cause complications, leave a splintered group. I feared this, tossed in bed fretting and thumping my pillows, pulling at my mosquito net, dreading the trip to the Maharaja's summer palace in the morning. I needed sleep yet could only lie there cursing my unruly emotions and the effort I'd have to make to meet eyes and appear normal. We needed a strong united front in order to rescue Felix, but I had shamed myself in front of these good people, lost control of my emotions and thus lost my self-respect, and probably theirs.

My companions put me to shame. Instead of pity and embarrassed glances I met a family-like sympathy and warmth, and almost as fierce an interest in bringing those officers to justice, as we had in finding Felix. It was Beatrice Chayle, not Mrs Broadbent, who shared confidences as we shared the open carriage on our journey. Sir Cuthbert and Ada Broadbent chose to follow behind in another purloined government carriage. We made quite a display as we drove in procession to the Maharaja's summer home, for Sir Cuthbert had arranged a uniformed mounted escort. We looked official and impressive, a ruse to emphasise the political and convince the Maharaja that he should take action if he wished to keep British favour.

"Excellent flimflam," Ada Broadbent had said as she settled into her carriage seat. She was correct.

Miss Chayle tactfully and politely did not enquire after my task, or chide me for my attitude to India. She talked generally first, about travel and the places she would like to see. As I had spent time in Europe we managed a reasonable and civil conversation until nerves overcame her resolution and she began to talk of Felix, clasping her hands and twisting them around each other.

"We will look foolish, Mr Ackerman, if Felix is not at the Maharaja's palace." She moved from her seat opposite me to take one beside me in the open carriage, half turning towards me, lifting her face to look me in the eyes.

Her eyes were a dark shade of blue, a moody sea blue, not full of sweet expectancy. They might be lovely eyes, with thick lashes, but they showed no respect, only an alertness, intelligence, and extreme worry.

I'd been having the same doubts but managed a quick smile. "Won't we just. It's a logical conclusion though and I am fairly sure we will find Felix there." I dared to tuck her hand under my arm to brace her over the bumpy road. "Miss Chayle, we have searched all possible places in the town, we have not been sent a ransom note and we know only a Club member could have removed Felix. We also have reason to believe that Major, the Honourable Aubrey Wulfsige, is the key figure involved. His wife has access to the zenana." I didn't go on to talk about the other officers participating, or the murdered door keepers.

Beatrice Chayle stiffened, firmly removed her hand, and returned to her seat opposite. "A process of elimination then, rather than definite knowledge."

"Yes, but a fair guess you must agree."

"Oh, I hope so." She clasped the fingers of one hand around the fingers of the other and squeezed them until her knuckles stood out like snow topped mountain peaks. "And why that threat about 'men who appreciate little boys'? What does it mean? "

I should have expected Beatrice Chayle to say something like this but she caught me unprepared. My ears burned, and the blush spread to my cheeks.

These were not my loving Aimée's eyes. Aimée I could have spoken to, explained the kidnapping and the note, cloaked the facts of sodomy and catamites in terms which allowed her the idea but not the details. But Aimée was going to be my wife, we could have discussed matters sexual, this prickly young woman was not.

Beatrice Chayle…well, I dreaded what would come next. She had read the note. If she began to question me regarding men and boys I did not know where to start or how to answer her. She had intelligence enough to understand, but how could I explain when sexual discussions were not just frowned on but forbidden.

Sodomy was not a topic for general discussion, not in polite society, nor was it thought fit for the ears of gentle ladies. I eased my collar, which now threatened my Adam's apple, and wondered why mothers didn't warn their daughters about such things. But how could they if they did not know? And such ignorance, as my mother warned, was dangerous. Oh, good lord, where to begin? And should I? The warmth of my embarrassment popped beads of moisture on my forehead. Perhaps I should simply keep silent?

"Mr Ackerman, please. I am certain you would not have me ignorant."

"Miss Chayle. It is no easy task to explain. I am a stranger, not your father or husband. These are things I cannot, should not, speak of to you."

Her eyebrows rose. Conjecture showed in her eyes, then serious thought. A faint flush darkened her skin. Instead of accepting my stammered explanation she began to berate me.

"You men. You claim to honour, revere and protect us, yet those so-called gentlemen officers felt free to violate innocent young girls, and many men visit brothels of which, I am told there are several in town, and about which I am not supposed to know. I don't think that is respecting and honouring us."

I opened my mouth to protest and explain but was cut off.

"We are told our husbands will teach us what we need to know on our wedding nights. Wouldn't it be better to know all that before to protect us from all these predatory men?"

If she had been my sister I would have wrung her neck. I seized on an excellent excuse for silence. "We are in an open carriage. There is a driver listening. How can I discuss anything of such a serious matter?"

"How can you not?" Beatrice Chayle placed her hand on my forearm. "Our driver does not understand more English than he needs. They are chosen for their inability to speak much English or understand it." Her eyes narrowed and she glared at me then removed her hand.

The desire to wring her neck grew. "Miss Chayle." I broadened my shoulders, placed my hands on my knees and leant towards her, into her space, blocking her into stillness. "Miss Chayle, this is not the place or the occasion to speak of such matters. And that," I said, setting my spine and bracing myself, "is all I am prepared to say."

Beatrice Chayle smiled with her mouth only, and continued to glare. "Truly?" The acid in her tone would have etched glass. The smile turned into a look, the sort you write with a capital L. "Do you fear to make me less respectful of men?" She smiled so sweetly, eyes downcast that I thought perhaps I'd convinced her and the conversation was finished. She raised her face, the sweetness vanished. Tempered steel would have been soft in comparison.

"I would like to know what the threat in the note means. You can close your eyes when you tell me."

"Miss Chayle…" I flung my hands up, clenched my fists but kept my curses trapped behind my teeth.

"Why can't you explain to me what you fear? Do you really believe that this topic is not one for a lady's ears?"

Now that was difficult for I knew how my mother, and women like Ada Broadbent, wanted such information to be available for all women. My mother would have expected Beatrice Chayle's mother or older sisters to speak to her on matters sexual. I fell back on safe repetition. "It is not my place to speak to you."

Beatrice Chayle gave a defiant sniff and attacked again, hack and slash, determined to make me speak. "Stuff and nonsense. What of your task here in India? If more ladies knew how some so-called gentlemen might behave surely we could prevent such incidents?"

"I concede that the ignorance of young ladies is part of the problem."

"Yet you will do nothing about it. How like my father you are. All men are the same. Even Julius Northrop…." Here her voice faded, she shook herself. "No, he does right to spare my poor cousin at this moment." Anger flared again in her face. "Why do you men have to try and protect us? All that does is leave us ignorant and vulnerable."

I kept my tongue firmly behind my teeth, and my teeth clamped shut.

"Well, Mr Ackerman?" It was a demand. "Do you not protect your mother and sisters?"

I sighed. She would have an answer. I smiled ruefully at her. "If you had been part of my family you would not have been ignorant of such matters."

Her face said she did not believe me.

"Wealthy Quakers like my mother's family are not bound to your usual upper middle class social customs, they believe in practical Christianity, and education. They use their educated minds to work for prison reform, hospital reform, education for the poor and in abolishing poverty and sickness."

This was new information to Miss Chayle. If her family was typical of their social group she had probably only heard the general misinformation about Quakers.

"Quakers also believe in education for women, Miss Chayle. They do not fall prey to ridiculous ideas, like, for example, the belief that a woman's brain will be damaged by studying subjects like mathematics, science and logic, the kind of education men have."

Beatrice Chayle's blue eyes widened. She was surprised and forgot herself. "I understood you were Jewish…oh, I beg your pardon." She blushed right up to her forehead, a soft pink shade under her remarkable translucent skin. Such beauty, even in her tired and distressed state. I gazed at her face until she blushed even more.

"I wasn't gifted with your kind of beauty," I said, knowing it would provoke an indignant sniff or withering glance. I received both. "Actually I owe my darker skin, black hair and this beak of a nose to my mother's family. My father is very English looking." I tried another smile, for the irritating female looked mortified. "Jewish beliefs mean that women are educated too and not kept ignorant." I thought of my father and mother insisting that my sisters sit in on university classes, that they learn to think for themselves.

'Quaker and Jew? I understood that…" her words trailed off. She blushed again.

"You may ask, Miss Chayle. I am accustomed to ruder questioning. I truly do not mind. What is it you wish to know?" I was not a product of her world, and I would have protected my Ami from much of the world's nastiness, but Beatrice Chayle was different. She burned with a deep anger I recognised. She needed to know and understand more of the world, she had been denied so much.

"Can a Jew marry a non-Jew?"

"Not officially, no, but our Jewish family are merchant bankers, not rigidly Jewish, or strictly orthodox, and my father is gifted both mathematically and in making wise choices for loans. The stricter members of the family could not afford to lose him when he fell in love with my mother. Accommodation has been made for him, and now for my brothers, for they too were born bankers. Indeed both are taking rabbi's instruction and intend to convert to Judaism. It will ease the situation."

"And what of your gifts? You are part of the banking world are you not?" She managed a tired smile.

"Oh, I am useful because I am able to speak several languages. The family can safely employ me for our international banking affairs." I also had a gift, nosing out new banking opportunities for us, but one does not boast.

She was about to speak again. I could see the determined glint in her eyes, but I'd thought of a way out. "Why don't you speak to Mrs Northrop when Felix is safely home. I am sure Julius Northrop will have explained the meaning of the threat in the note."

"Oh, yes, of course." Temporarily satisfied, Miss Chayle placed one hand neatly over the other and mercifully held her tongue.

I turned my attention to the countryside and wished to see an elephant or two. Not their type of country here in the hills, alas. I particularly enjoyed watching them, ornately decorated, in a wedding procession. I never ceased to marvel at how silently and gently they lifted their feet and placed them down so smoothly and quietly. A picture of slow moving calm in soothing contrast to the whirling, screaming circle of noisy celebration around them.

"Mr Ackerman? Will it work?" Beatrice Chayle clasped her hands in a prayerful attitude. "Will our official looking arrival shake Felix out?"

"Mrs Broadbent has spoken to you. You know the plan. We must make it work. You and she are the ones to find him. We men cannot go into the women's part of the house."

She nodded. "We will find him." She spoke as though she believed it to be a done deed, and tweaked her straw sunhat, pinching the brim to move it further down over her forehead. It shaded her expression and sent a dried grass whiff of English summers, and a reminder of August harvests under my nose.

"Do you know why I love India, Mr Ackerman?"

The abrupt change of topic disconcerted. I shook my head.

"Freedom. I seek those freedoms you say your mother and father allow your sisters. Permit me to tell you a story."

I hesitated.

She stretched out a beseeching hand. "After what you have told us I think you will guess why I wish to speak of this, won't you please listen?"

It would have been churlish to refuse.

And so she began, as though telling a story about someone else, but I had seen enough young women these past two years attempting to hide their distressed fragmented lives, so I heard the pain, saw the flickers of anguish.

"Am I then a parcel to be so disposed of?" she demanded as she explained about her aunt, shut away for refusing to marry, and her father's threat to do the same to her.

"So your engagement was announced at your ball?"

"It was," Miss Chayle said, yet she wore no ring on her finger.

"Then how came you to India? "

Beatrice's face twisted into a peculiar smile. "The Northrops. My cousin, Charis. She had lost the child they were expecting and then their two year old daughter died in an accident. The Northrops blamed Charis, her mother-law in particular, behaved harshly. Charis became desperately ill. She needed me."

Poor Mrs Northrop, that poor woman. I noted my crush was over, Charis Northrop I now thought of as Mrs Northrop. Thank God. No more physical discomfort in her presence.

"When Julius insisted she accompany him to India, and Charis begged to go, the Northrop family requested that I travel with her. My father gave way. The Northrops are an old family, of honourable lineage my father would say." Miss Chayle smiled wryly as she spoke. "And being more powerful politically, with my father needing their patronage, it was inevitable that he had to allow me to go. I fled. Thankfully. And I will not marry my father's junior partner. He's a thirty year old fusspot," she shuddered, "with a bristly goat's beard, pince-nez, a squeaky voice and clammy hands. A man with a mind like my father's." Her face pinched up in distress.

"I see." And I did perhaps comprehend a little of her distaste. Women like Beatrice Chayle needed a husband who married for love, a man who would listen, share some of his life with her, allow her a more expressive life of her own than was usual for the upper middle class wife. A rare creature indeed in her social circles. She needed to meet some of my family's friends and relatives.

"I begin to appreciate why India means so much to you."

"And I understand now," she replied, "why you dislike this country so much."

We sat in a more comfortable silence for the remainder of the journey

Visiting the Maharajah

Dholpore 1872

The Maharaja's summer palace was only a large house. Disappointing, I'd been hoping to see an elaborate place of turrets and courtyards, marble floors and cake tier fountains. The house stood square, three storeys tall and rather dull, more British Colonial than Indian.

The gravel driveway turned into a circle leading to the portico. We trotted up, halted in formation, and descended like royalty. The Broadbents swept us up the steps and into a barricade of the Maharajah's guard. Speed was vital. The women had to find Felix before information of our arrival reached certain ears in the women's quarters.

"We have urgent business with the Maharaja." Sir Cuthbert waved a sheaf of papers under the noses of the soldiers.

"Immediately," I said, standing tall and leaning over the nearest soldier.

"Take the women to Lady Wulfsige in the zenana," Sir Cuthbert ordered.

The guards moved sideways and two Indian gentlemen hurried towards us.

"Minor relatives," Sir Cuthbert hissed. Their clothes, silk, and jewelled turbans told him that.

"Welcome, welcome." Bows and hand clasps. "Please come this way, his serene highness will be delighted to see you."

"The ladies are visiting Major Lord Aubrey Wulfsige's wife," I interrupted, "please see them escorted to the zenana."

The minor relatives demurred.

"Now."

They hovered.

I sighed but waited.

Fortunately the major's wife, the maharani, appeared, drifting towards us in a waft of exotic scent, with several pretty attendants jingling and jangling in her wake. She looked all princess, regal and royal, swathed in a dark blue wrap, wearing one superb emerald and gold bracelet which did not rattle and clash as she moved. Greeting Mrs Broadbent and Beatrice Chayle with a cool charm and perfect English she welcomed them and gathered them up in her entourage. They flowed away, a rainbow of colours and trailing fabrics amidst gusts of that alien perfume and the tinkling rattling anklets and bracelets. Ada Broadbent pulled a face at us over her shoulder as she went.

We marched off in the opposite direction through a high ceilinged hall and into a long room which must have run the width of the house. It was a traditional Indian room with great punka ceiling fans, the long windows with shutters, so like French windows, and soft matting under foot. We were announced and allowed to enter. The Maharaja sat, not on a peacock throne as I half expected, but on an opulent brocade covered divan centred on a stunning rug in shades of red and purple, with traditional motifs in black. Spine stiff, shoulders back and head high, he managed to look imposing for all that he was a short, slight man, a tiny old man in fact. There was a low table beside the divan on which a servant placed a very British, fine-china tea service.

"Come and take tea, my friends, in Indian style." His voice creaked, and as we approached to bow I could see that he was at least seventy, with a face crinkled and wrinkled round the eyes and mouth, but showing that serene expression which some old people achieve. "Sir Cuthbert I know. Mr Ackerman I have heard of."

We bowed and he smiled and clapped his hands. The servant began to pour tea. The Maharaja helped himself to a gingersnap, and beaming, he waved the servant to offer us one.

"I order them from London specially," he told us.

We politely declined. Sir Cuthbert stepped forward and presented his papers. I hovered at his elbow. The Maharaja scanned the papers, handed them back to Sir Cuthbert, nibbled his biscuit, and regarded us.

"I see your authorities. I do not understand what you require."

"Felix Northrop." I had had enough; I glared. "We could come with soldiers and search here." The words burst out. The major's wife, it occurred to me, might well be under her husband's thumb and prevent Beatrice Chayle and Ada Broadbent from seeing where Felix was hidden.. We needed to hurry, we must apply pressure. Our departure had not been as private as I'd hoped and the Major would be watching me. He might well send someone to take the boy or have someone here ready to remove Felix.

Sir Cuthbert gave me the magistrate's stare, but this was no time for political dithering.

The Maharaja merely lowered his eyelids, hiding his expression.

"This four year old child is Julius Northrop's son. He was kidnapped." Sir Cuthbert patted my arm, hissing warnings. I shrugged him off. "He was brought here."

The little man lifted his head. A regal glare.

"It is time for him to come home. The Northrops are extremely distressed."

An expression I could only call smug, skittered over the maharaja's face.

"We know he has been brought here. You can have him 'found' and we will say nothing, or we will invoke the wrath of her Majesty and her government."

"For heaven's sake, Ackerman," Sir Cuthbert, puce cheeked, looking near to exploding, clutched his papers, crumpling them. "You can't start an international incident."

I shook my head. "I do not care. If that is what it takes to restore Felix then so be it. No more politics. That poor woman has suffered enough. She needs her child returned to her."

The servant searched our faces, anxiety written on his. His master spoke a few soft words in his own language and the servant padded away, glancing back several times to check on our behaviour.

"Be seated and explain."

Now how to convince this quiet gentleman sitting comfortable and serene in his own home that we knew his daughter's husband, a British officer, had stolen Felix Northrop and had brought him here. For we had no proof of any of the tale because the Club doormen had been murdered and the soldiers weren't talking. I need not have worried. He had no intention of being convinced.

Sir Cuthbert tried. He explained his signed and sealed documents carefully and promised secrecy and great discretion if Felix was produced and allowed to leave with us.

"This story, can you prove this tale?" Despite his solemn countenance and polite voice I felt that the maharaja was laughing at us. He knew the truth of it. With one of those inexplicable flashes of certainty, I was convinced that he had seen Felix. I could have struck him. Indeed I rose, moved forward.

"Ackerman, no, sit down. Restrain yourself."

"He knows, Sir Cuthbert. He has seen Felix."

"Then I will turn the soldiers and my magistrate's men loose here."

"You dare not." The maharaja sounded positive and secure. He had not moved from his seat and looked serenely unconcerned. He turned his head to watch the servant padding towards him.

"My daughter?" This time he spoke first in English, repeating his comment in the Bengalese tongue.

With much bowing the servant assured him that she came. And she did, she stood waiting in the doorway.

The servant dismissed and out of the room, the maharaja beckoned his daughter.

Kalindi Wulfsige quite dazzled the eye in a glorious sari of rich plum with silver thread decorations. She bowed reverently to her father and faced us with her eyebrows raised

"Where is Felix?"

This time Sir Cuthbert supported me. "Come, my dear. We know that your husband snatched him and we are giving him and you a chance to restore the child without recrimination."

The maharaja spoke, a few crisp sentences. His daughter bowed again, deeply and stood with head lowered. He turned his face to us. "No recriminations, Sir Cuthbert?" He expressed amusement again, looked at me. "And you, sir? Do you agree?"

"No, I'd have the Major cashiered and flogged, and his cohorts with him."

Sir Cuthbert gusted an exhalation of angry breath my way and glowered at me.

The maharaja beamed, now all affability. "As would I all British soldiers. But the maharani, my daughter begs me to be kind. She is like her mother." He stood up and pattered towards us, his fabric shoes scuffling over the soft matting.

"Come now, gentlemen. Once I discovered the boy do you really believe that I would allow him to come to harm? Indeed not." He stopped in front of me and looked up, twinkling at me. Had I not felt so furious I might have laughed. "Young man, you are dangerous, like a tiger. You go with my daughter, she will sooth your beast, and you will have your little boy to take to his grieving parents."

He pit-patted across to Sir Cuthbert, took his arm. "This way, Sir Cuthbert. You can sit and tell me how you discovered that the child came here. I know my daughter's tale of a mistake, of finding the boy in their carriage. Perhaps you can tell me the truth."

His command of English amazed me for he spoke the language far better than many Englishmen. I bowed and crossed the room to Kalindi Wulfsige. I gave her a polite bow and offered her my arm. "If you would be so kind as to escort me to Felix, Lady Wulfsige."

She showed me a puzzled face, hesitated, finally laid her hand on my arm. We left her father conversing with Sir Cuthbert as if they were old friends.

"I hope your father will not remain displeased with you, but Felix must be returned to his mother and father or there will be consequences none of us would enjoy."

Kalindi Wulfsige halted. "You care very much for the boy and his parents?"

I nodded.

"Let them know that if you had not been here we would have been silent. My father knows he can control Sir Cuthbert, but you...." She shook her head at me and strolled on, her hand warm and firm on my arm. "You would have turned your escort loose in our house, and wreaked havoc."

She lead me down a long passage bordered by the verandah, the windows shuttered and closed, the ceiling high, a cool dim place. "You, Mr Ackerman are unknown and dangerously unstable. You attacked and imprisoned my husband's officers."

"They deserved it." I wondered how she had that information so quickly.

We reached the end of the passage, where a sweeping curve of staircase, inset with nicely carved wooden panels, all diamonds and squares, faced us.

Kalindi Wulfsige set one tiny foot on the bottom step. Her sandal bore a jewel which caught a stray beam of light and winked at me as its owner tipped her head to view me again in perplexity. "Why should you care about these people, the child? What are they to you? They are not family."

How to respond without being offensive. I felt like telling her she should care, we all should care when a child was hurt or a mother distressed. Perhaps it wasn't the Indian way, I knew nothing of their customs, and telling her that good Christians should be concerned about their fellow men was not wise either. I shrugged.

She returned the shrug with a graceful one of her own and stepped onto the first step. "You may come with me to the top of the stairs but no further. We are now entering the zenana. Please to stay here."

"I understand, Lady Wulfsige. I have no wish to cause an international incident. I am not going to burst into your women's quarters unless I have to fetch Felix myself."

She laughed and transformed herself. "No, your women have already found Felix and he is showing them the wonders of our zenana." She reached a hand out to touch mine. "I would never have wished this to happen. I am sincerely distressed for the mother." As a loyal wife, she could say no more. She whisked round and up the stairs, her sandals peck-pecking on the treads like a little woodpecker.

I hesitated, then followed with care for the steps were narrow under my large English feet. At the top she turned abruptly. I paused, balancing on the last step and feeling most insecure. I swear she knew, her eyes told me, but she kept me teetering. "Do you have a son?"

"No." Startled by this rapid change yet again I made the last step and found myself too close to Kalindi Wulfsige with her lustrous black hair, long eyelashes and liquid bright eyes. She was sensual in the way that Charis Northrop or my Ami were not. Even her scent from her hair and body, could arouse me. Little wonder that the major wanted her. Yet if I had not been told that her mother was an English governess I would not have known from her appearance that she was Anglo-Indian. She was all dark skinned Indian to my unaccustomed eyes, yet most appealing sexually.

"Do you want a son?"

"One day I hope to have sons and daughters."

"Do you, like my husband's family, demand a son and heir, insist on your wife having sons?"

"I would like a son to inherit after me, yes." That had been Aimée's sticking point.

Her eyes flashed, her temper flared. "Oh you are so polite, so English. You have behaved to me as if I were the major's proper and English wife, not an Anglo-Indian bibikahna. Would you dare to in England?"

"I would hope so. Have you been to England?"

"Oh yes, indeed I have." The memory caused her to stiffen her spine and raise her head like a queen. "They insist on sons, light skinned sons. I must give them pale sons to be brought up by them." The sheen in her eyes turned to liquid, brightened, overflowed. She flicked the tears away.

"I will not have sons for them. Nor see my sons measured by the colour of their skins. They want sons but not mine, not boys tainted with my blood. They forget my mother was English, and that I am married under British law."

She turned away, but I'd heard the dreadful hurt in her voice and the pain in her eyes. Everywhere I went in India I found people who had been affected by this wretched major's actions.

"Remember please to wait here," Kalindi Wulfsige called over her shoulder.

I waited, and waited, and kept silent.

Finally I trod down the steps again hoping to find one of the guards or a servant to send into the forbidden harem. I had started off along the silent and empty hallway when there came a roar and a smashing crashing clamour overhead.

I whipped round and raced up the stairs. Hesitating at the top I heard running footsteps, then another crash followed by a scream.

"Run Felix!" I thought it was Miss Chayle's voice. I bellowed for assistance, heard behind me the thump of footsteps, but before I could leap through the archway and smash down the door I was firmly grasped from behind, my wrists twisted painfully. I tried to lash out, found my elbows gripped in a punishing pincer hold.

"Wait, Ackerman. Think." I did not know the voice and struggled as two Indian women hurried past, opened the door, and ran through. More servants came, crowding up the stairs and round the doorway. The grip loosened, but only enough to turn me to face the holder. It was that captain, the Honourable Major Aubrey Wulfsige's captain.

"Let me go."

"No, wait. You can't...." but loud screams interrupted him and the two women returned, scrambling through the door towards us, their eyes dilated, their polished brown skins overcast with a greyish tint. From their mouths came a babble of language.

Incomprehension gave way to horror as the captain uttered 'Dead?' then grasped one woman and shook her. "Who is dead?"

She burst into wails, tears stopping her voice. The other woman flung herself, prostrate, at his feet.

I attempted to barge between them, but was prevented by an elderly Indian woman who appeared from the zenana. She stood in the doorway and spoke firmly, but her hand shook as she caught the captain's arm. She pulled him through the door. I followed.

Murder most vile

Dholpore 1872

Blood. Blood spattered everywhere. The stench of hot steaming blood. A body on the floor, a scarlet halo round its head clashing with the rich plum on the body. Cushions and hangings lay scattered in disorder, furniture overturned. Someone moaned, a struggling heap under a torn down curtain. No Indian women in sight, no one offering help. And no Felix, no Miss Chayle or Mrs Broadbent.

The elderly woman pointed. We stood shocked rigid, like lumps of wood.

The captain called out, "Sevitri, Sevitri," which I took to be his wife's name.

The elderly Indian woman keened, pointed again to the body. The plum sari told me it was the major's wife. The woman wailed, high pitched ululations, the sound of mourning over the dead which I had heard in the city.

The captain, Richard Rankin, I remembered his name now, stepped between the pools of blood to lean over and gently turn the body face up.

I turned my face away, trying not to gag. Her throat was slit from ear to ear and her blood made a rich dark addition to the pattern on her sari before it pooled onto the floor.

"Murder." I breathed the word. The woman echoed my word and sank to her heels beside the body.

The person half smothered under the curtain writhed and muttered. I went to help and extricated Ada Broadbent. With relief I eased her to her feet, but she had a bump swelling over her temple, and her eyes failed to focus on me. I lowered her onto a seat, supporting her.

"What happened, Ada? Where is Felix?" But she had blinked, focused, moved her head and so seen the body. Her face drained of all colour. She panted, struggling for air.

"He is mad," she said, voice faint. "The major. He took Felix and Beatrice." Then she fell sideways.

Torn, I stopped her fall to the floor, desperately seeking help. I needed to chase through the rooms and rescue the boy and Miss Chayle. The major could only have had a lead of, at the most, ten minutes.

"We need some female assistance, Captain. Where are the women?" Mrs Broadbent was no lightweight and I could find no part of her to grasp politely. "For God's sake, man, get help. I must go after the lady and the boy."

He spoke sharply and the elderly Indian lady rose from her place beside the body and hurried back to the stairs. She returned in a moment with servants on whom I thankfully dumped Mrs Broadbent and fled through the zenana.

Footsteps pounded behind me, but I ran on without pause.

"Wait, man, wait," the captain panted out. "Two can search better than one."

I slowed as the passage divided, turned and stopped him. "Is the man mad? What is he doing taking the girl and the child?" I looked at the two possible passages.

"That way goes to the gardens, you search there," Rankin pointed to the right. "I'll take this way, it leads to several areas in the house. I know them all." He raised his hands in a gesture of futility. "I wish to God I knew what he's doing. Get on, man, get on. I know where he'll go with the boy. If you don't seize him now I'll bring them, or at least the boy, to the officer's headquarters."

He stormed off down the left passage as I fled down the right.

The passage led straight to a thick wooden door, an outer door. I yanked it towards me. It failed to open and I nearly smashed my nose. Locked. It would be. I turned the handle again and applied my shoulder. The door flew open. I fell through. It opened outwards not inwards. Cursing I clattered down the steps. At the bottom was a heavily decorated solid wooden door. I twisted the ornate iron latch and wrenched the door open. It led me into a walled garden. Now where would the man go with two unwilling captives? The stables? Some escape-way outside?

I bellowed. "Felix, Miss Chayle," then again, "Beatrice, Felix." He hadn't had time to gag them both. I listened, shouted again. This time I heard the grinding sound of stone on stone coming from the direction of the far wall. Then Felix shrieked "Cousin, cousin." Such a desperate heart call.

I ran as fast as I could and right into the darkness of an arched passageway. Before I could adjust my eyes a pitchy shape lunged at me, and I collected a crack on the cheek bone which knocked me sideways. A boot to my ankle brought me down to my knees and a shove in the back had me tumbling forward into space. A black opening, smelling of musty spices and rich damp earth, swallowed me up. The ground met me forcefully, driving my breath out with an oof and a yelp. The sound of stones grating together rang out above me and the darkness became an absolute of tangible velvet black. I swore, heaved myself up and heard a slithering. I do not like snakes and I stood quite still, fretting. Sweat prickled my forehead as I listened so hard I could hear my own heart-beat. Where was the creature?

I patted my pockets. Futile. This was an occasion where I wished that I smoked and carried a packet of matches. I could think of no way to make a light, and the fall had rattled my brain, which was now emptied of all but the urgent desire to see where the snake was.

The slither became a combination of rustling and swishing and I recognised that sound. If I had been tossed in here so might she. "Miss Chayle, is it you?"

"Are you unhurt?" or "Are you safe?" seemed an idiot's response to what had befallen her and as what I heard was a woman rearranging her skirts I knew she was reasonably well.

Her voice rose up from the floor. "Mr Ackerman? Thank heavens." She strove for control but her voice gave her away. "I saw a scorpion when I was dropped into this place. Do you think…I can't…I am afraid to put my hand…."

I heard her voice catch, smothering a sob. "Here's my hand, Miss Chayle. Reach for it." I stretched my arm in the direction of her voice and her hand flailed into mine grasping it with cold desperate fingers.

"I'm going to give you my other hand, Miss Chayle. Take that too and then I can raise you safely to your feet."

Another muffled sob and I had both her chilled hands firmly in mine. "Are you ready? Then up you come."

If she had been my Aimée I would have swung her up, around and into my arms for what that dear one lovingly called my bearish embrace. Beatrice Chayle needed more mannerly and circumspect manoeuvring so I pulled her gently to her feet. She trembled. I presumed to circle my right arm round her and steadied her against my side. Her legs shook and she leaned into me, sliding round so that her face was buried in my waistcoat as she clung, trying to stand alone and control her tears.

"My fiancée always said I was a useful prop, just rest against me for a moment, Miss Chayle, and then we must find a way out of here." I cupped my hands under her elbows, giving her support without the embarrassment of a close embrace. She still hid her head in my waistcoat, but her shaking had diminished to the occasional tremor and her breaths came without the catch that threatened tears.

She lifted her head. "Felix," she said.

Impressive recovery. I dared to pat her shoulder. "Brave girl. I am going to feel my way round this chamber and see if I can…"

"No, no, I saw, Mr Ackerman, when he dropped me in. Stretch up. I believe you are tall enough. The stones sealing us in are within your reach. It is only a small chamber."

She was correct. I could, standing on tiptoe, reach the slabs which covered the hole. The stone felt ice smooth, my hands slick, and I did not have full force of thrust from my legs.

"Hurry, Mr Ackerman."

My back burned, my shoulders strained, my calf muscles screamed. I felt the stone slab move. "It…" I began then my hands slipped and I fell forward.

I did not strike Miss Chayle but I did meet the wall and cracked my head. "Goddamn it!" I bent over holding my head.

"Swearing won't help, Mr Ackerman. Move that slab, please. For Felix's sake."

I tried again. This time I exploded upwards in a controlled leap, hands above my head, the thrust coming through my legs to my shoulders. Surely one mighty heave would knock the slabs sideways. If that man could move them I could.

I did, but one slab teetered and slid in towards us, letting in enough light for me to see and press Miss Chayle into the wall so that the incoming slab brushed my back and not her.

There was nothing soft or yielding about her, no melting against my chest, but she did lean against me and murmur 'Thank you.'

I stepped back. "Right, up with you. I am going to grasp your waist and if you jump upwards I can boost you through the hole."

I caught her firmly, felt her quiver. "Are you ready? One, two three and up you go." She jumped on three and rose like an arrow through the hole. In a flurry of skirt and flutter of petticoats she dived forward and kicked herself free of me, scrambling out of the hole. She didn't wait for me either, but rose to her feet and disappeared from my sight. I could hear her footsteps, running.

My head ached, my cheek throbbed, and I had a lump on my forehead. My palms smarted from where I had slapped them against the stone slabs. I guessed the major would have ridden off with the boy by now and fury raged. I swore at myself for falling for such an obvious reaction from the major and hoped the captain knew where he would be. I would have Felix safe and then that damned major's hide. Still if Beatrice Chayle could hurry to the rescue so ought I. A jump up, a heave over and I was in the passage, through it, and staggering out into the eye-watering brightness of another enclosed garden. Now where had Beatrice Chayle disappeared to?

The path led to a double gate, one of which was open. My stroll turned into a sprint as Miss Chayle's voice rose above a hubbub of voices. Her scream was unmistakably one of fury.

"Let go of me. At once." A command but obviously unheeded.

I arrived in a stable yard to see two soldiers desperately holding on to her arms as they avoided her kicking feet. I pushed my way through the lurking syces and outdoor servants to reach them.

"Take your hands off me. Let me go." Beatrice Chayle was clearly a handful, but the soldiers clung on.

I knew the men, the two trusties who had helped me previously. It appeared that they wanted to restrain her, not harm her, for they kept hold of her arms only and begged her to stand still.

"Ye canna be chasing the major, Miss. He's well gone and knows where to hide."

"The captain's after him, Miss. He'll have the lad by now or know where to find him."

Spotting me, the sandy one called out for help and I caught Beatrice Chayle round the waist and twirled her about to face me.

"Miss Chayle. Beatrice, Bea!"

But she was beyond listening. She knocked my hands away, hurled herself at me and slapped her hands against my chest, beating a frantic tattoo. "Felix, poor Felix. We so nearly had him. We must go after them."

"No, it's too late for us, but the captain is in pursuit." I caught her hands, pinned them against my chest, braced myself for worse. "Be calm. He will find Felix. He knows the major and the major will be less reluctant to hand over Felix to one of his own men." I cautiously released her hands. "We have to help Mrs Broadbent and sort out the mess the major caused here. His wife is dead." I held her away from me. "Be calm, Miss Chayle. Be calm."

She collapsed against me, her head just under my chin, and said something I couldn't hear. I held her firmly in a close embrace, rested my chin on her head and made soothing noises. Soon her anger passed and she wept. I found my handkerchief and passed it to her.

"Weep away your anger, my dear, then dry your eyes."

She ignored the handkerchief, continued to weep into my shirt.

"I am thankful the Broadbents' laundry servants can restore my shirts to new. Between you, Beatrice Chayle, and Mrs Northrop, my collection of shirts is reduced to soggy rags."

That did it. She raised her face. "How can you be so…so flippant."

I offered my handkerchief again and she snatched at it, mopping her eyes and cheeks. "That's better, now let us face the horror inside. I am as frustrated as you, but it is useless for us to pursue the major. We have no riding horses, and he has too great a start on us. He is familiar with the country, we are not. The captain is in a better position to know where he might go with Felix."

Miss Chayle steadied herself against me. I held her gently until she found inner strength and even managed a glare in my direction. Releasing her I offered her my arm. "Come now, Mrs Broadbent is hurt, and all is in a chaos we must help explain."

An unexpected friendship

Dholpore 1872

Chaos it was indeed in the summer palace. A squad of guards collected us the moment we approached the front of the house. Women wailed outside and inside. Servants milled about on the gravel drive forming knots and clumps which broke up and reformed aimlessly. As we were marched to the front door one of the lesser relatives appeared, stood on the top step and harangued us all. The servants fled. We trod up the steps and the angry relative greeted us in precise Oxford English.

"The maharajah demands your presence." He actually grasped Beatrice's arm.

I flicked his hand away. "Mind your manners, this lady is a guest, not some servant."

She sent me a swift grateful look. The relative narrowed his eyes but did not replace his hand.

"Follow me." He strode away and the guards urged us after him with fierce gestures.

The maharajah stood amidst the disorder in the zenana with his relatives and guards gathered round him. The men wore anxious or uncomfortable expressions, not used to being in the women's quarters. Three women servants sniffled mournfully as they scrubbed away the blood. The body had been removed. Mrs Broadbent reclined on the Indian version of a chaise longue, her face gently bathed by another female servant.

The moment he saw us the maharajah hurried to Miss Chayle. "You must tell me who did this terrible thing."

Beatrice was trembling, I felt her shaking and eased her into a low chair. She murmured thanks, lifted her face to address the maharajah. "Your Highness, I saw nothing. Mrs Broadbent, when we heard a commotion and the major's voice, sent me away to hide with Felix. That is what I did."

"Who killed my daughter?"

Ada Broadbent replied, raising her voice to be heard over the sobbing. "Her husband."

I'd wondered.

Beatrice Chayle shivered. The maharajah stiffened, disbelief gave way to fury. He uttered commands in his language to the guards. They bowed and raced out.

"Why?" he demanded, fierce as a hawk in a bate.

Mrs Broadbent raised a hand to her temples, winced and closed her eyes. "He strode into this room and his wife greeted him. I think she forbade him to enter." Ada sipped from the drinking bowl offered by her attendant, licked her lips and tried to clear her throat.

"He…" she tried again. "He demanded Felix. He ordered her to give him Felix. 'If you won't give me sons I'll take this one,' he said. She refused." Again Ada Broadbent sipped from the bowl.

"He gave her such a smile as I hope never to see again. She walked towards him, waving him towards the door and he took one swift step round and behind her. She had no time to move away for he embraced her from behind and a knife flashed. It was then I understood what he meant to do and tried to call out."

She raised her hand to her head, "I am confused about the following moments. He struck, your daughter fell, blood everywhere, then he came to me demanding Felix. He tore the room apart searching, then turned on me."

Beatrice left her chair and hurried to sit beside Mrs Broadbent, taking her hand. "At least Felix didn't see that, Ada." They both shuddered.

Beatrice Chayle finished the story. "I heard you calling out, Mrs Broadbent, and the major guessed that I was here, he knew Felix was here. He stormed after us. We ran. Felix tried so hard, but the major caught us. He is insane. He intended to take us both, but you pursued, Mr Ackerman, so he thrust me in that storage place, knocked you in too, and fled with Felix."

Tears slid down her cheeks. Ada Broadbent began to weep and I felt like doing so myself. What a bloody muddle. What a disaster.

Now the major knew that we knew who had the boy and had every intention of stopping him. We had been so close to rescuing Felix. What would his poor mother say?

Sir Cuthbert appeared in the doorway. He bowed to the maharajah. "Our soldiers are in pursuit. The major cannot hope to escape."

He noticed the tears and moved to sit beside his wife. His concern was affecting. He had no qualms about placing his arm round her. He touched her bruised face.

"You have been in the wars, my dear. Did the major do this?"

"I tried to…he was maddened…I saw him…" Ada Broadbent bravely attempted to explain, her eyes glancing nervously at the patch the servants scrubbed on the floor.

"I'll have him. How dare he strike you. Right now, you are…you both are," he amended including Beatrice Chayle, still seated at the end of the chaise lounge, "in need of rest and care at home."

The maharajah let us go.

We left him standing in the despoiled zenana, his expression one of animal ferocity.

Sir Cuthbert tenderly escorted his wife down the stairs. I found Miss Chayle in need of a strong arm as the events began to affect her now she had a moment to rest and reflect. Light carriage rugs were all we had to wrap the ladies in to stop them shivering. Sir Cuthbert actually held his wife. I dare not try that with Beatrice Chayle, she might prove a cosy armful, but only at her behest. She did however lean against me and rested her head against my shoulder. I sneaked an arm around her and held her firmly against the carriage's occasional jolts.

We travelled at a brisk trot towards home. I wished for the speed of the railway for Beatrice Chayle looked fragile, colourless, and she shuddered frequently.

"I should have hidden him, or been swifter to run into the house, not away from the house." Anguish and guilt combined in her voice, marked her face.

"No, don't play the guilt game. You should not feel any guilt," I told her. "You didn't know your way about the house, the major did. He would have found the boy if you'd hidden him, run you both down before you'd found us to help you. "

"Why? Why did he do it? What insane notion has he in his head? Felix could never be his son."

"I do not know, nor could I guess, Miss Chayle. The major is not the kind of person I associate with."

She snorted. There was no other word for the noise she made. "Oh, a plague on all men."

"Oh, not all of us, Miss Chayle."

"Yes, all." She bent her head so that I could not see her face. "Do you know why my father wanted to put my aunt, his own sister, away in a secure place? Not only because she refused to accept the man he wanted her to marry. She intended to take up a scholarship at a London studio and paint. That, to him, would disgrace the family, artists are socially unacceptable, bohemians." Beatrice Chayle swallowed a sob and continued. "My poor aunt, whom I never met, or even knew existed, shut up, never allowed to paint, and driven mad."

She shuddered. "He will do that to me. He will have the doctors declare me 'hysterical' and lock me away if I do not marry his junior partner. But I won't." She slumped against me, trying to find inner strength.

Damn it all. No sal volatile, no brandy, and the poor thing already deeply shocked by that goddamned major and the murder, never mind losing Felix. I pulled her closer, and tried to tuck the rug round her. At least she had cried herself dry.

She raised her head and glared at me, a feeble glare, but still a glare. "You're as bad. Why didn't you marry your poor fiancée? A plague on all men."

"Don't you dare talk about my Aimée, Beatrice Chayle." I rested my hands on her shoulders round which I had been arranging the rug.

She shrugged me off.

I grasped both her hands. "You are distressed, rightly so." Her hands felt clammy, chilled through. I held them between mine, gently rubbing them.

She struggled to pull them away. "Well? Are you going to marry your Ami?"

"She won't marry me." It was so hard to speak those words. They tore open the wound again and rage and anger poured in. Complete devastation. I fought for control.

She left her hands between mine but raised her face to give me a scorching look. "Couldn't you accept the child after all…?" then she stopped speaking as she looked into my face.

I released her hands. "Oh, you may be sure I blame myself, Miss Chayle. I'd told Aimée I would accept the child and raise her as my own."

Memory deceives, tricks and traps. The Indian sun became a sunny June day, one of those delightful days an English summer can provide. I could smell the roses. I held the basket for Aimée as she cut them, apricot and yellow ones heavy with scent, pearled with dew.

She gave me a glorious multi-tinted rose. "What if the child is a boy?"

I goggled at her.

"I don't understand." Beatrice had altered her tone from scorn to bewilderment. I returned from the past to explain.

"I had never considered that the child could be a boy. I'd always assumed that it would be a girl child. One who would grow up under the tender care and loving eyes of Aimée, my mother and her mother. The bad blood which the poor thing must inherit from her inception would never cause problems then when the child had been surrounded by such loving care, and shielded from any of those worldly evils which might stir her bad inheritance awake."

Beatrice Chayle pondered, looked at me, raised her eyebrows. "And?"

"A boy, you see, Miss Chayle, could not be so shielded and protected. He ought to go away to school, then perhaps the inns of court, university, places where he would meet evil and that bad blood might easily betray him, because we were not there to guard him and keep him safe."

I saw again Aimée's face. The love and the strength. I heard her firm 'No.' "Aimée refused to marry me because of that and because of family matters. My oldest son will inherit a small estate which has been in my mother's family since the 16th Century. My uncle, the nabob, will leave his fortune to me for my son and heir, and my daughters' dowries. Our family is proud of its lineage and Aimée would not have her bastard child take that from us, nor would she have him grow up blighted as the bastard hanger-on, watching as our true son inherited."

Beatrice Chayle began to speak, collected herself and her thoughts. After a quiet moment she looked at me. "And her child was a boy?"

"Yes. I had so hoped for a girl."

It was Beatrice Chayle this time who tried to enclose my large hands within her own.

Final pursuit

Dholpore 1872

The pursuit came more quickly than the major expected. Ducking amongst the rocks he muffled the child's face into his jacket and checked the horse.

"Halloo, Aubrey. For god's sake, Aubrey. Halloo, halloo."

Anyone might think the fool rode out foxhunting. The Major nudged the horse onto the road again just as Richard dashed past.

The way the man wheeled his horse round would have had the horse master swearing. Ham fisted oaf.

"Aubrey, thank God. You bloody fool. Give me the child then ride out of here. Ride down to the foothills, to the station, and catch the train. That curst magistrate has set his men after you. So has the maharajah. Leave India before the maharajah has you flayed and skinned. How could you kill her?"

His horse tossed its head and sidestepped beside the major's horse. Richard reached for the boy.

Too slow, Richard. The major backed off. "No, sir. I will not hand the child over." *I keep my word, you fool. I warned them, and that woman will know what pain is.*

Richard swore again. "To snatch the boy on impulse was crazy enough. To keep him in your father-in-law's zenana was madness. To fail to return him is insanity and you will suffer for it. Northrop will see to that. He's a government man, his family have power with political influence and more money than yours. Never mind that Ackerman's threatening to kill you."

So I am to quake before some half breed banker? Hah! The major's grip tightened until the boy squeaked. "I will leave the child at the barracks. He and I have been having a fine time, haven't we, Felix?" He joggled the boy up and down on the pommel but he squirmed.

"Gently, Aubrey."

The major watched as his captain manoeuvred near, his horse restricted to small side steps. *Too slow, captain, you'll never catch me.*

"What madness is it infecting you, Aubrey? Seducing a few maids is acceptable, to seduce and rape respectable society daughters and make a game of it beggars belief."

"Don't criticise me!" The shout echoed off the rocks and frightened the child to whimpering. The major felt only the mounting rage. *I must return home. I need an English wife, an English heir. What folly it is to think I could force the world to recognise half breed sons.* He ignored his friend and made his horse walk on. *I need to make my world right, as it had been and still should be.*

Richard swung his mount around to block the way.

"Your wife…why, Aubrey, for God's sake, why?" He made a darting attempt to grab the child.

Out of reach, you oaf. As the captain tried again the major snarled. "Back off, Richard." The boy tried to slide down and the major struggled with horse and boy. He settled both with a heavy hand and swore at Richard. "You goddam idiot. Stand off!"

The major yanked his horse's head round, nearly barging into the other horse. *Time to depart.* "Sons. I need sons to follow me. Don't you see, you fool. I'm last of our line."

Richard grabbed at the bridle and cursed the major. "Then why kill the princess?"

He will never understand; he is not a Wulfsige. The major stared him down. "Release my horse. I am going home. My family will make all right, we are the Wulfsiges."

The captain shook his head. "You blind, stupid fool, you…you irresponsible fool." His voice was full of pity. "You have no idea what you have done."

"How dare you speak to me in that way. We are Wulfsiges. No one dare stand in our way. No one." *And I am your commanding officer and you will suffer for that.*

Richard's mouth tightened. "You are insane. You have disgraced the regiment, caused a political upset and all you can blether about is your family name."

"Release my horse," the major roared. "The regiment can crush the maharajah. The regiment will want to avoid a fuss. All will be silenced to avoid besmirching their good name."

The boy cried out then wailed. *Snot-faced bastard.* The major hit him. *I must dump the brat where ….*

The captain cursed and reached for the child.

Enough. The major backhanded Richard across the face, slashed his hand with the rein ends and spurred his horse away crying, "Leave it to me, Richard."

The captain galloped after him bawling. "Commanding officer? The regiment will hang you, you fool." He fell behind. "Come back," he hollered. "Give me the boy. Your only escape is down in the foothills. You must get down there and take the train or hang, damn you."

They will have to stop me first. The major disappeared among the rocks.

Face to face at last

Dholpore 1872

I don't think any of us wished to face the Northrops. Ada Broadbent needed rest and care. She ought to return to their bungalow. Beatrice Chayle needed care and an escort to her place, which was with the Northrops. Sir Cuthbert had official business, to report the murder, the Major's actions and what we now knew of the kidnapping. Which left me bearing the news to the Northrops. I groaned inwardly as the carriages set us down at the Club. I foresaw a dreadful time ahead.

At the Club we transferred Ada to a palanquin and sent her home to her servants. Sir Cuthbert stormed off to deal with officialdom and find a doctor for his wife.

Beatrice Chayle refused a palanquin, said a pony and fresh air would help her recover.

"Brave girl." I dared to give her a supportive hug as I called for our ponies. She did not stiffen or push away, actually leant against me and sighed.

"Bear up, Miss Chayle." She managed a smile at me as I carefully set her on her mount.

Desmond Jury hurried down the steps towards us. "What news?"

I did not see the need to stay silent. " Major Wulfsige had the boy. He must be insane. He has stolen off with him again. Captain Rankin has gone after him."

Jury's jaw dropped. He tried to speak, failed. He flapped his hands, shook his head and returned inside.

My syce led Beatrice's pony and she did not protest, which was remarkable in itself. I followed on my clever little chap through the unique Indian noises, smells and crowds in the town streets thinking desperately about what I could tell the Northrops. If I left it all to Beatrice Chayle to report, the Northrops might not understand about Captain Rankin. After all he had been party to the kidnap and they knew it. A surge of rage, so hot and heavy it burned my gut, left me sweating and muttering under my breath as I thought of what I would do to the major. He surely was insane. He was driving me insane whenever I thought of his hands on Aimée and I owed him anew for that clout and imprisonment.

The pathway to the Northrops' hillside bungalow allowed for two ponies abreast, unlike the way to the Broadbents' home. I took the outer position and smiled across at Beatrice Chayle. Aim for optimism I told myself.

"Have courage. We know the captain will bring Felix home."

"Will he?" She shrugged, as though trying to chase away despondency and gloom. "How can I tell my cousin I had him, held him and lost him to that…that monster?"

"Miss Chayle…"

She shook her head at me. "My friends call me Beatrice, or Bea," she flashed a warning glance "but not ever Trixie."

We'd made a long journey together today. The journey ended, it seemed, in friendship

"Thank you…Bea," She nodded. "He tried to abduct you. You fought, you were tossed into a pit, shut in. What can you have done more?"

"I don't know, but surely there must have been something."

"No." Yet I knew her feeling of guilt. I shared it heavily. If I had not come here the child would have been safe. "We both lost Felix. We both were outwitted by the major's knowledge of the house and grounds. The man murdered his wife. He could have murdered you."

She did not answer but turned her face away so I would not see her tears. I hated to see her cry. "We will always feel this guilt, Bea, will always feel responsible for the hurt the Northrops carry because of our natures. Men like the major have no such feelings. He will never acknowledge his guilt. Accept your guilt as something to remind us of the cost of living and loving. Of being decent human beings."

Beatrice sobbed once. "I can't," she said and we rode on in silence.

My syce held both our ponies as I dismounted. I lifted Beatrice from her lady's saddle - there was no mounting block – and she clutched my arms, even rested her head fleetingly against my shoulder, as I set her on her feet. She stumbled and allowed me to support her while we walked through the garden.

Charis Northrop saw us first. She ran to the French windows, stopped, cried out and collapsed into her husband's arms.

Julius Northrop's expression changed from hope to despair.

"No, no," Beatrice Chayle cried, "we've seen Felix. He is well." She broke free of me, struggled up the steps and I followed.

"He was in the zenana, we found him." She clasped Mrs Northrop's hands, chaffing them between her own. "Have courage, cousin." She led her over to a well cushioned chair and sat her down. She perched herself on the padded arm.

"The major is surely mad," I told Julius Northrop. "He snatched the boy and Miss Chayle, dragged them off. God only knows what he intended but we forestalled him. His captain is in pursuit and should have your son by now."

"I do not understand." Julius Northrop ran his hands through his hair, pressed them down on the top of his head as if fearing his brain might explode from within.

"Let me try to explain what happened. It was a shocking affair."

Julius grasped my elbow and tugged me towards the ladies. I began the tale, Bea told her part, I finished it.

Charis Northrop had the awareness and selflessness to be horrified by our experience and distressed about Ada Broadbent's injuries. Such a remarkable woman. She could even say how sorry she was for the death of the major's wife whilst knowing what part that woman had played in hiding her son.

"Mr Ackerman, thank you." She held out her hand and I allowed myself the pleasure of holding it and even managed not to smile like a fool.

"You are a generous and forgiving lady. We did try and so nearly succeeded. I am sorry we could not bring Felix back, but he will return."

Bea put her arms round her cousin, a gesture of comfort. "If the captain has him he should be at the officers' quarters soon."

I wished she had remained silent. It was by no means certain that Rankin had done that and I had planned a different welcome for the captain, one not involving witnesses like eager parents.

Charis Northrop turned those lovely grey eyes to look at her husband's face, beseeching him. He nodded.

"Yes, my dear, I'm leaving now. Would you accompany me, Ackerman? And no, Charis, you cannot come. You are still too frail. Beatrice, my dear cousin, please support my wife."

Bea raised no objection. Astonishing. She had been more shaken by today's treatment than I had realised. Two brave but distressed women. Please God we would have the cure for them with us on our return.

We left the two planning food and a bath for Felix.

My syce readied the ponies again and we set off for the officers' quarters. He followed us at the trot as we bustled the ponies along.

Freed from consideration for his wife's presence Julius Northrop exploded into speech. "Kidnapping and now murder. To kill his wife, kidnap our cousin and son, harm Mrs Broadbent. I will have him cashiered, disgraced and in gaol for what he has done to Felix. Broadbent will have him hanged. Why? What in God's good name makes a gentleman of good family behave like that?"

"His family's overweening pride and arrogance. He believes he can do no wrong."

"But to steal our son? He cannot hope to keep him."

"No, but he can hurt those he envies and despises by removing their sons."

"Infamous. The man's action are not rational."

No, they weren't. Wulfsige had allowed his anger and frustration to overrule his good sense. Arrogance didn't help, the belief that his family had god-like qualities made things worse. I despised his inability to control himself, God knows I knew it wasn't easy, but without self-control a man could soon be a beast. We were better than the animals and should behave so.

My conscience woke, rose, and gave me a sharp nudge. Wasn't Wulfsige's rage and anger like mine? I began to think fiercely. Wasn't I as bad? I came to India driven by rage, righteous indignation, and frustration and not only for the young ladies. I had been deprived of my Aimée, who would not be my wife. I had lost something so precious it had turned me into a man full of rage, a man determined on revenge, and who seriously contemplated killing the one who had, metaphorically, killed my love.

Wulfsige had let his frustration over the problems in his life turn him into a monster. Did I stand in danger of doing the same thing?

The monkeys began their afternoon hoots and chatter. Birds protested in whoops and shrieks and I winced at the racket. My pony tossed his head as if in sympathy. The syce slipped beside Julius's mount and guided him away from the path edge and the ravine below. Julius did not notice, he actually shook with desperate indignation, kept muttering Felix's name.

I remembered what Aimée had told me, about what the major had done to her, how he'd touched her, how he'd treated her as a thing, robbed her of her humanity and left her feeling worthless, a soiled object to be used. But this time, although I cursed the wretched man, I retained control of black rage and thought of the damage he had done to himself. So many lives broken by the actions of one man. God rot his soul, but what of his soul? What damage did he carry and how could he ever be a decent human again? Well, that was between the man and his God. I must be concerned about the people whose lives he had wrecked, who deserved to, needed to, see him in court, shamed in public as he had shamed them both privately, and in some cases, publically.

We began the descent into town. "To the Officers' headquarters," I told the syce, "to the rear, their stables please, and guard our ponies carefully."

He bowed his head. "Sahib."

He took us down the path leading to the military quarter. The officers, of course, had a palatial building. We passed the porticoed front and rode along the side to the stable yard.

I looked at Northrop. "You should enter the front door as a representative of Her Majesty's government. I will investigate the stables and rear entrance."

Northrop demurred, then gave way. "Yes, damn you. You are correct. I'm here employed by the government and must follow procedures."

We dismounted and he thumped my shoulder. "Find my boy."

"You go and raise the regiment's commanding officers with your wrath and indignation at their major's behaviour. I will get the captain."

The stable yard stood empty, but my syce indicated that the captain's horse was in a stall. I strode into the rear entrance as though I knew the place and had every right to be there. People hesitate to stop a man who looks as though he knows what he is doing and where he is going, certainly the doorman opened the door for me smartly.

"Captain Rankin," I demanded.

The doorman flinched, pointed, gabbled something in his language. I flung a nod at him and strode up the flight of stairs and along the corridor. At the junction of the corridors, as I decided which way to go, the quiet splintered round me in echoing cries, voices reverberating from the ceilings, weird metallic crashes and a banshee scream of rage that ricocheted off the walls to deafen me.

"Rankin," I bellowed, racing towards the racket. As I skidded into the doorway I saw Northrop stumble up the top step of a flight of stairs at the end of the corridor. "In the office," I yelled, then tried to stop. I was sliding into a fight. A sword fight between Rankin and the mad major. For heaven's sake, shades of the Three Musketeers. Anyone might suppose we lived in the 18th century.

The mad major cursed, lunged with his sword straight for my heart. Captain Rankin sprang between me and the sword. His own sword slashed, knocking the plunging blade upwards. I thanked God for school rugby as I dived under the swords to tackle the major's knees. I felt a blade scrape my shoulder blades, hoped my jacket hadn't been cut, as the major staggered backwards into the desk. I let my weight pin him to the desk and rose to my feet, using my size and elbows to block his arms. Swords are no use when the opponents are chest to chest. He swore and tried to smash my face with the sword hilt. Footsteps thundered along the corridor, Northrop charged in with three officers at his shoulder.

"Where's my son?" He hurled himself into the muddle and yelped as Captain Rankin's sword swished past his chin.

I had the major by the throat with one hand, bent backwards over the desk, and I wrapped my other arm tightly round his body. His strength amazed me for he continued to struggle. I hauled him upright, crushing him against my chest so that he could not move.

"Where is Felix, you murdering bastard? Where is the boy?" I squeezed and battered at him but found, to my amazed fury, that the other officers were prising me off him.

"What…?" I thundered. "This man has kidnapped and murdered…take your hands off me." I kicked out backwards and tightened my hold on the spluttering major.

"Gently, Ackerman," Northrop, still restrained by Rankin, spoke from behind me. "Don't cheat the hangman."

I controlled my raging wish to break the major's back, remembered control and self-discipline – I was not like the mad major - and eased my grip, releasing him, but grabbing his sword as I did so. The officers, aides to the colonel beside me, took hold of him and held him firmly. He could not stand but bent over, wheezing, his face a purplish-blue.

Northrop grasped my arm and nudged me round to face the colonel. He was a big man too, our eyes were on a level, but he was lean, with brains enough not to try the 'I am the great colonel, Lord so-and-so' superior manner on a justly provoked and angry man "You are cognisant of the fact that your major," I inclined my head towards him, "has murdered his wife, the Maharajah's daughter, and created a most dangerous political situation. The Maharajah's turned his private army loose."

"Yes."

"And has Sir Cuthbert Broadbent spoken to you about the legal matters pending back home in which your regiment is involved?"

"I have been told."

We stared at each other. The colonel's nostrils flared.

"And what about the boy?" I roared, making the company startle. "Where," I demanded, turning to the captain, "is he? Rankin, where is the boy? You promised to fetch him."

The major began to laugh. "I warned you, interfere with me and you'd regret it. Find him if you can."

Northrop launched himself at the evil bastard. I prevented him with a quick grab at his shoulders and swivelled him round to face Captain Rankin.

"You promised to catch the major and take the boy. Now tell his father why you failed, you bloody incompetent scum."

The major released another explosive round of jeering laughter.

His colonel and the adjutants sniffed in disdain until their nostrils pinched and raised eyebrows at my language. They formed a group behind the desk. Like a pack of jackals they huddled, each supporting the other.

The captain flushed a dark red and raised his chin.

Julius Northrop's look of contempt scorched the captain's pride. He stuttered about not catching up 'til too late.

"Where, where did you catch him without my son?" Northrop made to throttle him.

"Hold hard, Northrop. The boy can't be far away." I held him back. "Call out your men, and hunt now. Tear this building and outbuildings apart. Search every officer's house, stables, everywhere."

The colonel stiffened, grew three inches and glared.

"You, sir." I addressed the colonel . "Get the whole regiment out hunting for the boy."

"I will not. There's been enough scandal."

"Ah, he speaks again. Another complete sentence. I began to wonder if you were as wooden of tongue as you seem of intellect." I pushed Northrop towards the door. " Go, Julius, make haste man. You must rescue Felix. I'll fix these idiots."

He fled. The colonel stepped aside. His officers moved, easing the major with them.

I stalked across the room, filled the doorway. "You let him go," I indicated the major with a tilt of my head, "and I'll ruin the lot of you."

The officers measured my determination, the lack of an exit, and stood still, retaining their hold. The major sneered.

"Find the boy. Get your men into every military building and all the bolt holes known by sodomites. Your major made threats to give the lad for a catamite. Fail to do this and I will not only drag the name of your regiment through every court in this country and England's and then fill the newspapers both here and back home. I will join Northrop to petition his party in government to disband such a disgraced regiment. I personally will ensure that no bank ever supports loans to your officers' mess or any of you personally."

"I doubt you are able," the colonel did not sneer but curled his upper lip in a contemptuous smile.

"I can and will. Your regiment is now in public disgrace, your personal reputation will be in tatters. You cannot cover up what the major has done or what your junior officers have been involved in, not when they appear in court. Your men forgot that they can be tried here in India for those crimes back home. 'Vengeance is mine, saith the Lord,' and so it shall be."

I swung a fist at the major. The officers moved to protect him. "Now, where did you leave the boy?"

He would not say so I rounded on Rankin. "You useless looby. Did you follow the major, did you journey the same way to town?"

Rankin nodded.

"Then where could he have left the boy?"

The major laughed again and I hit him, hard, an open handed blow across the face.

The colonel stepped forward. "Enough. Rankin, begin a search along the route the major took. You too," he ordered his aides. They saluted and departed, Rankin turned to follow. At the door he spun round, bowled the colonel into me and shoved the major through the door.

"Run, you fool, run."

The arrogant swine stood there, wiping his bloody nose whilst the colonel and I sorted ourselves out. As I got to my feet he snatched his sword off the desk, lunged at me, then fled.

Rankin moved to block the doorway.

I nearly throttled Rankin shoving him out of the way. Would have done, I think, had there not been an appalling outcry from the front of the building. At first I thought Julius Northrop and his men had seized the major and I ran outside.

"They've found him," someone cried. "They've found the boy."

Thank God. I crashed into the street and saw Julius and his men, followed by a rag tag crowd of native people, racing down the street. A small bewildered boy stood watching them approach. Even from where I stood I knew by the dark hair that it was not Felix. I whirled round, back through the double doors, running to reach the rear of the building, determined to catch up with the major.

He had reached the stables.

"Put your sword down, Major." I made it a polite request. "It's finished. Over."

He snarled and lunged towards me. "Keep off."

"You can't spit me like wild boar." I stood firm, four square, in control of myself. "Where is the boy?"

He flung his head back and laughed, a raucous bellow. "I told you what I would do."

"But the Maharajah's brother has not yet arrived, and you had not been in this little town long enough to find anyone else. You dumped him and ran here. Where is he?"

The major advanced slowly, sword full stretch.

I did not move. I wanted him to lunge at me.

The arrogant major believed he could run me through any time. He believed he was invincible and I was not. With his lips raised in a snarl, his flushed face and wild eyes, he did not look particularly sane. Certainly not a notable member of the English aristocracy, more a mad dog.

"Are you aware how many lives you have destroyed?"

He laughed, a triumphant crow. "Good."

"What harm did those school room girls, not yet out, still children, do that you and your fellow officers should treat them like brothel bait?"

He had almost reached lunging distance.

"You killed a fourteen year old, her name was Alice."

He stopped.

"Another died in childbirth, almost all those young girls lost their comfortable homes and places in society. "

"So they should." He jeered and, fast as a striking snake, he drew back the sword to thrust it at my gut.

I saw the flicker in his eyes, leapt sideways and forwards, dodging the sword, and catching him stretched out on the full lunge. I smashed his sword hand with one hand and chopped his elbow with the other. The sword drooped. Now my body was too close, beside him. He had no room to move a sword and I knocked it away. It clattered across the stones.

I spoke as I wrapped him in a wrestler's body hold and crushed him. "I have been waiting for this moment for a long time. You touched my fiancée. She told you I would find you. I have. I want to kill you, but I am not a mad dog like you. You are going to hang. The law will kill you and the women you harmed will see justice done and you and your family disgraced. You will be shipped out to Britain as a prisoner in chains, and you will be tried in London. And neither the regiment nor your aristocratic connections can save you."

The major tried to struggle free and I continued to squeeze.

Footsteps pounded behind me. "Release him." That was Captain Richard Rankin with his trusties.

"He is my prisoner. He will go home to hang. And you are meant to be hunting for Felix Northrop."

"He will not be freed. I give you my word. My men will hold him. We must make an end of this."

I looked at the lanky Scot and the sandy haired North Country man. They marched either side of the major to grasp him firmly by the arms. I gave him a final squeeze and let the soldiers take over. They shoved the major towards the captain.

"Come, Aubrey, you didn't have the sense to flee to the foothills and take the train. There is only this way left. You must. For the regiment."

It took a moment for me to realise what the captain demanded. "Oh, no. You'll not avoid the noose, you coward." I started forward, but the sandy haired private blocked my passage.

"Best this way, sir."

I struggled with him, trying for a hip throw so that I might heave him out of the way. He held on. The other blocked me in.

The major, snarling like the mad dog he had become, snatched the captain's offered service revolver. He pressed it to his temple, laughed that jeering jackal laugh, and pulled the trigger.

The mess was incredible and disgusting. I wrenched free of the trusties, turned from the shattered corpse, and stormed over to the captain. I slapped his face, one side then the other, with considerable force. "There are people in England who needed to see him hanged. Young women who require justice, whose lives cannot mend without seeing a proper punishment meted out."

Rankin raised his fists but restrained himself. "The regiment comes first." He stormed off, his cap all but sliding off his head. That reminded me.

"Don't go, you two. I want a word with you."

The trusties hesitated, obviously debating whether to run or not. I jingled the coins in my pocket and they paused.

We walked as far from the corpse as we could, the two soldiers looking sideways at me. "I might pay for information."

They bridled.

"Beer money as a reward for your help?"

They looked at each other and measured out two paces closer.

"Felix had a soldier's cap. Did you give it to him?"

"Nay" and a head shake. But Sandy Hair's head shake had a tentative start, and headshakes were not quite lies.

I rattled the coins in an absent minded fashion. "Gave it to his ayah then?" I directed the question at Sandy Hair. He shook his head.

Two orderlies with a stretcher arrived, followed by the regimental doctor. As they dealt with the remains of the major I leaned over Sandy Hair.

"Then how did Felix Northrop get the cap?" I removed a handful of coins from my pocket. "I'm still not familiar with the coinage but I hope there's enough here for a beer for you both."

The Scot edged his way beside me, cupped his palm and I poured the coins in.

"The major wanted…." he began, stopped as the orderlies picked up the stretcher and whipped a salute for the doctor as they passed near us, raised his voice. "Just holding the civilian until the colonel arrives, sir."

"It was the major," Sandy Hair confessed. "He wanted soldiers to get friendly with the Northrop lad."

I tried to keep a still face and a quiet voice. "So you were asked."

"Bloody ordered!" The Scott's face expressed his aversion.

"So you gave the cap to the ayah instead. That way the boy would have it and you would be able to say you'd given it."

"We didn't know," Sandy Hair insisted, "we didn't know what he was up to, but he aint…weren't… called the mad major for nothin'. We wanted nowt of it, dumped the cap ont' Archie's ayah."

"Aye, that major. He'd spit on us squaddies, kilt his own with his loony ways. Our wee captain saved us. He's a bonnie man. Major and his junior officers they did the snatch, but we weren't there, captain saved us, had us on sentry go in camp."

"And what about the Club doorkeepers?"

"The natives?"

"Yes, who killed them."

"Och, we knew there'd be a fussing about them, special trained natives they were."

Sandy Hair broke in. "We don't know, we didn't say. We haven't told you."

"Aye, we canna trust ye, best keep mum." The lanky Scott winked. "But we reckon 'twas our mad major's orders and some of his junior officers. They cared nowt for owt if it were native."

"They cared nowt for owt if it were not titled, English and a 'gentleman'!" Sandy Hair said. "We know what they'd do to us squaddies if they could,"

My head thumped, the smell of gun powder, blood and guts still lingered and my stomach revolted. "And where would he dump the boy before coming here?"

"We canna think. We'd fetch the laddie out if we could."

"Enjoy your beer." I turned on my heel ready to leave the yard. There had to be some hiding place where the major could be sure of threatening or bullying someone to hold Felix.

I swerved round and back the trusties. "You didn't give the cap to the Northrop's ayah. Who is Archie? Which ayah did you give it to?" One the major's men his officers employed?"

"Nay, she's the one at Madame's…." Lanky's voice trailed off. His mouth fell open but I had already turned, sprinted away.

"Find Julius Northrop," I bellowed over my shoulder. "Bring him there."

Finding the lost

Dholpore 1872

I ran, feet slapping the ground, darting, zigzagging round people. There was no breath for more than the occasional bellow of "Northrop," as I shoved and pushed my way through. I made a wrong turning, spun back and had to physically catch people and whirl them out from under my feet. Darting down the correct lane, led by the smell of those Indian pickles and chapattis, I burst out into the road again. There it was.

I hit the brothel doors shoulder first, running hard and charged straight in. Madam from Brum appeared at her doorway as I sped past seeking the servants. "You've got the boy," I managed to puff out as I raced on down the long corridor.

Kitchen on the right, servants' rooms further on, verandah and little garden on the left. I swerved left and halted myself by grasping the verandah post. Now where…? She hadn't much time to hide him.

No, the ayah crouched by the water barrel, the two brothel children splashing water on flowers nearby. She scrubbed at another child tucked firmly under her arm, its head bent as she washed dark water over the hair. She raised her face, eyes wide, mouth falling open at my arrival. She threw a towel over the child's head.

"Felix?"

Not a sound. Perhaps the ayah held him too close.

Madam arrived. She said something sharp to the ayah.

"Felix. Felix you are safe. Your father is coming. I'm the friend, Mr Ackerman, do you remember me? I played the vicar in your mama's play."

The ayah settled back on her heels and released the child. He wriggled out from the towel and raised a scared and hopeful face. It was hard to recognise him. His hair and skin were dappled with brown patches. The ayah had been trying to disguise him.

I stepped towards him and held out a hand. "You're safe now, Felix, your father is coming."

He hesitated, trembling. Then I understood. He was afraid. Beatrice Chayle had rescued him and he had been retaken. He feared and hoped.

The ayah rose. "The major is coming." Her voice expressed not fear but relief.

I glowered at her. "He's dead." I spoke again to Felix. "The major is dead, Felix. Your father is coming."

The ayah wailed.

Madam spoke to her chief manservant and he advanced on the ayah. The other two children watched as he marched her away. Felix stood.

I crouched down and stretched my hand towards him. "Your father is coming, Felix, he should be…."

We all heard the door banging, the shouting.

"Here he is."

Felix clutched at my hand and I drew him up the steps and along the verandah.

"Felix. Felix, where are you?"

We could hear Northrop clattering down the hallway. I hurried into our end of the long passage and there came Julius, gibbering and skidding in his haste.

"Felix, oh dear God what have they done to you. Felix, thank God. Oh Felix…."

I gently shoved the boy at his father, who finished his run with a staggering scoop and grab as he hoisted his son into his arms and enfolded him in a great hug. The child encircled his father's neck with his little arms and tried to bury himself into his chest, pressing as close as he could in the strong grasp.

"The ayah here hoped to camouflage him as a native," I explained. "Probably on the mad major's orders."

Julius Northrop heard not a word. He simply leant against the wall, and wept into his son's hair, crooning silly nothings to the boy. I left him there returned to the garden and spoke to Madam from Brum.

"Where is the ayah? She needs to be escorted to the magistrate. And don't employ her again. She's too bribable."

I received a magnificent down-the-nose haughty glare. Madam from Brum gathered up the two children and disappeared into the servant's quarters. My pretentions had been depressed. I grinned, stretching aching muscles, and went to find Julius. Sir Cuthbert could deal with the judicial aspects of the ayah's behaviour.

Julius and Felix had not moved. Julius spoke to Felix in a soft tone, almost a whisper. He spoke of what we had been doing to find him, and Felix had calmed, his shuddering ceased.

Time to leave. "Julius, we must go. We must take your son home to his mother."

The boy raised his head and whispered "Mama."

Northrop shook the nightmares out of his head, blinked at me and came back to the present. "Yes, indeed. To your mama, Felix. She will be ecstatic to have you home. We have been so worried." He wrapped his arms firmly round the boy, straightened up and we walked down the passage and out of the brothel.

The two trusties, Northrop's men and some of the regiment cheered us back to the Club. Desmond Jury offered baths, clean clothes and food for the boy, but Felix would only cling to his father.

"Best get him home," Jury said, so we did.

Rediscovering hope

Dholpore 1872

I don't think I've seen a happier or more emotionally satisfying scene than when we returned Felix to his mother. If such joy had the power to illuminate more than eyes and faces it would blaze like a firebrand across the night sky.

Charis Northrop enfolded her son, gently rocked him and sang something in a soft murmur, a cradle song perhaps. He knew it, for he melted into her arms, safe at last. My eyes filled, my throat closed round a lump and I all but bawled.

Beatrice Chayle and the weeping ayah started organising baths and food. Amal arrived to organise the household for us. Sir Cuthbert and Ada came later, in the evening, and we dined, but without Mrs Northrop. Charis stayed with Felix and slept with him all night.

"We will have to watch over him carefully, he is distressed," Beatrice told us.

Desmond Jury had said "Thank God, it was all over." but it never was as simple as that. Unpredictable consequences always followed. One could perhaps predict that Felix would be disturbed, not that his night terrors were such that his mother could not sleep. Thank God for Beatrice, who let Charis sleep during the day, and stayed with Felix occupying herself and him with sketching and painting. She made a series of portraits of the boy as he lay in bed dozing or occasionally scribbling on her art paper. One particularly fine portrait showed him as the brave little soldier boy. He smiled at that, but he was a faint image of the cheerful and clever lad I first knew. How long would it take before he recovered?

The regiment held a magnificent funeral for the Major. They would. His death was reported as an unfortunate accidental discharge of his firearm. Sir Cuthbert and I attended. Julius Northrop did not. Nor did the other parliamentary delegates which, considering the family name and lineage, said much about power and fading glory.

"No sons," Sir Cuthbert murmured as rifle butts crashed and feet stamped. "No more Wulfsiges, not even a daughter or two."

We watched the men march away and followed the officers to their mess.

No one could have predicted Julius Northrop's collapse. His wife and Beatrice Chayle supported each other, with Ada Broadbent and Amal running the house and coping with all the gawking visitors. Charis Northrop returned to England in two months' time, but Julius had to stay on and sort out the mess with the regiment before he could write his parliamentary report. Charis had her son to save and the move back to England to prepare. It gave her a future.

Beatrice told us all firmly, and with fierce intent, that she would leave. "I will go before my 'not a fiancé' comes to collect me as if I were a parcel from the left luggage office."

"We can't help, Bea dear," Charis said. "If we hide you your father will soon find you and we can't prevent him taking you, you are not yet of age, won't turn twenty one until the end of the year."

I offered help and a place with my relatives. Bea refused. She also refused to tell me her plans although I coaxed, begged and eventually threatened.

Ada Broadbent shook her head at me. "Let her be, Bryce. Give Bea her head and stand back."

It was hard to do so.

But Julius, poor Julius who had stood in that street holding his son and roaring for the major, had no future yet. He had planned on revenge, and when the soldiers announced the major dead, was struck dumb. He actually took to his bed. He could not speak for several days.

While the others dealt with callers and made each as day normal as it could be in the circumstances I sat beside the stricken Julius and constructed the legal cases and shared the letters from those afflicted families on whose behalf I'd come to India. I hadn't intended to do this, but Julius, realising that I now had all the information from England, from families as troubled as his, had held out his hand, begged with his eyes and struggled to speak. At this, the first sign of being sane Northrop had shown since he heard of the major's demise, I could not refuse for I understood what Julius Northrop felt when the major pulled that trigger. Somehow helping these families to their fair share of justice eased his frustration, allowed him to speak.

"How could a father," he asked of the families, "behave in such a fashion to his daughter?" His hand trembled as he passed the letters back to me. "These girls were violated by visitors their fathers allowed into their homes." He dropped his head onto a supporting hand. "To throw them out, claiming their disgrace their fault and shame to the family…."

"Come, Julius. It is common practice, a belief that the girl or woman is at fault. You know that as well as I do. And such scandal, a soiled daughter, for the family is not to be borne. The whole family would be regarded as tainted as well. Rape is not a topic for discussion in our polite social world and no one wants as wife a young woman who has been raped. How many fathers dare be loving and kind?"

"But where is a father's natural feeling for his children? What about their mothers? Surely they supported their own children?" He sat up, glared at me, sank back onto his pillows. "And what happened to those girls? Alice was only fourteen."

I found it difficult to answer. I'd wanted to marry Aimée, but not rear her bastard son. She had saved me by refusing to marry me. These families had to live in their censorious communities, maintain their social standing, protecting their other children. One 'soiled' daughter infected all the other daughters in the eyes of society. It was not right, fair or just but that was our society.

I looked at Julius's indignant face. "The consequences of those officers' actions have devastated every family, ruined once happy marriages, divided husbands and wives, left bewildered and scarred siblings and caused several deaths."

"What happened to those young ladies, Bryce?"

"Sylvia Courtland, the M.P.'s daughter. Oh, I could wish the major alive every time I think about her, so that I could flay him. She lost her family, her young man, and all hope. Her father cared for her deeply, but had to care more for her sisters and the family and his position and work. She never had the chance to speak to her John, because her father whisked her away to a private home he knew of, similar to the one my mother supports. She and her little girl are still there. Trapped, unable to return home, no hope, no future, just a pittance from her father. Sylvia refused to give up her child to a baby farm. Rightly in my opinion, knowing what my mother and her Quaker group say of baby farms. Her mother begged us to free her, but she cannot return home. Where can she go and what can she do?"

Julius muttered.

"Yes, our society is far from perfect but we cannot change it overnight. The problem is that these were young girls. Older ones we could have turned into widows, or have them return from abroad where they had been for their health. Alice and the other schoolroom misses would never have been sent abroad without their mothers, and were too young to settle, with good enough reason, with caring relatives at the other end of the country. These were not ladies able to become a widowed housekeeper or companion for some old lady."

Julius scowled. "What happened to those young girls?"

"Alice we could not save. "

Julius looked his question.

I frowned at the memory of my failure. "Her father flung her out of the house without even a coat or purse. The distraught child cast herself into the river. The information from my mother about a private place for girls in her situation came too late. Her own mother collapsed and faded into a decline, the older sisters blamed themselves for encouraging the young men to visit. The old family servant carries the guilt of not staying when the officers took tea in the summerhouse. Two others as young as Alice, flung out by outraged fathers, disappeared. They may be dead too, they may be in a poor house or a brothel. "

Julius's face reflected my feelings. I hurried on to a more cheerful report.

"My own Aimée is safe, married to the doctor in charge of the Quaker home my mother's group support. Her little boy is accepted as his."

Julius searched my face, nodded and swung his feet on to the floor. "And I must go on too, making something good grow from all this evil."

I left him to his servant's assistance and went out to sit on the verandah steps. How do you go on, make a new life, forget, heal and put away such pain? How do you live life as you had previously lived it after such an experience? I had had anger and rage to move me on when I lost Aimée. I'd had a task, to bring those young officers to justice and charges of rape, and it wasn't enough to remove the pain. What had the Northrops got to help them? And what would Bea do? Her whole life decided by others, against her hopes and inclination. I disliked that. She had been brave, loyal, and deserved the right to learn to paint well.

Ada sent her out to join me. "Take a little fresh air, Bea, now Felix is asleep with his mother."

She arrived with a tray of fresh made pakoras, one of my favourite Indian snacks, and a large jug of milky Indian tea. She and I sat on the Northrop verandah enjoying the pakoras and the tea - Ada Broadbent would not allow alcohol near the despairing - and discussed the future.

Bea passed me a full cup and I nibbled and juggled a couple of the still hot pakoras, onion and ginger, delicious. "You have nearly finished, so Sir Cuthbert tells me. What then?"

I shook my head and we sat, silent, taking stock of the last five days and trying to take hold of our lives. Some flower or creeper in the garden filled the air with a heavy scent. Bee Eaters flashed through the garden shrubs, their coloured feathers eye-catching bright, their calls almost melodious. I sighed.

"I could leave now. I have fulfilled my task. Sir Cuthbert has all the details and has begun the process of officially finding and punishing those other young officers…but…." I looked into the house where the Northrops sat together, holding hands, looking everything at each other, yet saying nothing.

"You told me not to accept guilt for…for… Felix." Beatrice stumbled over his name but checked herself firmly. "You have extracted justice for those unfortunate young ladies and a measure for yourself. Julius and Charis will either find the strength to go on knowing this and move away, start again somewhere else, or collapse and wither away." She touched my hand with her cool hand. "It is not your fault if they fail."

But I knew it was, for if I had not come here to the hills they would still have the Felix they knew, not this shattered fragile shadow who would always carry a wound.

I reached out, snagged her hand, turned it over and stroked her palm with my thumb. "No, no, Bea, there is not enough justice for me. I wanted revenge, to beat the major and his men to a pulpy mass and make him grovel, apologise for what he'd done, especially to Aimée. Instead my actions, my seeking revenge, have damaged more people." I gathered up both her hands into mine. "Not an intelligent, wise or civilised wish you see, this revenge." I looked at her and she looked right back.

She was afraid. I saw the real Beatrice, the beautiful young woman afraid to be forced into a life she had not chosen, wanting so much more, determined to fight to have it, but terrified of trying. I enclosed her hands within mine.

She freed her hands, but gently, slid her cushion closer to me, leaned against me, hesitated, then clasped each of my much bigger hands as a child does, tugging at them gently. "But if it was revenge it was also justice you sought, and through the law. You have gained it for those families back home in England."

I kept looking at her hands. They were small and soft. Her fingers wrapped round mine and gripped them gently. "You did the best you could, Bryce Ackerman, you should not feel shamed because the mad major was a destroyer, damaging all he touched."

I shook my head, but gently, and returned the pressure of her fingers. "Eventually I will believe that, you wise woman." For it was true and I knew it, in my more rational moments. "Each one of us chose and directed our actions and those actions made good or evil. People like the mad major and his officers, who thought they could behave as they chose, without legal consequences, must eventually face the consequences of what they had done to themselves."

Beatrice tutted, but sweetly. After a moment she tugged at my hands again. "Will you tell me what happened to Aimée?"

Surprised, I raised my head and met her gaze. She tilted her head and raised her eyebrows, her eyes full of something I didn't dare to name.

"I hope she is happy and well in her new life. She is married and living far away from her beloved Yorkshire."

Beatrice scanned my face carefully. "You don't sound distraught."

I managed a rueful laugh and dared to ease my arm round her waist, snugging her close so that I could murmur in her ear. "Aimée is married to the doctor who cared for her and the other unfortunate young ladies. She and the boy are in good hands."

Beatrice did not stiffen or pull away. She merely turned within my arm to give me a searching look. "Do you mind still that she would not marry you but would marry the doctor?"

"Yes, but I should not. When she made her decision not to marry me, if the child was a boy, then we both had to think about another future. I think I have begun to see mine." I smiled at Beatrice. "I know Aimée has found hers."

Beatrice frowned slightly, settled herself so that her head rested against my shoulder. "Which poet was it said that first love was for breaking hearts and last love was forever? Perhaps that is what you will go on to find."

I didn't know, but hoped she meant more than she'd said. Greatly daring I dropped a kiss on the top of her head. She might be right, irritating aggravating female that she was.

Beatrice, a becoming flush of pink brightening her lovely but still pale face, made no rejecting move, rather nestled closer, and I allowed myself to kiss her hair again. After all, we both needed some comfort.

"I suppose I must return home." I had no wish to stay in India. I tightened my embrace.

"Home to what?" Beatrice wriggled round to face me.

I did not know, back to the bank of course, certainly work on the problem of the baby farms with my mother's Quakers. I must raise money for those poor young women and others in the same situation. I wanted to help Sylvia especially, she deserved so much more than the narrow life she was trapped in. Yet she never blamed her father for bowing to society's attitude to protect his other children. Such problems before us in our society and I had so few ideas about how to solve them. "I'm thinking." I told Bea as she nudged me. "I'll tell you when I know."

Beatrice had solved her own problem. "I am going to paint and sculpt. I am going to the Art School in Dunedin, New Zealand." She gave me what is called A Look, daring me to disapprove.

I blinked, bit my tongue.

"New Zealand!" Julius had come onto the verandah to enjoy the last of the day before night fell so abruptly.

I finally managed a polite speech. "You've been talking to the gentlemen from New Zealand. So there is an art school?"

Beatrice, blushing again, nodded as she attempted to disengage from my arm. I held her closer, feeling cheerful, something I'd recently forgotten how to be, and remembering. I missed the mirkning, the long dusks of Yorkshire summer nights when I'd sit, holding Aimée close, on the big garden swing. What, I wondered were New Zealand dusks like?

"New Zealand?" That was Sir Cuthbert, standing on the verandah step to watch the night fall. "Who's been talking to those fellas with that scheme for half pay officers taking up land in New Zealand?"

"Beatrice," I said, still refusing to let her slip sideways out of my grasp, "is going to Art School in New Zealand."

"How?" Typical, blunt Sir Cuthbert, that question.

Beatrice raised her chin, prickled up. "I have a little money and I'm travelling with those officers and their families. I am going as companion to one of the wives."

That did trouble me. "You won't enjoy that kind of employment. It could be drudgery. Let me help…."

She silenced me with another of her Looks. I had to be careful not to rush her but allow her to find her own way. I closed my mouth and let her speak.

"Not this couple. I have the upper hand with this husband and wife. Captain Richard Rankin is a captain no longer. He has been forced to resign, leaving under a cloud. The regiment is a proud one with an honourable history and he has been part of the events which dishonoured it. He is going with this group to New Zealand. His Anglo-Indian wife will need all my assistance."

"Ah…clever girl."

The clever girl elbowed me sharply in the ribs. I squeezed her closer to my side and she gave a faint squeak but did not resist. I shook my head at her. She leaned against me.

Ada Broadbent appeared. "New Zealand? Who is talking of New Zealand?" Her husband answered with one of his sideways questions.

"Wasn't it one of my father's friends who went to New Zealand? From India. What was his name?"

"The major from the Bengal Horse Artillery? Richardson? Yes, he did rather well for himself didn't he? Became a politician and wasn't he made chancellor of the university?"

"And, what's 'is name? That family near us in Cheshire, who all went to New Zealand, made themselves a nice estate and meddle in the national politics?"

"Atkinson? The brothers who went together first and then the family…."

"Yes, Yes," Sir Cuthbert sounded testy. "All done well you see," he said to Julius. "New start, fresh country, something to think about."

Charis drifted to her husband's side, Felix asleep in her arms. "Beatrice and I have discussed New Zealand. It is her best chance of escape and I will be happy knowing she is safe with this group of wives and officers."

Julius took his son into his embrace and Charis sat at his feet. Still warn and distressed she had begun to find a way through. I saw hope in all their futures.

"I should like to tour New Zealand, Julius. The gentlemen spoke of thermal hot pools, boiling mud, and pink and white terraces. There are natives, who cook food in the boiling pools, strange trees and birds. Could we visit before going home?"

"And avoid my mother until her spleen is old and dry? An excellent idea."

Beatrice gripped my hand. "Would you travel to New Zealand?"

I smiled at her. "You go and become a world famous artist. I must return to England and report to all those families as well as my own. Then I shall take a trip and see if my family could benefit from a bank in New Zealand. Where shall we meet?"

She dropped her head into her hands and made an indistinct comment. Everyone else managed a smile. I kissed the top of her head again and she looked up with a laughing expression.

"One year's time in Dunedin then," she said. "I'll write."

"I will too." I smiled down at her. "I promise."

"To New Zealand then." Julius raised an imaginary glass in a toast.

"To New Zealand," we replied.

And new beginnings I thought. A way back to life, another kind of life to be sure but one which might include happiness again for us all.

USEFUL RESOURCES

'Plain Tales From The Raj' BBC Publications

'The Raj: the making and unmaking of British India' by Lawrence James

'Begums, Thugs and White Mughals' by Fanny Parkes and William Dalrymple

There are many excellent books on India and many collections of letters and diaries available which give a writer of historical fiction a real taste of the Raj.

DVD 'The Story of India' with Michael Wood

DVD 'National Geographic: Empires Of India'

READING GROUP QUESTIONS.

1. Sexual attitudes. Is Bryce correct in his condemnation of India as erotic?
   Why does he say this?

2. The novel is set in 1872, attitudes to women were meant to be protective and respectful.
   How does that apply today? Has anything changed?

3. Why did the young officers feel that they could treat women as they did?
   What was it that allowed them to treat the women as objects and not people?

4. Could this type of behaviour – a rape competition – happen today?

5. Do you believe the major is mad?

6. Bryce Ackerman has to make a journey from guilt, anger and hate to moving on with his life. Does he succeed?

ABOUT THE AUTHOR

p.d.r. lindsay is a member of the Writer's Choice writers' cooperative and when home in New Zealand, tutors would-be writers and promotes New Zealand novels and their writers, especially the independently published ones. 'Bittersweet' is her third published novel. Born in Ireland, educated in England, Canada and New Zealand and having lived and worked in many different countries she calls herself a citizen of the world, writes about many cultures, and prefers to write serious historical fiction.

Chat with p.d.r. lindsay on social media:

- Twitter:
- Smashwords author page:
- Linked In:
- Google plus:
- Goodreads:
- Amazon author page:
- Blog:
- Pinterest:

Writer's Choice a writers' publishing collective

We publish quality fiction for readers' enjoyment

Thank you for taking the time to read Bittersweet. If you enjoyed it, please consider telling your friends or posting a short review. Word of mouth is the author's best friend.
Thank you again. p.d.r. lindsay.

90% of our readers went on the enjoy another Writer's Choice novel. Order them through Amazon or Smashwords or the local bookshop.

There are also some other Writer's Choice novels you might like to read. Check them out at our website: www.writerschoice.org

'A Woman Transported' by Sharon Robards
'Unforgivable' by Sharon Robards

'South of Burnt Rocks, West of the Moon' by G.J. Berger
'Four Nails' by G.J. Berger

'Jacob's Justice' by p.d.r. lindsay
'Tizzie' by p.d.r. lindsay

Short Story Anthologies
'Blokes Muddling Through' by p.d.r. lindsay
'Woman Waking Up' by p.d.r. lindsay

Short Stories in the Writer's Choice Shorts collection.
by p.d.r. lindsay

www.ingramcontent.com/pod-product-compliance
Lightning Source LLC
Chambersburg PA
CBHW031234120726
479C5CB00002B/598